MOTHER'S DAY

MOTHER'S DAY

a novel by
Robert Miner

Richard Marek Publishers, New York

Copyright © 1978 by Robert Miner

All rights reserved. No part of this book may be reproduced in any form or by any means without the prior written permission of the Publisher, excepting brief quotes used in connection with reviews written specifically for inclusion in a magazine or newspaper. For information write to Richard Marek Publishers, Inc., 200 Madison Avenue, New York, New York 10016.

Printed in the United States of America

First printing

Library of Congress Cataloging in Publication Data

Miner, Robert
  Mother's Day.

  I. Title.
PZ4.M6635Mo   [PS3563.I4645]   813'.5'4   78-1831
ISBN 0-399-90012-8

To Linda

Ideas are not necessarily better for being deeply planted. There is ancient folly as well as ancient wisdom.

—Rebecca West

CHAPTER I

Whatever you may think you think, I am a mother. Men don't often get this chance, I know, but I qualify.

If things had turned out different you might have heard by now. "White male," the report would have begun, "age about thirty, no previous record ... "

As it was ... well, I have something to tell.

It is about a kind of miracle—ignorance like mine in the face of far simpler disasters should have been lethal. It is about a process so fierce and unrelenting no one who experienced it has dared to tell the tale. It is about the undoing of the male of the species. And it is about that conspiracy of silence called motherhood that women have visited forever upon each new generation of mothers.

Only this mother happened to be a man. And this mother keeps no secrets.

Listen. Here is how it was.

Lies.

Later—too late—when you discover for yourself that the

world has been lying about children since Adam and Eve, you're supposed to be too numb to notice, too proud, too crazed to care.

No one tells the truth. Not even the workaday stuff. Have you noticed, for instance, that your children always wake up just as you're about to come? Maybe in the old days that didn't matter: Fathers didn't have children and mothers didn't come.

Tonight it matters. I can't speak for Cindy, my children's absentee female mother—these days what man dares speak for woman?—but their other mother, may he come in peace, I speak for. Why else do you think I'd be tiptoeing naked like this through the kids' nursery, frosting my pumpkin on this glacial autumn night, while my new friend Karen shivers alone in my bed down the hall?

It's just that any comings these endless lonely last months have been self-propelled, reflexive as a tedious French verb. Tonight I scheme for the real thing.

Do I go on too much about this? You think it a trifling matter, perhaps. But that is how I am reduced. My children sue for custody, an adversary proceeding, and I must fend for me. I am a soft and gentle man gone woman—hard around the edges.

Besides, coming is the way you get from where you were to where you are, you know?

My kids are slack-jawed, soodling their way through the brittle fall night. Thomas has drooled in his sleep, his blanket wedged between baby teeth that gleam like plankton in the moonlight. Times like this the beauty of this child hurts. It reminds me what I otherwise forget. I love him helplessly. I should know better. Right now he is some skillful plant, some changeling. Ruthlessly innocent behind those silent eyelids. Not a sign of life. Usually he's stirring by this station of my evening. His hair is stuck to his forehead in sweat curls. I reach across his crib to sweep them back. His skin is too cold to the touch.

Mother's Day

Suddenly I am not sure he is breathing.

For the nth demented time since I've had him, I seize up in fear. Two and a half years of this and you develop procedures. I pinch off his nostrils with my left hand. I cover his mouth with my right. He flinches. I relax. He's my firstborn, you know, the one I've had most chances to kill off.

I eggshell my way across the nursery to Keturah's crib. A loose board snaffles underfoot. I search for telltale changes in her breathing. She's just nine months off the umbilical and sucks her fist. She's a comfort to me. You can hear her breathing from the other room, steady and wooden like a metronome. When Thomas was this small he wouldn't frost a watchglass with his breathing. I'd have to wake at night to check if he was still alive. Keturah changes tempo, from 3/4 to 4/4 when she's waking up, but now she waltzes steady despite that loose board back there.

Good thing. If she woke now I could lose my grip. I'm a desperate man, I tell you. Last time I managed to lure a woman here like this, I almost killed Keturah for waking up. In the months I've been her mother she's developed flawless timing. Last time, I went off my head. When she started crying right on cue I squeezed her so hard to keep from slugging her, she almost fainted. It's all too easy to choke off that brief, tiny life, so tonight nothing must go wrong for any of us. No uncalled-for interruptions.

The stars are pressed against the window by Keturah's crib, grinning malignly. The celestial hyena. I look down at Keturah. Her food-stained sky-blue pajamas are grown small for her. They've come unsnapped across her middle. Exposed flawless skin. I reach to touch it lovingly as I never seem to now when she's awake. But I'm afraid my icy hands may wake her. Instead I cover her to the armpits—babies smother under blankets pulled too high—with one of those moronically cheerful quilts people who don't have children give you.

Past her crib through the hall and the door to my bedroom I can see my night-light. I pick my way across the nursery minefield. One false move and some booby-trap toy underfoot could crash and blow us all to kingdom come.

Which brings me back to my subject.

Karen's hair glows copper in the night-light. She looks asleep.

"Matt?" It is Karen uncoiling primeval in my bed. She snaps her eyes open as I tumble on the bed. I just lunged off balance through the doorway to avoid a loose board in the hall. "Is everything all right, Matt? Where'd you go like that?"

"Nothing. Just the kids. Had to check on them, you know?"

"Oh. . . . Ahh! You're cold. Here, give me your hands." Karen uncurled my clenched fingers and squeezed a palm at a time on each of her breasts. They felt warm and sleepy except for a wakeful left nipple.

"I didn't hear anything, Matt. Were they crying or something?" She shivered as she talked. I squeezed her hard the way you do a child.

"No. Not crying." Just unwholesomely quiet, I kept thinking. Too quiet. Like natives in old movies.

Poor Karen. She's worried that she did something wrong back there. I had almost goose-stepped her upstairs to bed after dinner, so anxious to lose myself in an adult body for a change. Karen had been anxious herself. She'd borrowed money for a baby-sitter. So dinner, though genial, had been almost a lunatic formality.

Upstairs in my religiously tidied room—I'd laid it sacerdotally, like an altar—we had grappled, clicked together like magnets, then pushed apart again and again to look, just to look. Then, playing by these rules Karen hasn't found out yet for herself, I had lurched out of what threatened to be a terminal ecstasy, so reckless were we in our need, to stalk bristling and suspicious into the nursery across the hall.

"Turn sideways, away from me, Kay. Yeah, like that. I need to curl myself around you. I need the heat." She flinched at my cold, then pushed back against me to show she hadn't meant it.

"Jesus, Kay. It's that bad?"

"No. I sort of like it, even. You feel like pewter or something. Here," and her voice smiled in the dark, "let me polish you up a bit."

She began a fluid, rocking swing of her hips that quickly broke down my resolve. That's the key, you see. Resolve. The way I've figured it, with kids you can't let yourself go—or come—too soon. You can't get fervent, else all is lost. The signals wake them and you drown.

But Karen was rocking me off guard, endlessly. For the first time in months only this flesh and blood mattered—not the rest of it there in the nursery. Tonight, I began to con myself, finally tonight they'd sleep the skirmish through. Not like those botched, ramshackle others.

I suppose I shouldn't talk like this about a fellow mother, but Karen has an ass—there's just no other word for it—to fault Michelangelo. The first time we met I was afraid it would turn me to stone, I stared so hard. Somehow it reminded me of St. Paul. When I thought about her later—when I thought about *it*—I kept hearing him, magnanimous to the Corinthians about it being better to marry than to burn. Only the burning seemed to apply, though. I might have offered marriage, you understand, but it's bad form these days among friends. New rules for new desperations. Abandoned mothers abound, and who wants to marry one like me with no money and two squalling, blood-sucking appendicles? Who, indeed? Especially if she can have it for free without the complications.

So I burned, as it were, for that ass. And Karen always knowing I'm available. Here in my forsaken country house, a mother crippled by her lot.

I must have slid off into sleep again because I am suddenly aware that Karen is sitting on me, her knees tucked high into my armpits. She is so thorough. She is shivering again but this time not from cold. She seems pleased with me, somehow. She seems to have so much time. Partly, I guess, because she's on her best behavior, still worried why I left before.

The point about my leaving, you see, is that during the last months alone with kids I've learned a thing or two. Such as the strategy of coming.

Nobody I know of talks about it, nobody tells you. I think they think it's not supposed to happen. Maybe once it wasn't. Maybe in that antique time when parents had a built-in mate and coming was the least of adult needs. Those times have passed, of course, but people still seem to think there's something indecent about a certified parent, kiddies in tow, trolling for some mere nulliparous gratification. There is. Especially the haste and urgency, the bitter quaking need for any ounce of unencumbered selfish childless fare. That's fucking indecent, all right. Single parenthood is one miserable extended dryhump.

But I was telling what I learned. Or rather that I learned. You have to. Natural childbirth there may be, but natural motherhood there is not. Not for me, anyhow. I had to learn it all from rock bottom, and it doesn't come easy. Sometimes I think that's just because I am a man and don't have anything to give my babies, simple and physical, like breasts.

Once in an itchy sleepy morning sensuality, Keturah, who was new and tiny and groping like a blind mole for something to suck, was worrying my perfunctory nipples. I considered giving her my cock. It would have been a mixed gesture, you understand, part loving and giving like a mother with her teat, part something else—a curious and tentative attempt to follow instincts rather than the head. I have come to distrust the head for mothering. Before this I have been a man of few instincts, all censored to preserve my theoretic armor against this world. The head was useful for that part— protecting the theoretics—but it has served me badly since that morning several lives away (and two and one half years) when Cindy expelled Thomas wrapped in gore into my hands. She had been shrieking and vomiting and spewing blood from all available orifices. Thomas was blue around the edges from eighteen hours of labor. And my head kept getting in the way, obstructing with peregrine irrelevance all I felt.

And here was Keturah, gentle, groping, wanting from me something my head was set against. People would be quick to condemn if they knew this—I was quick then to condemn myself—but I turned Keturah down to suck, surrendering.

I wasn't a great success. Men are so drastically coded to reproduce, even under the least likely of circumstances, that the damn machinery would not lie soft. It thickened—and Keturah, too, became uneasy. I pulled her up and held her flustered to my chest, suddenly protective, as if someone had meant her harm.

I often wondered whether, if I had been able to make it work, it would have been the kind of seemly abandonment you see with breast-feeding mothers that makes them so relaxed, after, instead of nervous, adamant, and theoretical like even the best of fathers. *I* am not the best of fathers, even if I had the luxury of being one, and procedures do not yet exist for mothers so equipped.

Anyway, I have learned that natural or no, the parent who lives the babies' lives with them has to watch himself. There is a kind of signal children tune in immediately. A concentration on the self. Coming is such a signal. Not that there's been much of it, but whenever it has happened. I mean whenever it is about to happen. I suppose their sleep test patterns switch into white noise that sets them off. Parents used to notice something like this at dinner parties. After hours of premeditated chicanery, the kids would finally surrender themselves to sleep. Then just as you were serving dinner the kids would start to squall, magically on cue. That was in the old days, the time of the cow. No longer. This is the year of the hyena. No parents have dinner parties now, except to prime a visiting bedmate. And since dinner isn't the climax of the evening, the children do not wake to it. They wait.

I don't know how long Karen has been ministering. Perhaps I've been asleep again. She pretends not to have noticed. I have been lying on my back, stroked into paralysis like a cobra. Offering nothing, self-involved like a child. She plays with me like a mother with her baby—teasing, soothing, seeming no intent. My arousal is endearing to her like that.

You could tell her by her touch even in some unthinkable paradise with more than one ministering woman. She has a way with a cock. She tunes it like a precision instrument instead of the vestigial organ mine threatens to become. I am swollen with love for her now, what feels like sacramental love, even though I barely know her. This is the second time we've been to bed together and we have never had a chance to talk. Kids frown on that.

Sometime in spring, just after Cindy left, was the first time we were here together. I remember she wore grey flannel pants that day, very prim, and an air of immanent surrender. We had met by dryer number 6 one day—the way dog people meet on city street corners—and promptly conjured up the usual subterfuge: our children needed playmates. All the while we circled each other like overwrought cocker spaniels.

Days later she was driving up the long dirt road out here, past the stunted apple orchard, to this rural slum I share with onetime friends. The house is split in half by ancient doors and lately by a mutual contempt. I hate them for their cozy nuclear integrity, their bovine sense of proper form. Me they hate for disarray.

Like slattern assignations of the sort that rode the dusty wake of Karen's beat-up yellow Fairlane, two kids peering from its windows at two kids here holding me as if in gale-force winds.

In minutes the kids had bonded like two strains of epoxy, forming a murky tenacious alliance almost scary in its intensity. Two babies and two demonic two-year-olds. "Play" is anyway a euphemism applied to children, but for ours it seemed almost a malicious joke. Lethal-looking cuts and bruises blossomed, especially on the babies' faces near the eyes. Then the two-year-olds settled studiously into the systematic evisceration of toys.

It became afternoon and the children were cresting. Karen and I were paralyzed with fatigue and unrealized desire. Between us we had pressed two thousand pounds that afternoon, heaving and hauling screaming children. Now the portage had slowed down, the babies settled into holes of quiet or despair, the other two less loquacious in their body semaphore. Like zombies, Karen and I had wheeled and tip-toe climbed the stairs to my bedroom.

I had backed her down on the bed that afternoon, finger to my lips, and strutted through my numbers like a pigeon. I did the buttons well, and the hooks, but from epidermis on Karen had steered us like a ship, catching each swell at the peak. She could make you feel mortal sin, that woman, and now this evening, remembering, I am ticking like a time-bomb.

She slides over me now, warm across my solar plexus. I try to move and she gestures me still. This won't do, I keep wanting to say. I've done nothing for her. If she doesn't stop soon I'm going to explode inside her and fall helplessly asleep, I know it.

She jams me hard up inside her, loosing my precarious control. I try to think up horrors—the neighbor drowning puppies when I was a kid, a friend impaled on his steering column, crib death—anything to queer this snowball rush to climax. Karen won't return, I know, if this is all she gets. It's happened before.

Karen enjoys my agony and teases it raw to watch. I am viciously biting my tongue but nothing helps. My breath won't come. Maybe this is cardiac arrest. I am thrashing my head back and forth on the pillow, sucking blood from my ravaged tongue. I am trying to push Karen off me, to save the day, when I hear it.

Distinct, clarion, ice. In her crib Keturah has begun to crank up a scream, like a siren. It will take perhaps a minute, then she will be awake enough to make it work. Karen freezes at my new rigidity. I don't think she can have heard it yet. Maybe she thinks I've come, or had that heart attack. I am backing out from under her. She is staring baffled at me.

In thirty seconds Keturah will get that scream out. It will wake Thomas. They will both squall, taking turns as I try to shut up one, then the other. God *damn* them. God *damn* children.

I calculate it takes me three giant steps to get to Keturah's crib. I snatch her from the mattress, almost wrenching off an arm she'd stuck out through the slats. I start running for the door to the hall, holding her head close to my neck so she can't get out that scream.

The Fisher-Price Play Family School, I guess it was, got me. I heard that idiot bell they hang on it. I thought I'd memorized every obstacle before I went to bed last night, too tired and hurried as I was to pick any of them up. Now the play school crashes against the dresser. I do my screech of Job—through the teeth and from the pit of the stomach. I look back at the other crib and Thomas clicks his eyes wide open like a doll, then rolls over for a better look through the bars of his crib.

Maybe he hasn't focused yet, maybe he's still part asleep. I ignore him and Groucho-Marx slow motion out the door. He isn't making noise yet. There's still a chance. Sometimes he does this—sits up wide-eyed, then settles back to sleep. But now he jerks himself bolt upright, faculties clicking over in his eyes like symbols in a one-armed bandit.

I have Keturah on one hip, trying to smooth Thomas's hair, talking quietly to him as I have since I did my pirouette and soft-shoed back toward his bed. I am squeezing Keturah so she won't make a sound. I give Thomas his blanket, which he dropped when he sat up. Its shiny border is wet and warm from being in his mouth.

"Here's your nite-nite, Thomas. It's time to sleep, Thomas. Here, chew on your nite-nite. N-i-c-e nite-nite, Thomas, nice nite-nite." He just sits there, staring at me. Something in my voice gave me away, I realize, something urgent pulling on the cords. I tried to keep it neutral but Thomas wasn't fooled. He looks at me now, aggrieved, and there are tears in his eyes running with moonlight.

"Thirsty, Matt. I want juice, Matt."

"Go back to sleep. Lie down, Thomas. I'll bring some juice after you go back to sleep, OK?" Tonight he is not falling for that, and the big quiet tears begin to spill faster. In a minute he will start crying hard, in spasms, and the exercise from that will wake him up for good.

"OK, Thomas, I'll get you juice right now. Stay here. Right here. I'll be back. Lie down."

I am striding for the staircase, moving Keturah to the other hip so I can clutch the banister. She rides me bouncing down the stairs holding fistfuls of my skin like a baby chimp. I take the stairs two at a time trying to remember where the stair-toys were, where I left that pile of downstairs dirty laundry last night. For months now I've promised myself a night light on the stairs.

Keturah's bottle and Thomas's cup are in the refrigerator right at the front so that fumbling blind for them like now I won't knock things on the floor. Now we are moving back up the stairs, Keturah sucking silent on her bottle.

I give Thomas his Tommee Tippee cup, which has a little plastic top with holes so that he can't spill everything at once. Thomas had been trying to crawl out of his crib and I had shoved him sharply back in with my knee when I got here. I felt my mind clogging with rage.

"Stay in there!" I hiss at him. My voice is ruptured steam. I shove the cup at him again and he drops it, scared. The tears are welling in his eyes. Then I am desperately patting his head. "I'm sorry, Thomas. You're a nice boy. It's time to sleep is all, you're tired. Please go to sleep. . . . "

Keturah's bottle is already running out. I was too distracted last night to make a second. Now there's no chance of propping her back in bed to suck herself to sleep. I'm flooding with rage again, cursing out of control to myself—bloodthirsty, antedeluvian epithets. And I am getting cold, naked to the starlight. Keturah is already wet, smelling hot ammonia through her diapers warm against my skin.

Thomas gave me a look of mortal pain and righteousness a second ago, packed his blanket back into his mouth, and lay back staring at the ceiling through fat shiny tears. Keturah has begun to wiggle off the nipple every time I stick it back in her mouth. Now she drops the bottle on the floor. She looks refreshed and begins to burble strange enthusiasms.

We are rocking on the rocking chair, Keturah and me. The chair was icy to my naked back and I jumped up when I first collapsed on it. Now I have eased back on it, my jaws set, and it is warming up. Keturah is snuggled close for warmth, watching the stars go up and down outside the window as we rock. She is wide awake and warm and utterly content.

The stars keep moving up and down outside the window, grinning, but I am hugging Keturah now, then kissing her so fiercely she looks at me surprised. And I'm cold and naked, limp, unmanned, undone. And I'm squeezing back acid tears and wanting to cry like Thomas for all my conflicted woes.

CHAPTER II

Long shiny tunnels. Why are they always shiny? Directions in tile. Arrows, hieroglyphs, and numbers. UPPER/LOWER LEVELS. TRAINS. As if you knew already where you were and so could understand.

Back there we had blundered through the steam threatening the platforms. I held Keturah on my left hip with an elbow, a bag of baby things in that hand. My right arm slowly cramped, turning to ironwood from the heavy suitcase. Thomas had to hold my sleeve. He kept disappearing in the steam and I wouldn't be able to feel him with me. Not that I hadn't thought of that. Back there on the train I held Thomas one inch from my face snarling that he must not loose his grip. But on the platform he kept falling because he couldn't keep the pace. Furious, I wanted just to kick him along the platform like a box.

Now Thomas has to pee. I am sweating with anger. We two-step ten minutes more of tunnels down to find the rest rooms. Park the bags on the tiled floor in the hall. I couldn't pick them up now again without a rest. And I can't leave them here alone. This is New York, I know that. Keturah is hiccuping, working up a scream. The elbow was too tight for fear she would slip under it. Maybe she needs her bottle. Thomas will have to go alone to pee. I hoist Keturah to my shoulder so she'll have to think before she cries. I shove open the heavy metal men's-room door, point the way for Thomas. This door is like a fire door on a ship. Will Thomas possibly be able to open it alone when he comes out?

We sit in the hall, Keturah and I, balanced on the luggage. The bottle stoppers up her screams.

Thomas doesn't come out. How long ago was it? The hallway stinks and the walls shine from oily air sliding along them, I see that now. Keturah looks green in the fluorescent lights. People pass in the halls checking their watches.

They'd snatch my bags if I went for Thomas. Besides, those loathesome types in men's rooms always look you over sick if you bring in a girl, even a baby girl like Keturah. Cocksuckers.

Some kids come crashing out of the men's room. They're running down the hall.

Where is Thomas?

"Watch these a moment, please?" The redcap leans indifferent on his handtruck and pockets the bill. That bill means we take the bus, no cabs today.

No one in the men's room. The floor is white tiles, wet and swirled with dirt. The stalls look empty except for one closed door with large motionless black shoes sticking out. No shoelaces. Another door is closed. Under it that looks like Thomas' hand.

"Thomas? Thomas! THOMAS!"

Keturah squalling on the filthy floor and I squirm under the locked door. Thomas' pants are down around his ankles. He is curled on the floor by the side of the bowl. His hands are in his mouth. There is blood all over his legs and a blunt, pulsing stump where his cock was. I am squeezing the stump to stop the blood and looking for the other piece. Keturah is swimming on the filthy floor out there, screaming scared alone.

CHAPTER III

I underestimated him, of course. Thomas easily managed the men's-room door. From across the hall where I crouched frozen with indecision, wrestling with the Horrors, I saw the handle turn first one way then the other, tentative. Then Thomas was squeezing past the heavy metal door into the hall.

He was excited and kept pulling at my jacket to go back in there with him, to see what he peed in, like a bathtub. He was showing me that he remembered to zip himself up. And there was a thing in there, he said, you could get combs and little toys from.

I was saying no in a kind of reflex, but gentle, then I found myself clutching at him, squeezing him to me with my free hand tight around his shoulders. He stopped chattering in mid-sentence and stared up at me confused, then impatient with the vagaries of mother love. He wriggled away and started a circle of little hops around us, like some obscure rain dance, while I tried to sherpa Keturah and the bags for the trek to the street. I kept stopping in the middle of things to reach out for Thomas, running my hand distracted over his scruffy blond head.

Have you ever seen a little boy's cock? Maybe this is just for mothers somehow, but it's so delicate, so heart-string minuscule and temporary-looking, like a graft that might not take if you're careless. In the tunnels of the stations hiking to the street I kept thinking of Thomas's tiny elfin cock and wondering why I had to have my men's-room horror back there. I kept thinking of that nightmare cleavered-off stump of it I had to live through while I waited for him in the hall. Why the free sample, the gratuitous agonies mothers get?

People on the street are looking at me. Women especially, who give you this quick appraiser's look. Then they search the kids again and give you a second sideways look, heads cocked like chickens, to determine if you're that pervert, that child-buggerer and kidnapper they know is out there.

Those looks are why I keep myself scrupulous in public, a *Family Circle* man. Never look too young, or old, is the secret. Never wear a raincoat. If you can't look proud, look stern. Jeans are not worn by such men, who also shave hourly.

Once at the beginning, years ago, I had to go unkempt with a sick baby for some medicine. I had to slink along the sidewalk like a stoat because of looks I got. I broadcast guilt like an underarm. Thomas was tiny then and I hadn't learned to hold him cocked on a hip. I carried him instead like a bag of wet garbage, at arm's length, as if afraid he'd drip on me.

Clearly I wasn't his mother that day. Only by abdicating their maternal duties did women fail to turn me in. I did see one woman approach a cop. I thought she pointed in my direction but nothing happened. I was probably invisible to him, being unthinkable. Only mothers run errands with sick babies.

* * *

I am carrying Keturah now, Sisyphian, trundling us uphill against the rush-hour crowds. Chanting. "No sweat. Just a few blocks. No sweat. Just a few blocks"—my mother mantra, to keep back the Hyena. My ligaments are fraying from the strain and giant spasms of backed-up bile are surfing over me.

"No sweat," they'd said. "Take the bus," they'd said, my bumpkin childless city friends. "Just a few blocks." Ever notice how the mind dries up when people remain childless? How insulated are the nulliparous, like the rich, from the intricate perversity of life's little corners?

Sometimes when I'm at my most absorbed I find myself chanting out loud. Mother mantra of the day. And people looking at me weird. But no one in this city is looking at me weird, no one is looking at all, I discover. They're deep in anaphylactic shock, apparently, staring cataracts ahead of them.

Ever see a frenzied parent and two children on a bus? The Hyena would be proud. You put down the suitcase for a free hand as the bus pulls up, shove the ambulatory kid hard enough to get him up the stairs. He falls, of course, pathetic and scared you pushed him so hard. People behind you sigh and shove forward. The bus driver stares like a grouper, clicking his change machine. You reach and wrench the kid upright by his fishbone arm, shove and lift him dislocated till he's perched by the fare machine. The suitcase now has people leaning on it as you reach back, then hurl yourself, the baby, and the bag aboard. You're wedged awkward at the top of the bus steps, scrabbling for change you couldn't have ready because you had no free hands. The door slashes shut, the bus lurches off. The standing kid flushes down the aisle, tottering, no one reaching for him—till he tumbles halfway to the back. You punch in the fare, off-balance yourself, lunge for the suitcase rocking by the steps, and

Mother's Day

tightrope down the aisle after the kid, holding the baby, hoping you won't fall. People are staring hatpins at you for discomposing their transit coma.

A dilapidated, marginally female senior citizen has struggled to her cane to make a seat. You crunch into the space too shamed to look at her, hissing at the kid to get up off the floor. The baby's shoes graze your neighbor's sleeve. You are looking at your own shoes. People work hard to trip over the suitcase as they rush the exit every stop. Keturah is crying because you are squeezing her instead of lashing out at them. You try to make comforting noises to her, acceptable in public. You smile molasses at her like Aunt Jemima and watch a warm, fatuous reflection from some gullible childless face across the aisle.

Thomas did not get caught in the mechanical door when he tumbled from the bus, but he did sideswipe dogshit in the gutter and walked on the sides of his feet, looking, for the next block. Then he started crying because he was tired and couldn't walk anymore.

"Just a few blocks," I was chanting at him. "No sweat, Thomas, no motherfucking sweat." But now Thomas is sniveling, ontogenies of self-pity shaking his suddenly hideous, simian face. I want again to kick him since I've no free hands. He knows it, debating, you can see, the tactical advantages of a continuous high pitch of attention, honed finer with whining, against the temporary moral credit of a received swift kick. He opts for the intensity, of course. Intensity, however venomous, any kid prefers to even the most benign neglect.

Keturah has either gone to sleep or suffocated from the pressure of my anger. At least she is silent as we wait for the light at Second Avenue. Thomas feinted into traffic for a while, watching me, then switched to gagging. I could kill him now without remorse. People with us here are looking to see what I will do to this noisome kid, discomfiting their self-absorption. They are outraged at such license. I am doing nothing, staring at the pavement, marvelling at the varieties of dogshit, city geology, underfoot.

This morning on the train in from the country, Keturah had begun to gag like Thomas now is doing. That time I thought she had inhaled something small and lethal the way babies you read about do. Trying not to look high-strung about it, I turned her discreetly upside down in the seat and slugged her between the shoulder blades. It hadn't helped much. She continued to gag. But since she began crying monsoons as well and had breath enough for that, I just waited and the gagging passed. Now I realize the smell of the city caused it. The particulate, oven-cleaner edge to the air is an insult to both kids, country kids who'd never noticed breathing before.

Myself, I become fine-honed by city air. Oxygen deprivation. It inhibits vital circuitry and the rush from deprived cells is a merciful, exhilarating suspension of standards. Even the smell of poached urine and hot oil that gutters up from Seventy-seventh Street today is like a tonic.

Not for Thomas. He is really hoking it up now, clasping his throat, screwing his healthy open Corn Flakes features into those of a well-preserved mummy.

If they'd told me it was a sixth-floor walk-up, I wouldn't have come. The utter unreasoning stupidity of childless people. Six floors? With two demented, jelly-limbed children? And six floors down and back for every diaper run out, spilled last milk?

I become particularly round-shouldered when the world looms large like this. Also I diminish in size. On the stoop of the apartment building, staring at the rusty fire escapes up the outside, I feel like a dwarf, shrunk with self-pity.

When we finally got here, I had slumped on the front street steps, abandoning myself to pigeon shit and the day's incineration. I had pointed high into the clambering, junk-encumbered fire escapes for Thomas to see where we were going. Maybe he would rise to the occasion, forswear his mime show for a moment and brave those marble steps, grey and Himalayan, that I had glimpsed in the hall beyond the security door. Now my left arm wouldn't work to ring 6B. Rigor mortis from the suitcase. If I tried to shift Keturah she would wake and cry. Finally the arm worked, feeble, and the bell went in silent. Did it ring up there? Then I heard my friends Basil and Joanne, far away outside it seemed, shouting my name down into the traffic clatter of the street.

CHAPTER IV

Even filtered through the traffic, their voices sound so young. I wonder if Cindy and I ever sounded like that.

Four years ago it would have been us high in a city place like this, buoyed by traffic, us shouting through open summer windows at visitors below.

Four years. That would be just before children. I'm no longer always sure there was a time before children. Everything these days seems more or less unlikely.

Four years ago you still made lewd remarks at passing women, for instance, particularly in stuffy Washington. We called it Capitol Offense, Pat and I, and points were awarded for high degrees of fluster. Pat painted houses for a living and said the fumes skewed his mind. His other game was looking local by the monuments, then making hideous pantomime of deaf and dumb when people asked him directions.

Cindy didn't fluster easily. And her friend one evening

going. Maybe he would rise to the occasion, forswear his mime show for a moment and brave those marble steps, grey and Himalayan, that I had glimpsed in the hall beyond the security door. Now my left arm wouldn't work to ring 6B. Rigor mortis from the suitcase. If I tried to shift Keturah she would wake and cry. Finally the arm worked, feeble, and the bell went in silent. Did it ring up there? Then I heard my friends Basil and Joanne, far away outside it seemed, shouting my name down into the traffic clatter of the street.

CHAPTER IV

Even filtered through the traffic, their voices sound so young. I wonder if Cindy and I ever sounded like that.

Four years ago it would have been us high in a city place like this, buoyed by traffic, us shouting through open summer windows at visitors below.

Four years. That would be just before children. I'm no longer always sure there was a time before children. Everything these days seems more or less unlikely.

Four years ago you still made lewd remarks at passing women, for instance, particularly in stuffy Washington. We called it Capitol Offense, Pat and I, and points were awarded for high degrees of fluster. Pat painted houses for a living and said the fumes skewed his mind. His other game was looking local by the monuments, then making hideous pantomime of deaf and dumb when people asked him directions.

Cindy didn't fluster easily. And her friend one evening

Mother's Day

shot us both the finger in response. Which seemed so promising we followed them six blocks in the rain to Tasso's Bar near Dupont Circle. Weeks later Cindy said she'd liked my legs—all that showed of me except my yellow slicker. I hadn't known that women cared about the legs, I said.

Her friend called Mimi cared about the lewd remark. After whispered altercations by the ladies room, Cindy announced to me that she and I were staying at my place because Pat and Mimi had pressing business at hers. I remember walking late from Tasso's up New Hampshire Avenue. The rain had stopped and the streets were slippery with fallen chestnut blossoms. When the blossoms underfoot change to broken glass, I said to Cindy, you knew you were near the apartment. She laughed with just the proper mix of spleen and unconcern that in those days passed for worldliness. Pat's word for it was "carapace" and though, provoked, it earned no points, it was something tangible to ponder in your solitary moments.

I did, I think, ponder most of that night alone and several after it. Cindy'd said she'd sleep, thanks anyway, on the couch, and I listened to the breaking bottles on the streets below, the sirens, the hilarity, the curses, and I thought about that tempered laughter, cool and thoughtful in the empty midnight streets we'd seemed to own.

"Sand" was what I said to Pat. "Remember your Huck Finn?"

"As a matter of fact—no."

"Well, never mind. But she's got sand. Not like Mimi, who's a can of worms."

"Always a fucking moralist, eh Vole?"

"You're the one who said that first—"

"Maybe, but what I say is jest, not earnest prolegomena. And anyway, it's not the sand but tits you like of hers. Don't try to tell me otherwise."

The tits were, yes, a factor, as was the laugh and easy

elegance. Fine auburn hair, cool to the touch, and a firm long body that glided as she walked. In other words, I'd found myself a focus for the lazy loneliness of being twenty-five. And some ballast for the lopsided piss-ant earnestness of graduate school. Huck Finn, for instance, was for a seminar in humor, to be taken seriously indeed.

Cindy never did, seeming to my eyes profound in her silences, listening and laughing to my tales of school, seeming to have known it all already.

One thing she didn't know was how much someone in that silence wanted a baby. She didn't find that out till she'd mysteriously miscalculated once too often and found herself back from her doctor one morning, distracted.

"Well," I remember calmly saying, "I think we're ready. Don't you?"

"I don't know, Matt. I really don't know. I could always go back later to finish up, I guess. Maybe I'd even like it better then. Think my scholarship'd still be good?"

Ah, what a wondrous adult I thought I made in those days. Things were so simple. I'd read the treatises, the tragic tales, the statistics. I knew about priorities. ZPG be damned, this was real life and in real life you make the human decision—right? Humane, of course, as well. We men must embrace our responsibilities. No bounders or cads need apply.

"And besides, Cindy, maybe it's time we got going. We aren't minors, for Christ's sake. I can finish graduate school and you can cultivate the future. Our future."

I believe my voice matured decades that speech. I remember listening serene as I talked, nodding gravely to myself at the wondrous wise words. We wouldn't be like those couples before us. No harsh, recriminating words. No family cringes. No coat hangers, kitchen clinics. You don't destroy life just because it might be inconvenient. Yes, now there'd have to be money for babysitters, we'd have to postpone hitchhiking in Europe, but then having babies was what grownups do, like giving dinner parties.

We didn't even tell the parents, so grownup we were. They'd only fuss. Our generation is so much more realistic, so informed. This was, after all, *our* decision, and anyway Cindy's parents would object for typically old-fashioned, irrelevant reasons. Also they would sulk. No way she could still be a virgin, now, and I was somewhat left of Mr. Right.

I had wanted, actually, to tell my parents. They would have approved. But since we weren't telling hers we couldn't in all fairness tell mine. But I knew what they would say. My father would look grave and speak of the necessity for doing the right thing by Cindy. My mother would look a little sad. She had always felt children were too serious this generation. "You never dance, for instance. We used to have such *fun* dancing," she'd say. But she would have smiled bravely after a moment, then started raiding her clipping file for useful childbearing hints.

So it was the Criminal Courts Building, at nine-thirty one genial October morning. Mimi came as witness and giggler. She did the nervousness for us. She put the clerk straight about the "will-this-be-a-one-or-two-ring-ceremony" stuff, then almost ended married to me when she stood in the wrong place as we were paraded in front of a harried judge, third party in a string of eight.

"This is what the Middle East calls 'pastrami summer,'" I said as we left the gloomy chambers into the hot autumn sunlight. Mimi shrieked with laughter for some reason. Cindy said nothing till we reached Tasso's. Then she said we ought to have Bloody Marys, because she needed fortification for the future.

"And tonight I'm having champagne," Cindy announced. "I'm not sure it's good for my teeny fellow traveller here"—she described a generous semi-circle with her right arm from her breasts to her knees—"but what the hell. You think so, Matt?"

"You have champagne and I'll have hemlock. This scares me all of a sudden. Maybe we could just drop this course late in the trimester?"

"But you're our grownup," said Mimi, trying to look outraged. "You can't say stuff like that. You can't even feel stuff like that. If you think today is bad, wait till the parents find out."

Thomas was born in April in Connecticut. Washington is no place for babies. I had a graduate paper due in three days. I took my notes with me to the labor room and coached Cindy through her breathing. Psychoprophylaxis.

It was all so solemn. My paper was on the roots of Celtic literature and after eight hours of Cindy's labor I began to feel that birth was a druid ceremony. Primitive, incantatory, sacrificial. White robes, ritual, blood. Cindy lost control sometime around then, too, and began crying out like other women in the curtained stalls around us. A nurse kept giving her shots that didn't work, finally one that set her adrift into a private world of pain and annoyance. She talked passionately about the broccoli in the freezer at home. She talked a kind of labor-room demotic, absurd and ungainly, like opera in your native tongue.

The nurses talked baby-talk to me. I was talking to them about contractions, dilation, show. "Oh, yes?" They'd say. "Then we're making progress, aren't we, Mr. Vole?"

I outlined three versions of my paper before it was time. Then some new kind of nurse was walking a green gown on me from the front, smiling phisohex. Then an OR mask and Ben Casey hat. Cindy had finally stopped it about the broccoli. Now she was grunting like a wild boar. After everybody's rubber fingers had been removed from her and the nurse lurched her bed toward the delivery room, she called out my name, blurred and far away.

Why am I telling you all this? It's all more painful than I thought. Progeny recapitulates phylogeny—maybe that's it—

Mother's Day

and the stages each have unseen dues to pay. You think that makes sense?

If so, you need to know about the doctor.

Here was this little man. He had always looked big enough behind his desk before, but here he was, this leprechaun of a man in white, checking his watch.

He waved me to a stool at the head of the delivery table. Cindy's knees were propped up and the gown rode the top of them so I couldn't see anything. The magic doctor. I was angry with him and asked if they could please adjust the mirror above her so I could see. I felt like some pervert. The drug was fading, I mumbled, this way Cindy, too, can see. I soothed her forehead, which was slippery with sweat.

"Those forceps, Doctor Blake? There in the rack?" I wanted him to know I knew. I'd read the books. He liked the question for some reason. He looked at me for the first time.

"Yeah, but we won't need them. She's doing good work, aren't you, Cindy? Now push hard with the next one. Don't hold back."

There was some mumbling down there with a nurse. And the doctor, like a stage magician, hiking his cuffs.

"Oh, and give him gloves, too, please. Thank you. Want to come around now?" He looked from under his eyebrows at me as I picked my way round to the working end.

I got to watch the episiotomy—why did the doctor arrange that?—which looked like scissors cutting a stretched pink balloon. I watched the head bulldoze through. Then the face turning up. No one I knew, more like someone's puppy, or a baby seal.

"Here," the doctor said. "Put your hands behind the arms. If you drop him I'm in trouble."

Actually the doctor was holding, too. I was trying to concentrate on the awe of the moment but couldn't. I was looking for signs of breathing—didn't that come next?—and worrying about the cord, which looked like fish guts. "What are we going to call him, Cindy? Huh? It's a him. Yes."

The nurse at her head repeated. "A boy. Got all his outdoor plumbing, too. See?"

I don't know if Cindy saw. She looked passed out. Someone hooked a gadget into the baby's mouth for mucus while the doctor cut the cord. Clamp. Cut. Faster than you can say it. I winced but no one connected seemed to feel a thing. The baby was wrapped in a towel as the doctor took quick stitches in Cindy's split vagina. All I could think of was a fisherman mending his nets.

What I have been wanting to assure you is that we did it by the book. How you did things then.

I was greedy. I wanted part of everything. Cindy had no milk for days so I helped feed formula. When they came home I did every other feeding at night. I wanted that. I held the baby when it coughed and cried and puked and snorgled and garphed and whistled like a dolphin. Sometimes I fell asleep feeding the baby. Sometimes the baby fell asleep, and I watched him amazed at the intricate throbbing machinery, working, working when there seemed nothing substantial to keep it going.

After Washington, this isolated farmhouse in the Connecticut woods seemed to be floating in silence. Late at night I thought I could hear the baby's heartbeat. Only the fussing of the wind in the pine trees or fluid ticking in the refrigerator.

When Cindy fed Thomas at night—he became Thomas in about a week—she turned on the light in our bedroom for some reason, energized as if it were day. She also took pictures and I have one in my wallet here of me asleep with my arm on the baby. I am unshaven, fagged out. The dog is also on the bed, staring flash-cubed at the camera. The baby looks out of proportion, small and rather pointed like a Martian.

There was snow late in April and there is also a picture of

the baby, buried in red swaddling clothes, being wheeled by Cindy in the carriage. You can see carriage tracks back and forth across the white lawn behind. Contrary to what your mother-in-law would tell you, said the books, cold air was OK for newborns.

Spring days that I didn't teach or have seminars, I walked with Thomas. Cindy would sleep. I would perch Thomas in the back-carrier and hike. You couldn't see the baby up there behind you but you could feel him warm against your back, riding, and soon falling asleep, bumping gently against you with each step.

We lived on the edge of old woods and I walked for hours some afternoons through the pines and scrub down to a long thin lake that in winter had deer tracks across it in the snow like punctuation. I remember sitting on a rock in the sun one hot blue spring day, watching a striped grey snake work off his skin against a fallen pine. Thomas slept the whole time and I have never felt quieter in my life.

Old timers call them weather-breeders, such days. Mercifully few such memories.

Weather moves counter-clockwise, so it becomes difficult to talk of chronology. Irrelevant almost. What we ought to speak about is choreography, a kind of antique masque. I sometimes think what follows should be accompanied on harpsichord—formal, baroque, touchingly clockwork like our lives. Other times, bitter ones, I think of myself then as a pawn, one of those emissaries who thought he understood but instead was being used in far more elaborate, Byzantine plots.

Either way, I will spare us as much of this as possible. Already I haven't told you of my fatuous telegram home when Thomas was born. Or about my skinhead strutting at school when my colleagues heard about the baby.

And there were endless scenes, excruciating now, of Matt

and Cindy cooing in unison over the cradle, pecking and rocking like parakeets.

Shudder if you like. I do.

In a way I suppose this has a fine cautionary line and I should just get on with it. Life is anyway practice, most of it, for the few important moments. Maybe we can excuse this whole period, pass it off as practice. A dry run. There is a kind of DNA about what follows, conclusions lying foregone all over the place. So read it with compassion. Or kid gloves.

If it hadn't been the sixties, I might never have taken the necessary risks. A few years earlier and I'd have left Thomas to Cindy. A few years earlier and Cindy wouldn't have known any better. We might have survived—if that is not too grand a word for ignorance perpetuated. But in the sixties you were expected to liberate yourself from such ignorances.

New opportunities nurture new risks. Mothering, for instance, is contagious and I spent more time with Thomas than I should have. Most men are protected from overexposure by their work. But I was home for days at a time between classes, then constantly through that first summer.

I studied with Thomas, the baby crooked in one elbow, a clipboard in the other. I'd wait for Cindy to go to bed, then haul Thomas from his crib for warmth and company while I read late into the night. Thomas would sleep propped up next to me in an old overstuffed green rocker, waking from time to time to smile secretively or babble at me or drink noisily from his bottle.

Twice we had gigantic thunderstorms. The skies around us turned black in the face with storm, the dog slunk nervous under a bed and Cindy became edgy. I don't quite know what propelled me—maybe the atmospherics pressing on the glands—but both times I wrapped Thomas in a towel and rushed out into the crashes of thunder and the thrashing of the rain. I'd whirl and shriek with him like a witch at sabbath, Thomas wide-eyed and breathless with terror and pleasure. Cindy said she worried we'd be struck by lightning.

At first Cindy seemed pleased with my attention to Thomas. She said my coming home between classes was a relief from the unexpected strain. "I seem to carry him more now," Cindy said, "than when I was pregnant. How can that be?"

"Maybe it's because he rests when he's not working. We work."

But that work, even the most menial of baby chores, was tonic to me after the majestic boredom of graduate school. Besides, one of those things nobody tells you is that children earn their way. Maybe women don't notice—they expect it—but tend a baby and you reconstellate your responses. Babies are strange radioactive creatures whose effect is elemental, mutagenic. Tend them enough and you develop new molecules, new glands.

Before, I'd always found babies hideous. That disquieting smell, that awkward, flabby helplessness, that obscene urgency. It was a mystery to me why women homed in on these creatures, why they cooed and purred over them the way they do nothing else. Some helpless infantile closet part of me resented it: why weren't they cooing and purring over me?

Pressing the flesh was all it took. Caring for Thomas only a few weeks, I grew new possibilities of intimacy. Caring for babies is a physical language. No wonder no one could tell. I caught myself in strange involuntary Mona Lisa smiles. I learned to relax a baby by caressing it. I found myself secretly touching parts of Thomas I'd never imagined I could.

You speak to babies with your hands and I became fluent and uninhibited. So much touching, so much naked tactile honesty became profound relief—a living syntax of feeling always before mute. Before Thomas was born I worried what feelings for a male child might be ominously homosexual—that's how abstract men are brought up to be. Now as I kissed Thomas' body, nibbling and nuzzling him into shrieks of pleasured laughter, I thought only that baby skin smelled as clean as pebbles in a stream.

Sometimes Cindy and I brought Thomas to bed with us, a naked baby between naked parents, confirmation of our arrival as adults. When Thomas was restless or uncomfortable warm flesh calmed him. We found ways to lie in each other's arms with Thomas secure between us. Sometimes Cindy offered me one breast while Thomas worked the other. I was far less fond of mother's milk than Thomas—it was watery, as I remember, almost sour—but I welcomed Cindy's now rare moments of carnal interest in me. Most of the time we seemed to mime at sex, at best, and I felt increasingly confused, guilty about my needs. My arousals made me feel ugly and sophomoric.

But Thomas at Cindy's breast pleased me. Appropriate ritual replacement, I told myself. A proper family portrait. An ancient satisfaction, a kind of profound orderliness. Suitable for framing.

Think of a see-saw. Childplay. One goes down so another can go up. Who exactly is up and who exactly is down and where those places might be is not always clear in this case. But they are opposite. The force that drives the machines produces opposites.

There was the day in November when I got back from work early. Cindy was tired and Thomas had been in his playpen, screaming, when I came in the door. In a rush of affection and sympathy mixed with indignation at Cindy's indifference, I scooped Thomas from his playpen and started tossing him high into the air. Thomas was first scared, then screeching with delight, drooling and smiling. His eyes shined with relief and trust.

I caught Cindy looking sideways at me.

"Cindy? What's wrong?"

"Nothing. Nothing. You watch it though, throwing him around like that. He's been sick all day. And if he pukes again you get to clean it up. Understand?"

I don't think I did understand till just recently, when I felt some of the same anger Cindy did. One of my effusive single women friends. You don't mind help with the kid—most times you think you crave it—but you resent doing most of the work, then watching someone else give him the play you didn't have time for. And you resent the way the child loves that person, immediately, unequivocally, and doesn't even notice you are there.

I suppose it was also about November when Thomas became feverish about an hour before I was due at school. The university was a half hour of country roads away and the pediatric clinic fifteen minutes in the opposite direction.

"He'll be all right till I get back. It's probably nothing."

"But he's got a high fever, Matt, I can tell."

"He's had them before and they've just gone away. It'll be fine, Cindy. I can't miss my class, can I? That's how I pay for all this. That's how I pay the goddamn doctor."

"But Thomas is *sick*, Matt. I know it. Are your *students* sick?"

I drove to work in a rage, shouting at strangers along the road.

The more I had to work, the more Cindy withdrew. I became confused and angry—often with no apparent reason. The more I involved myself with Thomas, the more Cindy resented me. The more she resented the more critical of her I became.

Increasingly, Thomas seemed to be screaming when I got back from work. Or when I had urgent work at home. Cindy couldn't seem to keep him clean any more. His playpen and crib crawled with crumbs, filthy toys, and soiled sheets. There was food everywhere in the house. His clothes were always filthy. He needed to be changed. I came to feel that I had to do everything at home and still be the one working to pay for it all.

For a while before Christmas things improved. Cindy started sewing again and made Thomas a blue terrycloth jumpsuit. She knitted him red mittens for his first Christmas, and a red pointed hat. Thomas tried to eat the Christmas-tree ornaments. He managed to snatch down a string of bubble lights. Cindy took pictures of him sizing up the tree or butting it with his head. You can see the lights reflected in the dark winter windows behind.

My parents came for three days. They seemed tired most of the time. I had a paper on Wordsworth but I kept Thomas with me in the study to give the grandparents some peace. Cindy kept the place spotless and sat next to me on the couch when we talked.

We needed more money after Christmas so I began spending more time at work. I begged another teaching section. Thomas interfered with everything I did at home so I stayed at the office. I started to go to university meetings where people like me argued about free schools, changing women, day care. You had to be in touch with yourself, people said. It would flow from that.

"I think—if you will forgive the expression—that's bullshit." I was angry about a lot of things. Cindy's mother was visiting and she had opinions. And all the sullen medieval fanaticism about spoiled children. I thought I now saw why Cindy was hard with Thomas at times.

"Matt!" Cindy was horrified at my anger.

"Your mother is familiar with the expression, I'm sure. Aren't you Mrs. Franks? And anyway what I am saying is that all these rules for kids were dreamed up merely for the convenience of petty adults, nothing else."

"But Matt. Mother's not talking about punishment. She's talking about discipline. Or didn't you hear her?"

"I heard. And the words sound the same to me. I'm not saying—"

"Sound the same? Now come, Matt. Cindy was given discipline as a child. I'm sure you were, too. That's how you grow."

"I'm not saying you don't grow that way. I'm saying you grow distorted that way. Warped and tidy, like an orchard. The way that's gotten this world into so much trouble. Discipline is fascism, dipped in bronze for mothers."

Later that spring Cindy and I had long discussions. Mostly I did the discussing. I spoke passionately about distinctions. This was my favorite at the time: "There are two kinds of people, Cindy," I would say, leaning earnestly toward her on my chair, already annoyed because she seemed so engrossed in her knitting. "Just two kinds. Those who prefer order over freedom and those who prefer freedom over order. Violence—call it discipline if you want—breeds fear and fear makes you want order. That's what the good folks of the Granite State seem to have taught you, Cindy. Fear."

Cindy never said much. Mostly when she did she sighed and said she agreed with me. She thought I was probably right. It made sense, she said.

"I *know* it does, Cindy. It has to. Look. Hitting a child just teaches him to hit. Disciplining a child just teaches him to discipline others, to keep *them* down when he grows up. We've had enough of that. Nothing will change till we're willing to hold back all our fascisms and let these children grow free."

I told Cindy it was hard for her because she was from New England. I smiled and said her Calvinism was showing.

After these talks, things would seem possible for a while. The willows by the stream were turning phone-book yellow. Cindy put the aluminum chairs on the lawn. Thomas took his first steps one day when we were talking so hard we almost missed them. He teetered from one chair to the other, digging his fat toes into the soft new green grass.

In June we decided to have another child. Thomas needed a playmate. An only child grows up weird, the books said.

We smiled a lot more after that. Cindy took her temperature each day to catch the ovulation. Lovemaking on schedule seemed clinical and delicious at the same time, like those adolescent fantasies about doctors' examinations.

I remember imagining an old family album, years later. We would have had a little girl who would cling to her father in ribbons. Thomas would be solemn the way little boys are. Cindy would be looking proud. She would be wearing her yellow Indian print, and her auburn hair would be soft and shiny like the night we were married. Cindy had put it up that night so she could take it down for me when we made love. Mimi had brought us three champagne glasses as a present and we had taken pictures of each other looking embarrassed. Then I climbed drunk out the southwest window and crawled along the thirteenth-story ledge toward the north.

There was a pressing reason for having another baby, but Cindy and I never saw it. How could we? You have a baby—or buy a new house—when your marriage is failing. Then you live happily ever after. It's called playing house.

By the time Keturah was born it only remained for Cindy to say the obvious, which she did one day eight weeks later, after a desperate argument that seemed to have something to do with my cramming for my Ph.D. exams, the unpaid bills, and the mess in the livingroom.

The second pregnancy had been awful. In its last two months I was not permitted a whole night's sleep. Cindy had gained forty pounds and her back ached constantly. I spent hours each night rubbing it, fighting massive spasms of sleep. I often fell asleep between strokes, dreaming I still rubbed, only to wake with a jolt and find Cindy sobbing quietly at my selfish unconcern. Twice during the pregnancy Cindy bled profusely and spent weeks motionless in bed thwarting miscarriage. Her biology may have known better than she did.

Thomas cried for the last three months straight. Or so it seemed to me, who always found him in his crib, or locked in his room, when I rushed back from work. Cindy would be asleep or lying exhausted on the couch. Thomas would be screaming spasmodically, puffy and wet with sweat.

Sometime about then I stopped trying to make sense of it. I began in fact to pretend nothing had happened. I would rush upstairs and free Thomas, soothing him and chattering to him, bringing him toys or lollipops or cookies to stop crying. I contrived to have errands away from the house each day, bundling Thomas in outdoor clothes and disappearing with him for hours. Often we would just park the car by some woods and walk, Thomas chattering in what now sounded like Armenian while I rocked him in my arms and rubbed his cool face against my afternoon stubble.

I began to skip most of my seminars, Cindy seemed so bad. I tried to comfort her but each time became enraged for reasons I couldn't place. We had bitter arguments about what Thomas should be allowed to do. Thomas would look on, crying at the hard words, crying when someone threw things, crying at my sudden menacing quiet voice.

When I could manage it I slept alone. Usually I took Thomas to bed with me, rocking him to sleep, soothing, calming us both. If I awoke at night and heard Cindy pacing slowly around the room, or crying quietly to herself, I would force myself to go into her room and offer help. Usually I fell asleep before I could do much good, only to be awakened again and again by Cindy's miseries. Sometimes, rubbing her back, exploring the muscles with my hands, I found myself stricken with unexpected love and longing for her.

"Cindy?" I would whisper. "Are you awake? You feel delicious, you know?"

"No, Matt. No. I feel like shit. That's how I feel."

Keturah was born premature, a tiny wizened froglet in a plastic bubble when I first saw her. No delivery-room charades this time. Cindy had wanted full anesthesia—much to the satisfaction of the hospital staff. They were tired, the nurse told me, of all those people pretending they knew a better way. I spent several hours in the fathers' waiting room with a beefy man in his forties whose wife was having her fourth. No, *he'd* never been in the delivery room, that's for sure. "If God had intended men to be in the delivery room"— he laughed—"he wouldn't have invented bars."

Cindy stayed at the hospital ten days. The nurses fed the baby, even after it was out of the incubator. Cindy felt mostly sick, she said, and she was afraid she'd give the baby some disease. I wanted to take Thomas to see Keturah but the hospital wouldn't allow it.

I rush over the rest because there isn't much to tell. Cindy returned with Keturah, coped a while like some kind of electric device. Abstract, efficient, distant. She was suddenly too calm with Thomas and me, silent and mechanical with Keturah. I noticed that she spoke very quietly, even when she was angry—which was often. Within days of her return she cleaned everything, washed under the radiators where little forests of food had grown from Thomas' scatterings. She stripped all the beds and washed them down. The nursery smelled constantly of Lysol. Once I woke at night to find her spraying shoes in the closet. She had turned on all the lights in the room and was methodically spraying each pair.

"Christ, Cindy! What the hell—?"

"It's OK, Matt. Go back to sleep." She spoke very quietly. "I'm done."

Two days later she was packing to leave. The argument had begun because I said I had to spend the day in the library for my exam in modern poetry. She had announced calmly that I would have to take the kids or get someone to stay with them. She wasn't feeling up to it.

"You're never feeling up to it anymore."

"I guess you're right, Matt. I guess so."

"God damn it, Cindy. I've got to go today. My exam is next week. Most fucking graduate students spend a year studying for this. I'm allowing myself a week. You have to cope. You have to."

"I can't."

"You can't. You can't. You can't seem to do anything any more. The goddamn living room is swimming in all the shit you can't seem to do. TV Guides. Kleenex. Ashtrays. Yesterday I found Thomas drawing circles on the floor in ashes and old butts. This is your family, too, Cindy. You can't just stop now, right in the middle—"

"Matt—"

"You've got to help. Now, first—"

"MATT! Listen one minute. You never listen, but listen. This was your idea. Thomas was your idea and Keturah was your idea and the noble savage is your idea and the Ph.D. is your idea and cleaning up the ashtrays is your idea. You do all this so fucking well and I'm no good at any of it. I am the child-abuser. I am the fucking Calvinist. I am always tired and you're always full of energy."

She stopped to catch her breath. Her eyes were dry but the sockets were purple and her face was an intense glaring gray like the light before summer electric storms. She had been sitting on the window ledge next to Keturah's crib but now she was walking toward the hall door where I stood, holding a handful of diapers in one hand and a large safety pin in the other. The head of the safety pin was blue with a white happyface painted on it.

"It was your idea, Matt. You do it all so well, Matt. You

wanted all this, Matt. Well, take it. Now you can do it just right. Your way." She straightened herself as she got near me. "Let me by, Matt. *Let me by!* You wanted them and now you got them. I don't want to see any of you again. I mean that, Matt. Now leave me alone. Don't pull at my god damned sleeve. You're always pulling at something, nagging at something, whining like my mother."

I'd like to say it was shock kept me quiet during that speech. But it wasn't. It was relief. And guilt at the relief, like you feel when something dies.

That was four months ago. A life ago. In nuclear physics there is a phenomenon called the Cerenkov effect. Radioactive material stored under water gives off an eerie rose-colored light. Radioactivity is decay, energy, which moves water molecules so fast they glow. When I look back on those last months of marriage I see it outlined in rose. It's more like somebody else's marriage, really—intense molecular activity, underwater.

Even to *say* energy tires me now. I haven't experienced energy in the last four months. I think Cindy took the last of it away with her in those two plaid bags that day. Since then there has been fatigue, despair, anger. Never energy.

No, that's not quite true. For some days after she left I felt a kind of fearsome strength, probably stored-up righteousness, indignation, and satisfaction. But that passed. It wasn't until we were coming down here to New York on the train this morning, just after Keturah began that gagging I told you about, that I felt what might have been energy. Maybe, though, it was just oxygen deprivation, city high. Anyway, now Thomas and I are looking straight up again through the black rusty fire escapes, trying to see around the old mops and flowerpots and stray boards to where Basil's and Joanne's voices have come down into the street.

CHAPTER V

Joanne oozed mother from the moment we got upstairs. I can read them now like books and Joanne was text perfect—birth-canal fever.

Keturah was whisked away from my arthritic right arm, jounced and dimpled and pinched to distraction. Thomas clung sullen and downcast to my left pant leg, silent after bassoons of weeping in the stairwell moments ago. At least four separate tenants on our way up opened their doors to see what inhuman monster was torturing children on the steps. Galvanized by the noise, then the attention, Keturah had awakened as we marched up, brightly squeezing out tears for each apartment in turn.

In the lobby when he first saw the stairs, Thomas had dragged at my sleeve, crying, then regressed into a jellied coelenterate sprawled on the dirty marble steps at the first floor. He had bawled in surges like a pulsar. Joanne clattered down to the second floor and took the bag—Keturah had screeched in outrage when Joanne first tried to carry her

49

away. Basil, whose grand idea it had been for me to come seemed already to be suffering second thoughts. He had barely dragged himself down as far as the fourth floor, but he did hoist Thomas kicking onto his shoulders for the ride up.

But now Joanne is cooing with Keturah on the couch. Basil is talking and I am looking at Joanne, doing a checklist. Good eyes, brown with a touch of Tartar interloper somewhere along an otherwise faultless Jewish line. Nicely turned breasts, it looks like, though Keturah obscures the view right now. I like the way Joanne tucks a leg up under to make a lap for Keturah. Long friendly brown hair. It matches Joanne's eyes and furls gently over Keturah's head in her lap. Basil has never had anyone move in with him before so I find myself thinking that Joanne's got to have talents.

Though you can't tell about talent as you could in the old days. Or I can't. It's not so simple, and in a peculiar way it doesn't even matter so much any more. Motherhood subverts.

This is somewhat vague and complicated, but I have begun to experience what I can only describe as lesbian alliances with some women. This is no androgyne surrender, understand, no shift to the platonic. More a kind of license, an abandon. A thaw.

It seems to go like this. In the way men often find themselves attracted to the tomboy (who seems relaxed, unmanipulative, one of the boys), certain child-bearing women are attracted to me, a mother. Even if they haven't actually had children yet, these women who labor toward it in their dreams, whose ovaries tingle with anticipation each month—these women get contractions around me. And I around them. I claim no feminist credit, however, since I don't understand or control the process, and since it makes me as much unquiet as enhanced. Anyway, somehow the gynarchical trappings of my daily routine with children triggers something deep in the female pituitary.

As it did for Joanne. For her, nurturing me and the children in her barren singles apartment was like coping with a sister's unexpected pregnancy—conspiratorial, delicious, intimate. While Basil talked of John Lilly, Mayor Lindsay, or the abstract mysteries of contemporary sexuality, Joanne and I exchanged seismic oscillations.

The kids and I had ventured into New York on a kind of quest. I had become crazed alone in the country. I had alarmed my neighbors, with whom I shared a brooding, prim New England farmhouse with meticulous stone fences and paper-thin walls. At first gently ("Don't you think the kids should see their mother in New York?") then less gently ("Was that the TV last night, Matt? All that shouting? And where are the kids, anyway, this morning?") my one-time intimate friends next door had begun urging me out of their sight.

Liberated and radical as we thought ourselves in 1969, a lone man-mother turning mad housewife was more than ideology could bear. A token male in day-care? Fine. Share the diapers and cooking? Better. But no one, least of all me, was ready to tolerate the symptoms of modern motherhood in a man, where they showed.

In women those symptoms had become invisible, because traditional. In a man they were disgrace. "Here," as ancient maps say at the edges, "be dragons."

Women with little children have been going mad for generations. No one pays attention as the mother declines into ontologic disarray, alienated from common adult behavior by a ragged, high-pitched festinating demeanor which at any other time would end her in the state home for the bewildered. During her mothering years she can canter ramshackle about, talking in tongues, belching fire at tiny, helpless children, ululate in public places—and the world looks on nodding sagely, content at ritual reenacted.

At me it looked daggers. Most of the time I didn't see them looking, too preoccupied in disbelief in myself. Soon I took down all the mirrors in the house. I told myself it was because the kids might break the rest as well, like the one down in the hall they destroyed by forcing me to throw a toy at it. But really I removed the mirrors to avoid that eye-bagged hairshirt visage staring goitered at me as I plunged by on nocturnal missions. During the day I mugged myself in them unthreatened, but by night, unprepared, I found Dorian Gray.

I think most of all the vocalizing did my neighbors in. Mothers have a coded tot language that threatens only children, but I didn't know it. Adult epithets directed at children carry special currency, like translated idioms. You hear them literally and are appalled. Children just read decibels, the smoke, and assay the risks. Adults listen to the words. My tidy neighbors, soft and literal in their domesticity, listened and were afraid.

"Now! Or I'll kill you. Break you in little pieces and flush you down the toilet. You scum! You snivelling little shit"— followed usually by an agonized, increasingly hoarse, incantatory "Fuck. Shit. Fuck-shit. Fuuuaaaaaaack!" and the ricochetting clatter of pelted objects.

My neighbors dreaded the mornings. From where they lay in their connubial, crenelated bed they would watch me scramble for my car in the driveway below their window. Always the children spared no effort to make me late, and always by the time we reached the driveway I had reached critical mass. I had to be at work by eight and it was an hour's drive to the babysitter and my teller's booth at the Montville Bank and Trust.

I found out later that one fine spring morning the neighbors were watching as I waded to the car through the debris of creative childplay. Hurdling playpens, rocking chairs and

Mother's Day

ride-em toys, dragging shoes, diapers, epithets, and two children turned paralytic by my haste, I looked behind in time to spot Keturah's baby bottle now rolling in the dirt. Her only available bottle, the fruit of fifteen ransacking minutes of search before we could leave.

I apparently stopped dead like they do in old movies, stared disbelieving, then whirled round to scoop it up and hurl it full force against the side of the car. I don't remember that part. I do remember that the morning was gentlest spring. Between curses and terrorized screams from the kids I noticed babyskin air, cucumber green from a night shower. As we straggled toward the car the maples by the front porch was oozing lubricious in the first morning sunlight. The door on the passenger side turned out to be locked, of course. I tripped on the garden hose as I flung myself around the car front to try the other side. Somewhere above me I could hear a starling calling liquid metal to its mate.

Both children were wailing harder by then, Thomas from a knee scraped on the driveway, Keturah from her usual bug-eyed terror at my urgency. For all she knew we were fleeing enemy attack. I remember upending her over the front seat into the back among the cookie shards and wall-to-wall used Kleenex. Thomas had to be heaved, like a side of New Zealand lamb, into the front. I couldn't put him in back with her. There was sure to be something pointed back there he could drive into a handy eyeball. Once in fatigue at the house I'd watched him take a number 2 pencil to her left eye. She hadn't even blinked, so tiny and trusting and pleased with the attention. Frustrated so often before in his practice runs, Thomas' aim was off and the only person hurt that time was me. I had taken a flying dive at him from the toilet where I'd been trying to complete a twice previously interrupted digestive maneuver. I tackled him away from her with my arm, slamming my back into the door jamb in the process.

On good days my car had one start in it. That morning

there had been rain and my chances were shaky. Everything had to go Indy perfect. I was screeching at the children for silence and listening like a test pilot for signs for life. Twenty thousand miles earlier the battery had begun to languish. Now it was terminal. Each cell could turn the engine one revolution. Period. I turned the key and the engine slurred to life.

I was backing frantically, peering bitterly at my watch, when the neighbor kid's tricycle got me. I heard a screech, a rough dragging collapse. The car stalled in surprise and I found myself exploded out my door in fury, pushing hugely at the back bumper, hauling on the mangled red and silver tricycle.

It wouldn't budge. Choking back sobs for air and lost innocence, rolling my eyes for celestial witness, I ran for the driver's seat again. I'd have to release the handbrake and let the car roll with the kids in it while I hauled from behind at the tricycle. If I did it right, my mind told me, I would sprint for the door as she rolled free, jump-start the car on the driveway hill before it levelled out. Brutal sobbing curses echoed hollow off the spring foliage.

Anyway. Maybe it had been that tricycle, I don't know, but after that morning the neighbors became urgent in their solicitude. I should go now to New York, they thought. Get out from under the strain, linger awhile among friends. Other friends. They were right, of course, and anyway the insinuation was clear: either I get out now, for awhile in New York, or very soon after for good.

CHAPTER VI

"OK. Out with it." Basil looks amused and his gray eyes crinkle at the corners. He's reaching for a cigarette from his shirt pocket, and his spikey black hair stands up at his cowlick, giving him a boyish look quite out of keeping with his carefully tailored Madison Avenue blue suit. "Out with it, I said."

"Out with what?"

"Vikes, Matt. Vikes."

"Now *that's* right, Keturah. Good girl—*vikes*?" Joanne has dislocated her attention from Keturah to squint animatedly at Basil. Keturah is stiff-arming a breast.

"Gimme the lighter, would you, Joanne? Thanks. Yes, Matthew, as I was saying: vikes. V-I-K-E-S. Secret male code word, dearest. Now cough up, Matt. You don't think I invited you here for nothing."

"Well. Let's see. Ahh. There's for instance Frances. I tell you about her?" I'm wondering what sister Joanne is going to think of this. "And oh, Joanne? *Joanne!* Forgive me for tearing you away, but Vi-Car-iouS thrills. Get it? You know, the stuff of raw experience for the sexually underdeveloped like our friend here."

"Fuck you, Vole," said Basil, interrupting a drag on his cigarette to protest.

"Fuck me? OK, if that's the way you want it—no vikes."

Keturah all this time has been methodically mauling one heartbreaking breast after the other. Joanne seems not to be noticing. I am peering at Basil, then Joanne, who are not noticing. They are waiting for the awful truth about Frances.

"Frances was my first rape. Late, I admit. It was this January and me past thirty. I'm at this normal party and this large crazed woman in double-knits starts to slap the make on me—"

"Matt, she have diapers? She's wet, needs to be changed."

"Yes, Joanne. Sure. You two'll have to hold your water about Frances a second —and you, my little wet rat, Keturah. How's my little wet rat, huh?" Keturah begins to drip down the side of her chunky left leg as I carry her to the bedroom to change. A golden shower for the Bigelow. I am holding her at arm's length so she doesn't drip on my pants.

"Turah got caca?" Thomas has a keen interest in such things. "Caca" he picked up from my Europeanized neighbors in Connecticut. I am teaching him to say "shit," but he has trouble with his "sh"s. I am dissecting Keturah's melted Pamper, peeling it like skin from a burn victim. It smells like hot asparagus. Basil started to follow me into the room, then remembered why I was going there and thought better of it. Fastidious, these single types. He looks slightly nauseated as he pretends to study some tiny object underfoot.

"I mean, Jesus," I say to distract him. "I think I'm not unduly uptight. But here was Frances without warning doing stuff like snaking her tongue into my mouth in the midst of some casual ice-breaker of a conversation—a couple of times right in front of certain pillars of the community. And then in the hall on the way to the kitchen one time she unbuttons her blouse and scoops out a breast. Eye of round. Anyone could have walked through—"

Mother's Day

"Cut the shit, Vole. You're lying through your gap teeth, I know it."

Just at that moment, as I was reaching away for a clean Pamper, Keturah did a gymnast's kick from prone position and almost managed to roll off the bureau top I used as a changing table.

"Actually, Basil—and I'm ignoring that last remark of yours—I think she had been drinking hard and must have heard from someone that I was easy. After all, here I am—abandoned mother Siamesed to my children like some social freak-show. Pinned down. Horney and frustrated, no doubt, what with no culturally acceptable outlets—no iceman or delivery-boy thing. And I know my neighbors fantasized me a wanton life. Women were rumored to have been seen entering the premises at odd times. And mothers are not supposed to have sex, especially with other women."

Basil is amused. Joanne tried to look appreciative but was more studiously intent on watching me powder Keturah.

"So did she smoke after or what?"

"I didn't—is that the way it goes, Basil?—notice. But what are you meaning by that? You don't perhaps like my vike? No more details? That's a synopsis you want then, not a vike."

"OK, Matt. Bore on."

I hand Keturah back to Joanne, who tucks her foot under again and holds out her hands. Just then I notice Basil check his watch and lunge his way to the TV in the corner of the living room. I was just beginning to bask in the pleasure of adult company when I notice suddenly that Thomas is nowhere to be seen.

"Thomas? Tho-mas?"

No answer. Off the living room and master bedroom, which are combined in the center of this apartment, and opposite from the bedroom where I changed Keturah, is a small bedroom with an even smaller, sort of Alice-in-Wonderland door. I am tiptoeing toward it like a cartoon cat after a mouse. So quiet, Thomas can only be up to no good.

I suppose in the good old days, when they built this low-rise tenement, people were shorter so they had to have windows closer to the floor. I hadn't thought to check the windows when we first got here a couple of hours ago—unaccustomed, I guess, like those Puerto Ricans in jokes about basement windows and suicide.

The window at the end of the room is open. I am looking through the hot summer air to the street below. I can see his fine blond hair waving in lazy circles as he begins to fall, slowly twisting, six stories slow into the garbage cans and smell and pavement. I am r aching desperately for his baby feet. Will a leg come off like a lizard if I snag him by it before he tumbles out of reach?

I am shaking him now high in front of my face, staring crazed at him in fear become rage. I'm standing by the window and his silhouette blocks out the light. I am so angry I think of heaving him through the glass. That'll show him.

I turn to put him down, studying his face. He is bewildered but not surprised. He's learned a basic children's lesson: anything engrossing, anything that gives you unfettered pleasure will make a parent angry. He reaches up his arm to shield himself—any sudden movement of mine these days and he does that.

He wasn't even teetering, really, when I came crashing through the doorway. There's a red curtain of some sort slung over that space to make a door and I was tangled in it just long enough to convince myself that he would spring up and out the window before I could get free to stop him.

I knew a kid that quiet couldn't have been up to any good. I realize that for some time during the vike session I was being nagged by a feeling something was wrong. By the time I began to do anything about the nagging I knew I was late and would have to pay.

Or, as is increasingly the case, the kid would have to pay.

Thomas is hiccupping in self-pity, tears running down his nose. The tears catch on the edge, curl under, and drip onto his extended lower lip. He senses it's too late for me to hit him now (we are back wth an audience in the living room), so now it's his turn to make me pay. I drag him with me like some balky piece of furniture.

"What's up, Matt?" Joanne is upset by the rough stuff—other people manhandling children always seems unpardonable—and by Thomas' tears.

"Nothing."

She looks at Thomas, then at my iron face. Thomas has trapped me into looking the ogre and I'm mad at her for falling for it. She doesn't understand and looks away, hurt.

"It's just that he almost saved me the price of a college education, Joanne. That's all. He was two-thirds out the bedroom window, hanging by his knee-caps." Thomas tries to wiggle loose from my hand and I jerk him toward me again. "Now stay away from the window. *Away!* You understand?" Thomas looks at his shirt front and fiddles with a button on it. I yank his arm to make him look at me. "Away, got it? Got it?"

Basil is embarrassed and angry. The news is on and he's probably never had his news interrupted before, so fastidiously perfect is the singles life, so rich in earnest self-indulgence. He snatches a theatrical last look at Reasoner's hound-dog face, then heads for the front hall where he starts rummaging noisily in a closet.

The adrenalin is gone and I feel my shoulder muscles slacken and my arms dangle at my sides. I realize I am very tired. The kids always seem to do something dumb or suicidal when I am tired.

Now Basil is standing in the hall with an armful of grungy window screens, opaque with years of black clotted city air.

"Thanks, Basil. Thanks. I'll put them on in the morning. OK? I'm too bushed now." I can see from his look of impatience he can't comprehend how anyone could be so tired he'd risk a child's life rather than put up screens—especially after a person has interrupted his news to get them.

"Oh yeah, Basil—sorry about the melodrama a minute ago...." I wanted to say more but I don't know how you explain in civil terms to single people the difference between their inert and your biodegradable—child-degradable—chemistries.

That night the kids wouldn't sleep they were so wound up in strange surroundings, so we all watched television for the rest of the evening. Keturah dozed on Joanne's lap, then fussed when Thomas crawled into mine. So both kids shared my lap and fussed at one another till I got angry and shoved Thomas off for kicking Keturah. He cried a bit, called us all caca a few times, than sat on the floor against my leg, just out of reach of Keturah's feet which she seemed to keep swinging at him anyway.

Frances at the party had shocked me. You think it might be heaven to have some women force herself on you like that—you keep telling yourself that it *is* heaven. But instead it's ugly. And a gigantic cringe. How do you keep from being humiliated in such a situation—especially with others looking on?

I remember that it was a misty January thaw night. Steam rising from the patches of snow left. Clammy, cold air. I was new at Montville Bank & Trust but even tellers were invited to some hospital fund-raiser. I'd come with the loan officer and his mentecidal wife, straight from work, and was on my best behavior. Bank tellers are not paid well but it was better pay than my other option, a dissertation fellowship that allocated no funds for second infants.

Anway, first Frances had whipped out that breast I told you about, tugging my left hand toward her. It could have been a limpet mine the way I jerked my arm away. She grinned at that—at least I think it was a grin—and sashayed into the kitchen pulling her shirt front back together. No one noticed her as she finished the buttons at the sink.

And the thing is she didn't look bad. If I'd initiated all this

Mother's Day

I would have considered her a presentable poke. Instead I was cowed. And I was flustered at the thought of going back into the rooms full of guests and having to deal with further Frances offensives.

She cornered me in the living room minutes after I thought I'd sandbagged myself in a safe corner. Pinned me over a Chippendale with her 36D. Nobody in the room could have missed it.

She was blackmailing me outside into the yard of this elegant but now suffocating house.

"Let's go," she kept saying a little too loud. She seemed annoyed and impatient—almost indignant. What was I waiting for? she seemed to be asking.

I don't remember a word exchanged outside or how we worked our way to the rocks by the edge of the old dam at the end of the yard. I do remember huge wet Irish Setter kisses and a lot of painful snatching at my marginally functioning private parts. Then even the marginality stopped. I couldn't get it up again. I kept looking at the steam rising from our white bodies and the white snow everywhere around us.

I know I must have drunk too much, nervous during the party, but it was more than that. She was clumsy, I kept saying to myself. Undignified. Then I was trying to flog myself erect with hortatory stuff about being so wanted. She was good about that, I admit. She kept at it doggedly. And if that thing down there could have stayed in her mouth, for example, instead of flopping repeatedly out like an overripe fish, she would have gotten high points for application and appropriate noises.

But nothing.

I think what finally happened was I got so cold and desperate my mind short-circuited like a possum's. They have such tiny brains, possums, that when they overload from stress, they pass out. In my case let's call it a suspension of disbelief. I stopped thinking, exhorting, lamenting.

And like a charmed snake the thing stiffened to her tune.

I turned her away from me so I wouldn't see that wild-eyed drunken face I was sure I could see in the reflected light of the snow. She was kneeling on all fours in the snow when I scooped myself into her. No sensation, like an overdose of Linger, maybe, or being sheathed in one of those slicker-thick condoms we got as kids. I might have been doing some obscene form of transcendental yoga if it hadn't been for her stage whispers.

"Come, baby. Come." I swear she said that, just that way, except "come" seemed to be spelled "caaaam" and the "baby" was Janis Joplin in whiteface.

I have always hated women who talk, who interrupt my sacred concentration. Was *she* coming, maybe? Is that what she was saying? I slapped harder against her titanic buttocks steaming ghostly in the night. I auditioned a few cries of my own. She speeded up. Maybe she really was coming. How do you know, anyway, with such women? Would she fake it like this tonight after all that work?

I would fake it. "Don't stop!" I hissed. Isn't that something you're supposed to say? "Don't stop!" I hissed again. Then I made noises like they make in movies for people strangled with piano wire. I locked my arms around her middle, iron for effect, exhaled hugely and crashed my chinbone hard against her upper back.

We were still for a moment. I pulled away and and backed off her, feeling used by both of us. She didn't make a sound, just knelt there. And I looked and saw she was smoking into the cold night sky.

I remember sliding off into sleep that night thinking about Cindy and how she never called. I'd asked Basil to tell her what day we were coming. He said she'd been emotional and pleased, saying she would call as soon as we arrived. I don't know whether I felt relieved—and righteous—or resentful that we seem to mean so little to her anymore.

CHAPTER VII

Joanne has been softened up like a beachhead.

This, you understand, I am only just comprehending. At first, if there was intent on my part, it was subcutaneous—the cloak and dagger of the species. Apart from the usual male spasms about woman propinquitous (a reflex I scotch automatically by now, like micturition), I noticed nothing overt on my part.

But never underestimate the family arsenal.

Those first few nights in New York, for instance. Keturah in Joanne's ample lap sucking that rubber nipple micrometers from Joanne's real ones. Thomas naked and finger hard in the bath as Joanne sponges him. Or a particular quizzical look from Joanne once, almost a look from behind a look, when our eyes met as I was soaping Keturah's toy vagina.

Most evenings Basil would watch TV, pater familias. Joanne and I would traffic children. Later, cocooned by TV and fatigue, we'd curl up on the couch, a child purring in each lap. I think Basil was glad to be out of the nuts and bolts of it, avuncular. But Joanne was shining inside like an isotope.

At first the kids wouldn't sleep alone. Nothing new about that. They'd slept with me in my half-empty bed in Connecticut since Cindy's unilateral withdrawal months before. It was warmer that way for all of us, and saved me having to haul myself to the nursery nights every time someone stirred in his sleep—or didn't stir enough. Besides, I have been lonely, I admit it. I'd miss them at unguarded moments in the night, when the strains of the day were hidden by the dark. And there were still lots of unguarded moments.

Basil and Joanne had arranged a separate room in the apartment for me—the one of Thomas' defenestration—but I didn't use it for some time. The kids would doze reptilian all evening in adult company but the minute we tried to ghost them asleep toward the double bed on the floor of their room, they'd click awake like electric eyes and plead eloquently, then hideously not to be left alone. Shadows rattled the walls at night from traffic on Second Avenue. Thomas said shadows made him afraid. "Afraid of *what*?" I'd sigh, disgusted.

But I knew, and he knew I knew. How he'd learned so early to sucker me, I'm baffled. He seems to know that when I was small I used to have to look under the bed every night after the lights were out. I'd stoop down on one knee and the balls of my feet, ready to spring out of reach. Often I'd have to look several times a night before I could go to sleep. And I always had to search the clothes closet, too, sure as I moved the hanging clothes aside that deep inside the darkest corner ... Even now I don't like turning off the light behind me and having to walk up the basement stairs.

Still, after a few days, I tried to shame away Thomas' fears. "Look," I said to him standing one night in the bedroom with them, "I'm here and I'm not afraid of the dark. You shouldn't be afraid."

"I'm not afraid of your dark," Thomas said soberly. "I'm afraid of my dark."

So they had me. Not that I wasn't mostly ready for bed when they were, God knows. Usually well before. My eyes glazed over when it became dark outside. I was like a parrot covered in his cage—a couple of clucking squawks about the hour, then profound relief. Except I wasn't allowed to collapse when I needed to. The kids got manic when it got dark, too tired to relax, so they buffaloed about, calling out for the coup de grâce of the day. But I was too supine and paralyzed to move them to bed.

Sometimes Joanne fixed them supper, but mostly they wouldn't eat it because it wasn't me who made it. Sometimes, most times lately, the kids just foraged for themselves among the shelf of Froot Loops, Sugar Crisp, and other sticky poisons. Keturah you could sometimes stopper with a bottle; the noise would tell when she'd sucked herself into a stupor.

Daytimes, the kids applied themselves to the apartment like termites—studious, creative, malign. First paint, then plaster whispered from the walls of their room. You'd find it under their filthy fingernails at suppertime and think about lead poisoning but be too tried to do anything about it.

What had been Basil's study now sported bedlam like a stew. The bed never stayed made. Uusally it looked like a savage sea, strewn with the flotsam and jetsam of miniature typhoons. Crayons, Tinkertoys, cereal bowls, half-eaten toast and bananas, old socks, diapers eddied around with the children's play. In that room you walked on the edges of your feet: there wasn't room in any one place for a full-grown human foot. Day-glo wax crayons pulverized themselves and were ground into the sheets and blankets. Keturah's talcum powder always spilled somewhere, along with juice or left-over cereal, all of it fastened to hard surfaces like glue. There wasn't much floor space for the kids to play, anyway, so within minutes of my almost continuous clean-ups the kids had used up the floor and begun to work over the bed like seven-year locusts, shredding as they went.

That was where we slept. I got so I just shook the covers

down at night, as you do for spiders in the tropics, scattering debris into the troughs formed by the narrow floor space around the edges of the bed. In the morning, I would tell myself each night, in the morning I will clean it all up. And in the mornings I just picked through the troughs for cups and spoons for breakfast, cleaner socks and underwear, a towel like a damp toad huddled in a corner.

You ever slept with little kids? When they are tiny you worry you will roll on them and break a bone or smother out a life. Even then they never sleep like babies. More like overbred dogs. They cry out in their sleep, flail about. Several times I have suffered a split lip or bruised face from runaway elbows or hands. Now that they are larger, Thomas and Keturah sleep quieter. But for some infernal reason—probably why those euphemistic child-care books discourage sleeping with children—their length at this stage makes for an unnerving problem. Keturah is shorter, being not a year old yet, but what she lacks in endowment she makes up for in ingenuity. Either way I get repeatedly kicked in the groin.

So I sleep doubled up—that is, I try to stay awake long enough for the kids to go to sleep so I can turn on my side like a fetus and untangle from around each neck the arm we all need to expunge the joylessness and rue that somehow monopolizes our days. Even as I do, and tuck my knees hard against my chest, most mornings I feel as I did after frenzied self-abuse when I was twelve—fierce forays against my private parts left them feeling battered by pugil sticks. Keturah at least varied her approach. Instead of your run-of-the-mill swift kick, like Thomas's, I'd find her feigning sleep, walking my privates like a treadmill. Or searching them out tiptoe, exploring almost simian the sleepy thickness of early morning.

I won't pretend this was always bad. Sometimes it was the only attention I received for weeks on end. But it was unnerving—for whatever reasons it is you feel unnerved by intimacy with children. They seem so savvy. They have a knowing look that belies all the sexual innocence we are supposed to protect in them. And then there's all that stuff in child-care books about antediluvian ramifications of being seen naked by children, or—God forbid—making more of them.

But I was about to tell you about Joanne, softened up. A week after the children and I had settled into her apartment Joanne and I began a strange amphibious dance.

A friend reminds me what I told her once about my erection. I can't remember quite how it came up, the subject, but she claims I found it was in the way, almost. That is anyhow the feeling I remember with Joanne those first days. My erection—or in that case my given masculinity, for nothing so unsubtle as erections had reared itself as yet—seemed an awkward intrusion and a barrier to a more perfect union.

Yet anything I did seemed to give Joanne contractions. I can't be held responsible for this. I had learned painfully enough—a labor of my own—to respond less guardedly to Keturah and Thomas. I'd learned to relax under the touch, to suspend judgment of it, to tell the body truth. The way a child does rubbing against you like a cat, or climbing in your lap to wiggle down, making a nest. Flesh to flesh.

I'm not breaking news, I know, but for Joanne the daily locomotions of this as I moved among the kids stirred her collective unconscious about children. I don't mean to malign her. The process is inevitable if you are open and unburdened by experience. Only after, the nerve endings cauterized somewhat, you watch a Joanne and cringe for what will happen next and you powerless to prevent it. Like watching that dog in your rearview mirror start again to bolt into traffic

Anyway, Joanne was being softened up, as I said. My special-effects crew at work. Then the amphibious assault.

You're around children and you touch. If you forget, you

touch adults who come into reach, too. Either they flinch or their skin ripples like a cow shaking flies. I suppose I touched Joanne a lot. Basil watched, as he does, then later made some dyspeptic remark about my "new interpersonal program." But he never understood and I don't think I did, either, at first.

You know how they say touching can affect the growth of a baby's spine? For Joanne touching translated into something like progesterone. Her cervix softened almost, and she told me later she'd felt itchy in her nipples, as if about to lactate.

Mornings she began to wander into the kids' room where I'd slept. Usually I was trying to recapture sleep I'd lost on my routine dawn forays to hush up squabbling children in the living room, change diapers, clean up spilt cereal, turn down the TV. Whenever possible I tried to keep the kids in bed with me, out of trouble and out of earshot of Basil and Joanne where they attempted sleep, high on a loft in the main room.

Joanne would wander in after Basil left for work. If I had been cuddling with the kids, or reading them a story, or telling what always seemed to become lies about what we might do that day in the city, I would stop when Joanne came in. The kids would resent it. They sense how an adult tenses in the company of other adults and they felt their privacy invaded.

But children are adaptable. Soon Keturah learned that Joanne would be physical with her, as I had, if she gave her a chance. So when Joanne came in and sat on the edge of the bed (there was nowhere else to sit), Keturah would crawl over and climb her like a jungle gym, a warm primeval-smelling animal with keen instincts about what to manhandle while it was close at hand.

Morning visits became ritual. Soon Thomas and Keturah learned to be bored by the talk. They forgot their resentment

Mother's Day

at the intrusion, seeing in it opportunities to entertain themselves elsewhere until Joanne left for work at ten.

One morning two weeks into our stay I was buried deep in lethargy after valiant attempts at further sleep. I was lying in bed staring out the window, vacant and dingy as the city sky out there, when Joanne appeared at the bedroom door.
"Matt? You awake?"
"Sure. Yeah. What's up?"
"I come in?" Uusally she didn't ask, assuming, I guess, that since the children were here it was a public occasion. This morning the kids were watching Mr. Rogers in the other room, so she asked.
"Of course. Basil at work?"
"Yes. It's late, just after nine. I'm playing hookey today, those bastards. I called in sick."
Now that I consider it, I don't think I have ever been the aggressor with a woman. No, not true. Once I was with a recycled old girl friend and I got what I needed, OK, but where do you stand later? After the rape, you seduce? I don't see how. Anyway that was years ago. Now I like to know I'm wanted. Especially after those grinding years in the fifties when they kept calling you greedy for wanting anything at all. Enough of that and you begin somewhere to believe it. Now I want to be the good guy, serving needs.
In the blue-striped button-down men's shirt she calls pajamas, Joanne is talking animatedly for the hour of day. She doesn't always sleep with Basil, she says. Last night in fact she'd slept in the other room, my bed which I wasn't using because of the kids.
Why is she telling me this? Can she know how loathsome to a man is the idea of other men's semen on a woman? You remember the smell on your hands as inexpert masturbator, the dried-phlegm snail's-tracks crinkly underwear and sheets. And if you've ever fucked a low-rent whore and

watched her squat to drip out come before the next man's turn you don't much cherish the idea of someone else's come, waiting for you. A woman friend of mine thinks that's why men hate condoms: you have to swim in your come that way, handle it and feel it yourself.

So Joanne is telling me she hasn't slept with Basil last night. "Yes. Your bed. It's nice, sort of private and cute, like a dollhouse bed. You should try it."

"I suppose so. I haven't really considered it. I just flop down here. And besides I usually tumble asleep reading them their rotten bedtime story—you know? I feel like I belong here."

"You do belong here. Really, you do. You don't know how lucky you are. I guess it's not a thing you talk about with people, but it's got to be special somehow sleeping with your children. So loving. So natural—I don't know . . ."

"Anytime, friend. Anytime. I'll rent you them any night you want. Give you them, in fact. Free of charge. But first gird your loins and pad the rest. They kick and pummel like street fighters. Cradle martial arts."

Somewhere in this listless talk the wavelength has changed to UHF.

Now at least where I come from—the fraternity of men— you don't mess with another man's woman. Whatever the provocation. It's not friendly and it upsets the order we created to protect ourselves. Once, though, years back when Basil and I roomed together after college, this thing had come up. A sweet girl named Stephanie he was seeing began moves on me I considered rather overripe. She'd engineer herself too close when we were in the same room together— but so casually, I couldn't be sure it was accident and didn't dare move for fear of innocent hurt feelings. So I'd sit frozen—her breast, say, snuggling warm into my arm. That kind of thing. I remember believing she couldn't be interested in me so I decided she thought me harmless and unthreatening, a friend she could have while Basil had her. Body contact with no strings attached.

But when Basil departed for a month's vacation that winter, the dust hadn't settled in our hallway before I called her. I remember that night carefully folding her clothes and hanging them in the closet—a kilt of some kind and a bulky pink sweater—before even undressing myself. It seemed to have been arranged, and I never worried, as I might have then, that any such delay might give her a chance to change her mind and run flustered from my bed clutching underthings.

I tell you this because until I had children and wrestled bigger demons I thought for years I felt guilt about that night. When Basil returned to the apartment she was moved in with me and everyone seemed content, but I have always felt there was an asp lurking somewhere, baring its tiny fangs between Basil and me. So when Joanne switched to UHF that morning I found myself thinking first about Basil.

But with a difference. Now I felt a kind of predestination, not agony of choice. After children, all that free-will stuff of the past seems vanished—vanquished, really, by the ubiquitous leer of the Hyena. *Choose* your sex? *Control* your life? A snare and a delusion. The Hyena speaks—that's all.

I do still like to go eyes open, though, and so what Joanne mistook for a kind of loving calm and acceptance of what happened next was really just a hiatus in time while I entered a new heading in the Big Tome. "Skullduggery," in italics—then a brief note: "All the usual complications will follow." Though probably, if you knew to enter truth in the Big Tome, I should have noted only "Here be dragons."

Women, we hear, love to talk. Nobody except women ever listens to them but what women love to talk *about* is substance. Not make-believe, like men. Since I've been a mother talking to women I don't think I've had a frivolous conversation. Substance is all, spiked with intimacy.

So I knew the drill by now. You hold up show-and-tell cards to determine subject. You nod as at an auction, signifying commitment. There are stages, of course, and an exit ramp at each one like a parking garage, but because participants all share a determination to get somewhere (women are so goal-oriented) it is bad form to duck for exits.

What makes all this confusing for me is that all other things being equal, I am clearly not the woman I seem in such conversations. I can talk like one now, take the risks. I know and sympathize like Mary Magdalene. But the corporeal body belies the spirit. So what transpires—at least so far—is a kind of shell-game. I am, but I am not, and we both know that and toy with it in a kind of delicious underwater ballet. And that means that while you pretend a kind of neutrality—no, not pretend: you *believe* a kind of neutrality—all along there are signals being passed, subsurface vibrations. Which is why I said a while back I feel lesbian in these affairs. The hurdles of gender have been unnaturally superseded.

OK. So we talk, Joanne and I, with increasing substance about my sleeping with children. About ... intimacy.

"I've never had that before—intimacy."

"How do you mean 'never,' Matt?" Her face was pointed at her lap and she looked up at me from under her arched eyebrows. "What about with Cindy?"

"I don't believe it ever came up. I'm not sure men and women can be intimate. Too much on each other's case."

"But you had babies with her—"

"She had the babies alone. I cared for them alone. The only levelling we ever did was of our marriage."

Cynicism and a dash of bitters. The mixture suits these encounters. Vulnerability and bravado women know about. I can't help the bitters, mind you. The cynicism is optional, I like to think, but lately it seems the only option.

"I guess I know what you mean. Basil and I are like that, probably. It's hard to tell with him. Or me, I suppose. He thinks what we have is profound but there are times I feel nothing, lots of times."

"Here, Joanne, I'll shove over a bit." She had been seated on the farthest edge of the bed, balanced half-cheeked as she talked. "Cold? My robe's over there by the window, there by the bureau."

"No. Thanks. It's OK. I ought to go in a minute, anyway. Leave you to your temporary quiet from the kids. It's just that . . . how long's Mister Rogers, anyway?"

I've learned to cherish embarrassment. It means conflicting emotions and that means possibility. Joanne was wanting to say something and blocked from saying it. We both knew it but were pretending we didn't. But by now I was sure enough what Joanne felt to risk myself a little. From where I was sitting, propped up against the wall with a pillow, I reached over very grownup for her hand.

"Joanne?"

She turned her head a bit, cocking it, and looked at me deadpan. "Yes? Matt, I—"

"If ah, if you promise not to kick in bed, Joanne . . ." and without planning any such thing I smiled my best sapphic smile. I hadn't let go of her hand and so I just pulled steadily on it and she let herself slide over across my lap.

I try to be delicate about these things—mostly due to early teen training when those anguished spasmodic homings on certain delicate parts resulted in nasty rebukes. But kissing is OK. Everyone agrees. So I was kissing Joanne while my neck creaked under the strain of reaching swan-like to my lap where she lay staring brown tartar eyes at me.

Too much could be made of this but almost immediately Joanne was hauling at her blue-striped shirt-tails. Under them she had blue spiderwork panties but before I could ponder what that meant Joanne was scrambling to sit up, working her shirttails over her shoulder. Then she was kneeling, straddling my lap caught beneath the covers. Her left hand moved up her rib cage and cupped a fulsome breast, pushing it toward me. Time slows down at such moments. Things seem more graceful than they are. Because while I remember it as a ballet, actually Joanne was in an awkward hurry and I was frantically trying to walk on my ass bones, like a restless kid on a church bench, to maneuver myself into position.

I know this isn't supposed to be so but the tip of her right nipple looked moist as it headed toward me. Poor Joanne. That is what I kept thinking in this slow-motion time. Poor Joanne. Why, I don't know. Why was I thinking at all, in fact? I am cursed with a hyperactive, noisy brain. Thoughts breed and split in there like amoebas. Can't shut them down. I miss a lot while that is going on. I don't think I fully appreciated the warm-skin fulsomeness of Joanne's breast. Nor the urgent approval of my tentative first mouthings at the nipple. She had moved her hands behind my head and was pressing herself against my face. Quite hard, come to think of it.

"Mmmmmmmnnngggphfff—" I felt a kind of rudimentary panic. Stifle is stifle, even by so handsome, baby-oil smelling a breast.

"Yes. Like that, Matt. OK?" She released my head a bit and I could see her chin above me pointed straight at the ceiling. Her voice was stretched thin at that angle.

"Here, Joanne, just a sec. I—" She was pushing again. I was afraid my talking teeth would snag a nipple. "Hold ummmnugg, Joanne."

I was afraid she would be hurt or embarrassed at my seeming reticence so I pulled her tightly to me anyway, ordered up a shiver and held her a minute like that.

What I should point up about that first morning is that it worked right. With a little help from Mr. Rogers. Not that I worry about my little monsters watching, but even the most worldly of women clam up at first under a kid's impersonal fish-eyed curiosity. So you have to pace yourself, break for breathers while you scan the door for tiny eyes, keep her

Mother's Day

facing away from them. I've developed a technique for squeamish women which involves my staring out of the corner of my eyes to catch the incoming child's eye, then flashing my eyes to the other end of the socket, wide-eyed, in the direction of away. But even this tenses so many odd muscles in the face that it only works about half the time.

Doing it right, as I was saying, involved eschewing the maleness that morning. It's always hard to gauge what punishment women want for their nipples, so I was tentative and oscular to Joanne's. She was not big on teeth, being as yet too respectful of herself, but pressure she adored. I arranged us on the bed so I could work her front my way. She was lying on her back now, shirt shed, and I was kneeling over her from midway, working those nipples as Keturah worked the bottle and sliding her blue panties out from under her.

Joanne kept pulling at me, hugging me down so hard, forcing me off balance above her. But she relented as I maneuvered my tongue past her bellybutton and along the edges of her pubic fence. She was easy to please that morning—so devout and concentrated, so electric.

I don't always understand about the labia and utensils down there, but whatever I brushed with my tongue quaked like a beach clam off guard. She didn't make noises, and I realized I'd never heard a squeak from her any night with Basil though we we were just a closed door apart.

By the time Thomas blundered in on us we were modestly embracing, head to head. I heard his footsteps coming from the main room and gently pulled a sheet over us. Thomas walked around the foot of the bed and stopped. Joanne craned her neck to see what he was doing. He looked at her blankly. Maybe a little sullen, like one of the three bears.

"Thomas?" I tried to sound neutral but I could feel Joanne's tension. "No more TV? Where's Keturah?"

"I'm hungry, Matt."

"Where's Keturah, Thomas?"

"I'm hungry. I want some cereal."

"OK, Thomas, in a while. Is Keturah watching more TV? Go tell her to come here, OK? Then I'll get the cereal. Go tell her."

Thomas trundled out and Joanne relaxed a little.

"What do they think, Matt? Have they seen ... this before?"

"Sure. You're lucky. The last person got to sleep with all three of us. She woke up in the early hours to find a tiny kid struggling to wedge its way between us. That was Keturah, who earlier I'd brought to bed because she kept waking up and it was too cold to sit around rocking her back to sleep. By morning the woman had been kicked, mauled, and peed on. She didn't come back."

"But what do they think? I mean, if they see—"

"They've seen it all. Boys don't give a damn. Thomas checks out the arrangement, such as it is at the moment. Then he asks for something—as he did just now. To reassure himself of his clout—and maybe to be sure I am OK, puffing and cavorting like that. Then he wanders off for a while. Keturah, though, studies the scene meticulously. She cocks her head to align herself, squints maybe. She doesn't say anything but she watches absorbed. Female all the way, she takes this stuff seriously. Often she insinuates herself into the arena."

"Doesn't it make you feel weird?"

"Not anymore. Annoyed like hell sometimes. They have jugular timing, you know. You're one of the first they haven't caught in rather exceptionally compromised positions."

Keturah and Thomas were squabbling in the living room. Well, at least Keturah was still with us. While Joanne and I had been talking I had been building toward one of my chamber-of-horrors routines, guilt clad. Keturah drowned in the toilet chasing the toys she drops in. Keturah under the kitchen sink force-vomiting that Drano I've been meaning to move out of reach. Keturah forcing down the last of those

Mother's Day

white tranquilizers I saw lying on the table by the couch early that morning.

We made love two more times that day before Basil got back from work. Joanne was tight for a woman of such lavish hips and breasts, and ingenious in her application to the tasks at hand. Talent indeed.

Forgive the reduction. It happens without my noticing. What I was trying to say is that I felt deep gratitude to Joanne for that morning, a confirmation of those sisterly conspiracies we'd shared from the beginning. Babies have undone me at both ends. I'm prey to tenderness and anger I've never felt before, and for every rage at them I need a counter tenderness I didn't used to need. A deepened sense of closeness Joanne could risk enough to give.

There is a strange feral kind of responsibility to intimacy that makes the risks more delicious. A kind of addiction, but no mere monkey on your back, more a magic kind of bird, kingfisher or pelican, preening itself casually, alert for some sign in the moving waters far below.

Cindy called. She's very busy, I am to understand, but desperate to see the kids. As soon as she can arrange things.

"Any possibility you can arrange money for them while you are about it? We're hurting."

"Matt, you know I can't. My expenses are already—"

"Forget it. So are mine. Only the children suffer, anyway. And maybe you should forget just rushing right over here for the kids, too. I'm not sure they'd remember who you are...."

CHAPTER VIII

"Yabba dabba dooo!"

It is seven hateful o'clock some morning. Thomas must have tracked down the TV plug and worked it into the socket. Christ. We can't last here.

We were all up late last night with good dope Basil brought home. The kids nodded off earlier than I did, probably stoned out from breathing the air. Then the adults just drifted for hours late into the music. Santana and the Dead. With your eyes closed the music conjured finger-paint hieroglyphics on the inside of the eyelids. This morning I have a headache that booms like pebbles in an empty well.

I have been up before now, of course. Keturah wet herself through the Pampers, rubber pants, and Dr. Dentons enough to wake me. That was before dawn. Then Thomas had to have cereal with the early bird. Yesterday—a score of yesterdays—I let him get it himself. No, that's not accurate: I snarled at him to get it his fucking self. So yesterday he spilled milk everywhere trying to pour a half-gallon container into a pygmy bowl of Froot Loops balanced on the corduroy sofa. This morning I got cereal for him, my hands knocking about in the kitchen like wooden spoons. Then the TV balooned on with some insufferable drone about the Antinomian Heresy. Insult to the brain. That time I had snatched the plug out of the wall, glaring at Thomas as he crouched up in a corner of the couch with his teeth working the wet corner of his blanket. It was cold and he wore just a T-shirt, shivering but determined to stay there.

Now he'd found the plug I hid, somehow failed to electrocute himself, and frantically tried to turn the volume down when the set warmed up. So it sounded actually like this: "Yabba DABBA dooo!" I got there by the "doo!" and punched the switch off. Thomas retreated further into the corner of the couch, jammed his blanket further into his mouth, and put on his poor-little-match-girl face. I grabbed the end of his blanket and led him back to the bedroom, yanking it furiously against his teeth.

Basil is supposed to be up by seven-thirty but I think he feels anyway in the mornings as if he has to pull himself out of setting cement. The children at seven making noise is almost terminal agony for him. He wakes up hunched together like a mummy. The children are sorry when they make him angry but they suffer no guilt—as if it had been an earthquake that woke him, demons that made them do it. I am *not* sorry for Basil—there's something gratifying about other adults also having to get up earlier than they want to. But I am clenched with guilt about it. Every morning I wake up with my finger to my lips, hissing silence at the kids.

I have to pass Basil's sleeping loft on my way to our bedroom from the TV and I notice Joanne curled up with a blanket over her head. Basil is staring rigid at the mirror on the ceiling above him. I can't tell if he's having a seizure or doing his TM. If you're lying on your back, is it most relaxed to push the eyelids closed or let them roll back open?

Now back in our room Thomas whispers that he has to

pee. I wave him out, annoyed. That means I'm going to have to wipe up after him in there, too, before I can get off this freezing gritty floor into bed. Thomas isn't much taller than the toilet bowl and he splashes all over the seat. Usually over whatever is nearby, too. Joanne thought it was cute the first time she saw him at it. I don't think Basil will be touched this morning to sit on a wet seat.

I didn't hear Basil leave. I must have slumped back to sleep, my frozen feet lying against each other like rocks in the bed. Thomas and Keturah I locked in the room with me by pulling the dresser against the door. Keturah is curled up in bed at a ninety-degree angle to me, her feet braced against the small of my back. She's got most of her left hand in her mouth and the thumb hooked under her chin.

I don't know where Thomas is. The door is still wedged so he's got to be in here someplace. The room is rectangular with high ceilings and just enough room for the double bed on the floor, a small bureau next to it on one side, and a built-in closet (a built-out closet, rather) just off the foot of the bed. Between the closet and the bureau is a tall low window. We don't have a curtain for it so it stares filmy with grime when I look up from sleep.

Thomas has gotten hold of my scissors and cut up every magazine in the room. Also his hair. He looks like a Nazi collaborator. How he missed his chance at Keturah's eyes I don't know. Instead he has made jagged confetti out of my *Newsweek*. He also worked on *Screw*, it looks like, but he likes the slicks best for the slippery feel of them and the hiss as scissors slice the ads. Last week he cut up a polyester shirt.

That was a day I had planned to begin looking for work. At least so I told myself later when I couldn't go because I had no clean shirt.

When I came to this city I smuggled seed money—$100

detoured from the bill collectors in Connecticut. I had had $150 but the power company sent a man over in a yellow pickup two days before I was to leave. Bad timing. He had two large cans of mace on his belt—"for dogs," he said—and I paid him the $48 to keep them there.

I don't know what I'd planned at first. Planning used to be my stong suit, but not since the Hyena. Now I specialize in fast footwork, sometimes on an extra good day a preemptive strike or two. A successful day in the life of a single parent is one in which nothing permanent happens.

In the beginning I kept thinking that thing about a houseguest, like a fish, beginning to smell after a few days. But Basil is an ancient friend and we had always had rules against limits to friendship. When we'd lived together as undergraduates all property (except women) was common, imposition a mark of friendship and trust. He'd carry me till the money ran out, then I'd carry him. It was unthinkable that things might have changed.

"Joanne would stay and do it, Matt."

"I don't think—well, you think she would? Maybe I could pay her—you think?—after I get work?"

"Sure. Why not? Check it out with her. Look: I think you'd be much better off in this city. Take a true-life job, make some loose change. I've thought it through. I'll shark you a loan while you look. You pay me back after, by degrees, if you can. Joanne hates work, anyway. She'd been talking of quitting since she began. She told me she'd been skipping work a lot. She's got the hots for those kids, anyway."

This just added to my guilt about Basil. It has increasingly little to do with sex, though. I'm learning from my fellow women their refreshing practicality about such matters. Two nights ago we went to a cocktail party at married friends of Joanne's, where the lady of the house and I had a talk about men's sexual conservatism. She ended by casually saying,

"Look, I'd give you head right now here in the kitchen if my husband weren't so uptight about this stuff. Why are men such assholes?"

And now Basil was loaning me money so I could stay on in New York and further ransack his life. We have already gutted it of almost all quietude and he doesn't know the half of it. I have noticed though that he stays at work later these days. He's even working Saturdays. He never did that before.

"I'd love it, Matt." Joanne is beaming from across dinner, looking first at me, then Basil. He had asked her about the babysitting so I'd been spared asking something no friend should ask. "And besides, if you think you can pay me—when you get work—then I don't have to face finding work sucking off executives someplace, do I?"

"Meantime," I said nervously, "Papa Basil shall support us all—right your eminence?"

"Up yours, Matt. And let us not forget the, ah, prerogatives. I expect my paper and slippers the minute I come through the door after work. And my smoking jacket. Droit du seigneur with Keturah when the time comes. Dinner sharp at eight, children tucked away for the night—"

"Fat chance. Unless you plan on my being tucked away with them. Or maybe ... maybe—goddamn!—that's exactly what you do mean, you swine. Taking on airs already, it would seem."

"Well, seriously, Matt. I know they need you and all, but we need you to ourselves sometimes. If you don't get some time off from them you're going to slip into thumb-sucking and baby talk yourself, perhaps permanently. Maybe that's what scared your neighbors in the country. Even bonafide anatomical mothers don't do this shit. I never saw one—did you, Joanne?"

* * *

First Joanne had begun regularly to call in sick. "Come and oil don't mix" is how she put it after she had hung up one morning with her boss at Exxon. Her regrets were scrupulously close to the truth. "Gynecological complications," she'd say to him. "You know how women are." Exxon doubtless muttered darkly to itself about the curse but I think it was only during her period that Joanne got to work at all. And that was only because of a misunderstanding. Basil was unmanned by blood and Joanne had become used to abstinence during her period. She'd assumed me equally fastidious.

Yet for Joanne her period was a kind of secret signal. Verification of the magic of motherhood she thought she believed in. She told me later she felt positively lubricious when she had her period, as if it were justification for all those unsavory erotic urges. Secretly what she wanted was to offer it up to a man, a kind of accomplishment—the way young children feel about their biologic functions. "See, Matt?" Thomas used to say proudly, pointing to the toilet. "See? Mine"—as if it were living proof he worked.

Anyway it was Thomas who brought the whole issue to a head. I found him one morning in a sea of Tampax on the living room floor. He had found the newly opened box in the bathroom while I was still asleep and proceeded to disassemble the contents one by one. They make good toys, really, and he played with them much of the day, feeding the cardboard mechanisms to Keturah to chew on. There was something apt about two babies surrounded by schools of sperm-like cotton projectiles with white tadpole tails.

When Joanne returned from work that day I apologized for the run on her Tampax and it was then I discovered her reason for abandoning me in favor of the office. I chided her gently for underestimating the effects of motherhood on even the most finicky of men. After that she went to work one more day—to claim a paycheck—then called in her resignation. From then on we had retired daytimes to Basil's sleeping loft, where we could have some privacy and still keep an eye on the children without such exaggerated interruptus as before.

Not that the interruptions hadn't been instructive. Children learn bladder control and eating habits from their network programming. Adults learn the telerhythm method, a kind of contemporary adaptive response for parents. For future generations it will come natural, with your DNA, but these days you have to work to learn the ins and outs of Captain Kangaroo or Mister Rogers.

I have found that single people experience something of the same phenomenon. Single working women I have met have difficulty lubricating until after Johnny Carson—as if their response were triggered by the monologue. For me it is Mr. Rogers' monologue.

Mornings are a time for local relief, as they call it in the better massage parlors. Time does not permit complete intromission, but I've found children's programming well suited to manipulation of the private parts. Something about Mr. Rogers' soothing tone relaxes kids into relief after all the adrenalin of cartoon carnage. Kids will give Mr. Rogers at least thirteen consecutive minutes of pure passive concentration before wandering back to check on things. Just time for organized adults to accomplish a little relief of their own.

The telerhythm method may be a stab at population control. Anybody knows that after a day with kids no parent has the spare energy needed for procreative endeavor. Only mornings might some parents delude themselves energetic— and children's TV comes on early enough to insure the kids are up before you, and to contain even the most prematurely ejaculative of parents. This forces various forms of onanistic behavior which while providing relief, locally, contributes little to the future of the selfish gene.

So Joanne had been introduced to telerhythm while I adjusted to local New York City programming. And in the process Keturah introduced Joanne to the joys of group sex.

What happened was that Joanne came to my bedroom one morning after Basil had left. Thomas, trapped in there by the bureau against the door, had busied himself mixing baby powder and Contac tiny time pills into a paste with my Yardley aftershave. He'd been so absorbed he forgot to torment Keturah awake so when Joanne squeezed her way into the room past the bureau, he'd bolted alone for the TV. It's risky waking Keturah when you're planning sex. She's apt to be playful in the morning—not yet slumped into sullen docility from watching TV—and likely as not to hang around. So as Joanne undressed herself before getting under the covers, I just glided Keturah asleep over to the far end of the bed next to the wall.

Joanne had been a little late that morning and we had missed our cue. So we were just winging it, toying with one another until after Thomas' expected first interruption. I was lying between Joanne and Keturah while Joanne worked her way discreetly down under the covers. She would surface for air and affection then move further down, playing and amusing herself. She had moved almost beyond fail-safe when I felt Keturah stir at my side.

I worried that if Keturah woke, Joanne wasn't veteran enough to continue. And I needed her to continue. Whatever demographic necessities isolate mothers with babies also guarantee the craving I felt at that moment for Joanne. Since Cindy left, my children's needs for me—and my needs for those needs—have inflamed a desperate counter-need for comfort from others.

Joanne cannot have heard Keturah stir, so with the grace of great practice I eased Keturah close to me, tucked her head gently into the curve of my neck, and began stroking her fine long black hair, whispering ancient lullabies.

Joanne continued her ministrations below but instead of the steep angular agitations of sex I had expected, Keturah's simple sleepy love as she snuggled next to me loosed an appalling tenderness that made me clutch her to me, kneading her shoulders and neck in an abrupt confusion of passion and heartsick regrets.

What would become of this child I seemed never to have loved enough? What would become of Thomas, the goat of all my miseries, when he grew larger than the imperfect reach of my protection? I realized that constantly, almost by rote, I asked myself these questions, but now so despairing of an answer that I'd ceased even to acknowledge them. Instead, numbed by failure, I'd merely congratulated myself when Keturah made fewer and fewer demands and when I'd learned to neutralize Thomas's anxious strategies for attention.

My skin began to sting and tears itched the corners of my eyes. I don't know what magic I had said to Keturah but she was asleep again, I realized. I kept kissing her, then as I squeezed my eyes closed to clear the tears I saw the kids sitting in some unknown place by a white barn in the early spring sun. The light was pale but alive, like the skin of a baby, and from a great distance I could see them peering up at it, squinting. They looked innocent and vulnerable, I thought, unprotected, deserted by the parents who should have been there with them in the sun.

Joanne seemed to have sensed something because she had become gentler, nuzzling her face against my chest, holding me softly, barely moving. I reached for her head and eased her to the surface.

Just in time. Thomas wandered in for his inspection, cast a cold eye, then pattered back to the TV. Next thing I knew Keturah was awake, crawling over me, trying to snuggle between Joanne and me—for whatever complex doctrinal reasons a young daughter does such things.

I don't remember the play-by-play, exactly, but since Joanne seemed secure and willing, Keturah stayed and Joanne and I proceeded. I was nuzzling Joanne's left nipple, I remember, when Keturah turned and began expertly to suck the other. Joanne never flinched. Her eyes widened a bit and that was all. Seconds later she was cuddling a still sucking Keturah to her while I had moved alongside Joanne's odalisque cocked hip and maneuvered myself ever so discreetly inside.

Good sex does not a wage slave make. I tried, though. So did Joanne. We tried the rhythm method—one day my looking for work, one day playing house. We tried total abstinence (during which Basil's sex life took a vigorous turn for the better, to judge from the thumpings and heavings high in the sleeping loft). We tried local relief between employment agencies.

But when Joanne took the children out so I could phone uninterrupted, I became paralyzed with sloth and fear. No calls got made. An hour away from the kids and I felt desolate and insecure. When I did manage interviews they went something like this:

"Yes, and what experience have you had Mr. Vole? Ah, I see. Well, perhaps library work or day care. We don't handle that kind of thing but maybe . . ." and he is pointing vaguely in the direction of downtown.

Several agencies thought me ideal fodder for door-to-door. "With those bedroom eyes," one breezy old crone told me. "Once in a lifetime opportunity. Learn the ropes, then right in to managment trainee. Commission sales—no *limit* on what you can make. Oh . . . You won't travel? Can't the wife take care of that? Wow. You *have* got a problem."

You know who were most buffaloed, most bitter, most intractable? Women. Women who interviewed me. Women at the agencies. They were the ones most impatient with my qualifiers. I needed working hours to jibe with day care. No overtime because there is no overcare. Heavy health insurance since children get sick at least once a week. They looked at me, these women, and set their jaws, angry at such intrusion. I kept trying to look behind that look, to ask them if they hadn't encountered this phenomenon, knowing all along that they, too, perhaps had secret children stashed away someplace. But without the qualifiers. It wasn't that they didn't understand—just that the question was irrelevant, somehow. Don't bring *me* your problems, Mister—ah—Veal. You just shouldn't have had children, that's all.

Even if there had been day-care jobs for me—and there weren't: every Joanne in New York was vying for them, clinging to a dream—I wouldn't have taken one. Being spelled by Joanne with the kids already made me unable to stomach them as much as I had—and stomach myself less for feeling that way. The thought of thirty or more children, sardined in some basement storeroom from seven in the morning to six at night was pure nightmare. And besides, I was already losing public control.

Three weeks had passed and my tantrums with my children began to horrify Joanne. How could any grownup human being scream like that at a nine-month-old baby? Hold her by the shoulders and shake her like a rag doll? Or lash out like that, knock a toddler down just because he spilled his juice? Already the children scurried to Joanne for safety when they feared trouble. I found myself muttering darkly like a mental defective.

It took Keturah and Thomas exactly thirteen days to bring Joanne around. Every time I left the apartment without them they wailed. Keturah developed a fine ancestral keen which cascaded down the stairs after me when I went out looking for work. I'd have to scramble back up flights of stairs for more kisses and empty promises. Thomas waited till I'd gone, then attacked Keturah for solace and attention.

Usually there is a watershed. One side of it they're just kids, the other ...

"I don't know what I'm going to do with them, Matt. They're ... *demonic!*"

"*Now* what'd they do? Thomas! Why is Joanne so upset? Huh? God damn it. She's doing us a—"

"Matt, don't. I don't know. Maybe it's just me, not them. But everytime I look there's a disaster. I can't seem to keep up. What's got *into* them these last two weeks? I mean, they were *sweet* before. All Keturah does is cry or suck her bottle. And Thomas—"

I can't say I was surprised. I was even pleased, in a vindicated way. So I wasn't the only one. Even a vigorous young motivated voluntary fallopian card-carrying female mother had become unhinged. And in less than the two weeks it had taken me to try to flog myself on the marketplace.

The threshold varies from day to day, barometric pressure to barometric pressure, but for most of us there is an act of inspired lunacy that alters forever the circuits of control. For Joanne it was cake.

I had left early that day. Basil was taking me with him to his magazine for an interview. They wouldn't hire me, we both knew, but things were getting hairy and Basil noticed the dulled hypothermia look in my eye and knew something quick had to be done. Joanne had been sleeping in the spare room at night. She'd been sleeping a lot more those days, we'd noticed, sometimes crying out in the early hours. So we let her sleep that morning, propped the kids still nodding in front of TV, and backed tiptoe out the front door.

About two hours later when she woke up, Joanne later told us, she had found both children in the kitchen.

"Cake. Cake," Thomas kept saying as Keturah mimicked the syllables. "Cake, cake," exhilarated at their focus for the morning. On the floor, mostly in the center but with occasional trails, footsteps and outflows elsewhere, were one and a half bags of King Arthur enriched flour; a dozen eggs with shells; three pounds of granulated sugar; milk to taste; salt and pepper; Froot Loops.

Keturah was caked to the elbows with it, her hair had gone bedlam white, as had her eyebrows. Thomas was mixing with a hairbrush and assorted knives and spoons from the drainer. Someone had spilled milk and orange juice inside the refrigerator.

Joanne's watershed. Her Waterloo.

If there is one thing a kid can't stand it's restraint. Joanne, she reported that night, had been a model of rectitude, a frozen smile on her face the whole time as she scraped the cake from the linoleum with a spatula and the whole time she was sponging the refrigerator. She did scream from time to time that day, she said, but not at the kids directly.

That smile was still frozen on Joanne's face when I got home that afternoon. Basil's boss had talked his precious minutes about "dues" and "commitment" and "technicians." He suggested I try a regional newspaper, get some writing experience, then reapply and see how I "stacked up" by then.

Joanne wasn't interested in Basil's boss. She had stiff-upper-lipped her way through the day's holocaust. She didn't cry now like they do on the soaps. She didn't even gulp and stammer. Her words to me were calm and orderly and few. The operative ones were "day" and "care." She kept repeating them, stroking at her high Tartar cheekbone. Slowly her smile sank at the edges till it disappeared into a fissure in her face where her mouth usually was.

I had to say something but everything I thought of was bound to lead to trouble. I tried a frozen smile of my own. "Kids will be kids, eh Joanne?"

"God, Matt. It's not the time for jokes."

"Still got to be better than looking for a job."

"Well you stay here, then. I'll gladly blow midgets in the photo stalls at Woolworth's rather than face another day of this. Something is wrong. ..."

"Nothing wrong, Joanne. N-O-R-M-A-motherfucking-L is what it is. I know how you feel."

"Like shit, that's how I feel. Like Gulliver pummelled by tiny multitudes." She smiled faintly at the image. She was beginning to get her spirits back and the color was returning to her face.

"Maybe you could take a break, call in sick, Joanne? Say it's your period. I could stay home, trundle out the earth-moving equipment—"

"You're just like the rest of them. Earthmoving, indeed. Look pal, after today I'm beginning to have serious reservations about the act itself. Look what it can result in, for God's sake. Je-sus!"

"Now that you bring it up, Joanne. I've been meaning to suggest an ancient unnatural variation which is one hundred percent childproof."

"Your sense of timing, dear Matthew, leaves something to be desired...."

CHAPTER IX

I am sensitive about my children. Not sensitive *to* them, I know, but sensitive about how others see them and what that means about me. I don't take lightly to criticism of the kids—despise them as I may at times—and Joanne knew that. I had told her my secret self-hate about my inadequacies as a mother, not knowing that women don't often do that. So what I told her was shocking news to her, further proof of my wanton intimacy. She had seen me rise up and strike back like a rattler when Basil had so much as hinted he thought the children excessive, so it was no casual undertaking for her to insist like this for day care.

And it was no casual remark I was making about ancient unnatural practices.

We'd known one another about a month. Sisterhood is powerful medicine and we found ourselves alternately drunk with excitement or relief. Sex had been reassuring mostly, a normalizing ritual when the spiritual questing got too scary.

Mother's Day

We would talk some dark secret then grab for each other's bodies like frightened children in the dark.

With curiously opposite results. For Joanne, I began to discover, such sisterly intimacy with a man urged her into sexual explorations she might never have tried—confident, I guess, that I wouldn't use her as a man might. For me, Joanne's increasing physical abandonment led me deeper into emotional intimacies I'd never know with anyone, man or woman. Both of us arose from such encounters giddy with possibility but confused and scared at our new vulnerability.

Now I know that Joanne was freeing me, as no man could have, from the obsessive entanglement with my children that the months alone with them had induced. What had crushed her in three weeks of baby-sitting had addicted me, so intense the sensations, so vulnerable my body's innocent receptors. Having babies is a continuous series of crises. Nothing else will produce the necessary changes, so intense are the adjustments you must make at each stage. Joanne had been having my current crisis for me—as Cindy had had an earlier one—forcing me to adjust to a basic, wrenching truth: the children would have to be abandoned repeatedly if I were going to be able to grow enough to keep pace with their needs.

I know this sounds like Dear Abby but don't despair: what I am leading up to is the 101 days of Sodom that follow.

I can hear him now, Basil in his tired, principled way, polishing the logic.

"It's perfectly simple," he is saying. "You owe Joanne money for baby-sitting? I'll pay it. Or rather the credit union at work will. So will the credit union pay for day care till you get work—"

"Now wait, Basil—"

"No. No wait. This is a job for super shark. I pay now. You pay—through the nose—later. That way I can assure myself of your continued attention during my lonely old age."

"You might be a prick, Basil, but you wouldn't do that to a friend, would you?"

"Friend? Friend? Who said anything about a friend? I want a vassal, a sharecropper, a peon, a mujik. And besides, think what happens if I don't cough up."

"The kids and I take to the trees again in sylvan Connecticut."

"No, that's not what happens. You don't get a job, the children starve, you feed them pieces secretly hacked off from hidden parts of your body. I have to pay funeral costs and adopt the orphans. Whereupon Joanne flees the coop and I begin feeding the kids pieces of my body."

"How very oral of you. I din't know you had it in you. I believe you are growing soft—a premature senility of the heart."

"Oh, cut it out." Joanne sounds angry. "You guys dance around a subject like medicine men. Medicine men on speed. I think it's a fair idea. You've got to get a job and survive here, Matt. There's no going back to mother Connecticut, you know. That never works."

So Basil paid me to sleep with Joanne uninterrupted. I tried to work this one out, endlessly, but all I could figure was that Joanne sleeping with me was her decision and didn't involve Basil, even though he supported us all, which allowed her sleeping with me to take place.

It's hard, this era. I have said already that women are matter-of-fact about matters sexual, shamming reticence merely to mollify men, but I couldn't shake off my guilt about Basil. Traditions die so hard. Which didn't, however, prevent Joanne and me from symbiotic new depths of intimacy and lust.

For a week after Basil's pronouncement Joanne remained dragooned with the children while I fellated any interviewer I could find.

Mother's Day

But I didn't leave Joanne unprotected. I taught her one of my most shameful tricks. Ever since she was present, Keturah has been apprenticed to the vacuum cleaner. Barely old enough to hold up her head on that fragile babyskin neck, Keturah could be charmed by the machine. She would come as close to it as she could, close her eyes and begin twisting her head back and forth autistic to the noise. I used to worry it would addle her brain or give her wry neck, but in emergencies, I told Joanne, place the baby in the embrace of the machine and throw the switch.

I had no tricks for Thomas that I was telling, but with at least one child immobilized you had two hands for the other to fill.

Joanne was contrite after her harsh words about the kids the day of the cake. She felt bad, she said, for all the things she hadn't done for them those weeks, for all the things never done for them. So for a week she forgot what she already knew and tried to be the mother she imagined mothers were. Maybe it hadn't worked, she said, to keep them home all day as she'd been doing. Maybe what they needed was to get out a bit, stretch their horizons.

Forgive me for sounding dyspeptic but Joanne's sudden mother energy seemed a transparent result of her impending delivery by day care. For a week anyone can be Mary, Joseph, and the Holy Ghost combined. Perfect parenthood depends on who's otherwise minding the store.

I don't know why, but I tried to tell something of this to Cindy, the weekend she took them. Not that she took them the actual weekend. Saturday morning she had to work and Saturday night a business dinner. So Saturday afternoon, as the city settled quietly into the heat of July, she arrived at our door flushed of face from the six flights up, maybe even from the emotion.

Thomas had become so starved for affection that he was instantly promiscuous with her, hugging and snuggling and pretending he'd never noticed that she'd left. Keturah hung on tight to my pant leg and sucked her thumb hard, looking intently at her shoes. Cindy knelt to kiss her and she looked the opposite way. This flustered Cindy—hurt her, I could see—and for a moment I felt her pain, her innocence, and tried to reassure her.

That was until I saw her looking about the apartment in disgust at the chaos, the pile of dirty laundry I'd assembled in the living room to take to the laundromat while she had the kids.

"Doesn't Thomas have any kind of shorts, Matt? It's hot as hell out there—"

"No. Buy him some, why don't you. If I cut off a pair of pants we won't have a change in the fall."

"Oh. Oooooh!" Cindy was looking at Keturah's finger. "Where'd she get that scar? Let me see the scar, Keturah. God, Matt—"

"God, yourself. Look. Even if I told you, you wouldn't—oh, it doesn't matter. What's the use?"

"I think I am capable of ordinary information processing. Come on. What's wrong. Where'd she get it, huh?"

"Lay off, OK? You want the children—scarred and inelegantly dressed though they may be—or don't you? Don't start probing yourself around in our lives. I'm not sure you've earned the right, exactly. Besides—" I saw the hurt in her eyes and I felt suddenly caught and angry at the same time. "Pruning shears—all right?"

"Pruning shears?" Cindy's face turned ugly with disbelief. "What in hell—?"

"A lesson in the facts of motherhood, dear innocent. Furthermore, I saw Thomas with them and was too tired and distracted to take them away. Now they have a notch in the handle. . . ."

That silenced Cindy and she hurried to bundle the children out as soon as she could wheedle Keturah away from me, and after we'd searched in the wreckage of this place to find a bottle to take along.

Thomas hadn't quite understood, because as they moved to leave he turned to me.

"Matt coming?"

"No, Thomas. It's Cindy's turn to see you."

Thomas looked at me, then at Cindy, who was nervously stripping a piece of gum for him. He reached for the gum and looked at me again.

"I'll be here when you come back for supper tonight, OK?"

"OK." He seemed suddenly to have thought of something. He ran to his room and came out with a small white truck. He handed it to me, then turned and walked out the door.

Cindy held out her arms for Keturah, who hesitated, torn, then succumbed and squeezed her arms tight around Cindy's neck. Cindy winced, then smiled bravely. Then she looked at me with what I thought was a mixture of triumph and disgust.

"We've got to go." She said this too quickly somehow. "This place depresses me—how do you stand it?"

"We don't. It stands us."

While Joanne coped with kids at home I foraged for work abroad. Our orbits changed. I came back nights to the touching animal affection of the children. "Matt Matt Matt," Keturah would chant, falling over herself in a rush to hug me. Thomas burst suddenly into tears of relief and suppressed anxiety at my absence now ended. They'd follow me everywhere in the apartment, pulling at my clothes, poking in my shoulder bag to see what treasures I'd brought back, pulling me to see their day's handiwork.

Joanne, who'd been their most important person all day, was abandoned without a thought. She'd look on somewhat disgusted, then resentful that I seemed to have no time for her either, monopolized by them. Petty annoyances would surface and she'd use them like wedges to split into the family.

"Matt, you sure Thomas is OK with that blanket like

that?" He had put it aside when I came in but now something in Joanne's voice and my tension made him leave my side and grab it off the couch. He was packing its wet corner back between his teeth, looking up at us. "I mean anytime there's a problem for him he retreats to it? How can it be so important?"

"I don't know—no, that's untrue: I do know. That's what he's had instead of parents...."

For the first few days Joanne would breathe a sigh of relief when I arrived and disappear into the guest bedroom for quiet. But after a couple more days she had become so locked into her role she just looked at me suspicious and resentful, pushed her hair from her face, and went back to her chores in the kitchen. A kind of exhausted sulk. Later, slumped before the TV, she would dredge up the horrors of the day, helpless to keep them from sounding like complaints, ashamed they sounded so petty.

"Are all babies stubborn, Matt? I mean, I can't keep Keturah from anything in reach. This was the third ashtray she's smashed reaching up blind to the top of a table. She pulled the whole cloth down, in fact, spilling my soda, the bowl of pennies, every goddamn thing. I say 'no' and 'no!' and shout at her and she cries or pouts and two minutes later she's pulling herself up on some other disaster. I don't know—"

"I know, Joanne. I know. Look. You've just got to clear the decks. There's no way to stop her exploring—"

"Exploring? That's not exploring. That's search and destroy. I think she's *trying* to break stuff, not just looking around."

"Well ... whatever. All kids seem to do it. Maybe it's just being cooped up with no place reasonable for her to operate. I don't know. Even in Connecticut where Thomas had already levelled everything once, she found stuff. But there at least I could just put her out in the yard to eat caterpillars and sticks and savage the flowers. Think of it this way. She's eliminating all excesses from your life, trimming the fat. A kind of urban renewal."

Joanne was infrequently appeased. Mostly she just fell asleep waiting for Basil to come back, looking harried and despoiled, slatternly. Her once-beautiful brown hair was strung out in all directions, unkempt. And her rest was troubled with little meteorologies of anxiety that swept across her sleeping face, smooth and metallic like alloy in the half-light of the TV.

While I looked for day care for the kids, day care for me with Joanne was suspended while she acted out the last reflex pantomimes of motherhood—what Basil in annoyed bewilderment one day called her "dial M for Mother syndrome."

The sidewalks of New York, apparently, are where kids are supposed to spend the summers. New York City takes its traditions dead serious. I did find some day-care centers on the West Side that operated through the summer for a ripened fee, but parents on the East Side—what few of them lurked there among the wall-to-wall singles—are apparently supposed to spring their kids for summer camp, Lake George, or the Vineyard.

If I lived in the West Village, one bird-voiced woman told me, and fit somewhere specific on the sliding scale, they might have room for me. I didn't. You can't have income without day care and you can't have day care without income. Anyway you had to live there to qualify. However, if you could pay, shall we say, $100 per week per child, there was a cheery brightly painted place one block from the UN that swore by Maria Montessori.

Who needed day care if he made that much money? You could buy a governess or arrange for your estranged husband to kidnap the children if you had that kind of spare change.

I collared innocent bystanders in the neighborhood, ambushed tip-toed East Side ladies with prams, but most professed not to know what I meant.

The Yorkville Co-operative Playtime Center is what I meant. Squirreled in the corner basement of a hospital residence hall, two medium-sized conference rooms divided by a sliding screen and peopled by beings who looked like plants you find growing, pale and transparent, under old lumber. The place smelled of latrines and the clammy desperation of small children.

"Yes, we do take the untrained. A year? Oh yes. And the other, she's—oh, *he*'s two? They'll go in different sections, of course. All or half day? I see. Yes, we're open eight to six sharp, Mr. ah Volld. Spelled that, would you? Oh. We pay by the month in advance, and with the discount for the second one that makes $240 for July, just begun."

Jayne Kripps was a martinet in double-knits, lean and tubular like machinery, one of those women who should be desirable but somehow isn't. Standardized limbs, no trace of fat. An eater of lean meat and bean sprouts. Her black silk hair was a bit too efficiently short and she wore a pencil behind her left ear when she wasn't tapping it on the laminated fingernails of her spread-eagled left hand. Her face ought to have been open and appealing but instead it looked blank and smooth like a subway slug. She moved as if she had no cartilage, rocks against hard places. That first morning there with Thomas and Keturah I kept wanting to summon up token distracting lust for her but couldn't. A finely machined tool is more seductive.

A couple months later, just before the kids and I were forced from New York, I would be talking to her about the money I owed, or the empty orange juice containers I forgot to bring and I would feel I was drowning, all these children were drowning, and there was Jayne Kripps, pencil on her ear, clambering steadfastly across on our drowning heads.

Co-operative day care is supposed to mean that you bring old egg boxes and they make your small children disappear.

Mother's Day

But the reason parents become addicted to such places is that they provide an oasis of despair in an otherwise mindlessly cheerful world.

The Yorkville, for instance, turned out to be an evil-smelling behavioral sink, forty-five children strong, where the walls were smudged to three feet high, the toilets backed up or misplaced, and the ion level intense. We arrived there mornings, we parents, mostly late for work and crazed-looking like horses in a storm. Children with us were galloped past the building's West Indian doorman, who daily tried to penetrate the private frenzy of the amputated families that passed him. Sometimes the children snapped alive and smiled as he bowed and clowned at them, but mostly they didn't, just quick-stepped their way past, touching down only every few steps as their parents yanked them along in the rush.

Keturah never touched ground at all. She clung to me from the moment we left our apartment the first day. She clung to my arm, then my hand, my jacket, my pants and my shoe as I tried to disengage myself from her when we got to school. I think she thought I was leaving her for good, so artificial and tense had I become as we neared the place. Thomas cried all the way there, more because we were late—parents are always late—and me furious than anything else, I think. We took a cab because people at the bus stop on Second Avenue gave me such dirty looks for allowing Thomas's crying to disrupt their A.M. absorption with themselves.

The school room was hot and smelled like a hospital specimen lab. Several children were crouched in a corner crying and sniffling while an overweight woman in some Indian peasant coverall tried to comfort them. She looked at me vaguely when I came in and proceeded to detach Keturah like a blood leech. Keturah was desperate and intense, fighting for a hold, while I tried to pretend nothing was wrong, that it was all play—we do this every day, folks, just a little game we have, father and daughter. While I tried not to break anything of Keturah's or pull anything out of sockets. I kept thinking that one time I will yank too hard, preoccupied or pissed off, and out will come an arm or leg at the ball joint: the child will be sitting there unstrung like an old-fashioned doll.

Other parents were crowding through the door with other screaming children. Some children, though, didn't scream. They didn't make a sound to their parent. And it was always one parent: I never once saw two parents with any one child at that school. Maybe there aren't two parents any more. Maybe it doesn't take two parents anymore to make children, I don't know. Anyway, parents set several children down like furniture, staring dead ahead of them. These children were usually the tidy ones dressed in matched sets with cute quilted animals attached. Same color sock on each foot. They were training to be stockbrokers or bankers, those kids, to wear their Chemise Lacostes.

In Thomas' class was one. Samuel Somethingorother, who never spoke the whole two months I took the kids there. Neither did his token parent, of indeterminate sex, who brought him mornings and came for him nights. I got to know the parent, in a way, because we were both always late in the evenings and had to compete for excuses with the martyred aide elected to stay overtime with the abandoned kids. Even the aide left sometimes—more and more as the summer went on—and we'd find the kids milling around the foyer of the building and a tight-lipped doorman trying to keep an eye on them.

I never knew her name, this parent, but she—and it turned out to be a she—mainlined starch and Clorox, I think, and an anti-wetness agent. She had rabbit-short hair, shaved neat at the back of the neck, and wore suits and ties and briefcases to and from work. Her steel-rimmed glasses glinted like surgical instruments as she moved. Samuel must have imbibed the starch with her antibodies for he never sprawled in the hall like the rest of our kids, he never acted anything out. I began to notice, though, that whenever I was early in the evenings, I'd find him crouched in his cubby—as they called the rack of blue partitions where each kid kept his belongings. The teacher of the day had banished him there, Thomas explained, because he was "bad."

Her usual late excuse was cabs and traffic jams, Sam's mother. I decided she was his mother when I found her with him twice on weekends slumped in the park in jeans and a scarf holding her head on. The second time Thomas found Sam and pointed to the mother, who was sitting on a stone bench reading a newspaper and stuffing the pages, one by one as she finished them, into a wire wastepaper basket. She looked bloated and unglued. Her workday demeanor seemed gone, maybe because she seemed to have left her space glasses elsewhere.

Sam and Thomas tried pushing each other off the slide, and throwing sand, then settled on an intense game that consisted of Thomas trying to climb the slide chute while Sam crashed into him from above. Keturah was eating sand in the play area, looking repeatedly surprised at its effects on her lips and tongue. I was hoping cat people didn't walk their animals there and thinking what to say to Sam's mother. I don't think she had seen me, or maybe anyone else, and I only saw her look for Sam once, craning her neck at him so sharply that he stopped mid-climb on the slide and walked directly over to her. She said something and he walked back across the tops of benches like a child performing in some school show.

Finally I went over to her and she flinched when I said hello. She tried to look at me directly and tried again and finally settled for staring at my right lapel. Devoid of all the flash and warpaint of her daily mask she looked awful. She had been reading the real-estate section, all she'd brought with her.

I said how long has Sam been at that school. She said four months. I said has he been at others and she said no. Do you like it? Does he like it? Sure he likes it, I guess. He can't come to work with me, can he? No, I said, I suppose not. Nobody does that, I suppose.

Then there was a silence. I noticed starlings in the trees that grew out of the cement park. You could hear them carrying on, like slide kazoos, clear and eccentric over the noise of cars on First Avenue. The park was at about Sixty-first Street, I think, quite near the Yorkville Center. That's probably why both she and I knew about it, having passed it weekdays and made a mental note. And there we were, me with the Help Wanted, she with Real Estate, trying to say something—anything—that mattered.

Something about that gesture I saw that brought Sam to her earlier, something about the puffed, shamed face filled me with almost maternal sadness for her. Really sadness for me, too, I guess, but directed at her. I wanted to touch her shoulder or the sad naked back of her neck the way people do to each other at funerals. But I couldn't. So I asked instead if Sam could spend the day with us.

"Us?"

"Me and my kids."

"Well, I don't know, now. I'm not. I'd have to—" She looked intently at some new thing in the park between each remark, as if the cement turtle she studied, or the bright-yellow jungle gym had some say in the matter. "I think maybe some other time, thanks. I just can't figure out our plans yet, you see—"

I said I saw and I did, but it just made me more depressed. I pretended I had just noticed Keturah eating sand and snatched her from the pit, brushing off her lips, which were frosted and crunchy like a margarita. She had pouches of sand back in the corners of her mouth near the tonsils and I hooked these out with a little finger, wanting to spit myself at the slurry noise it made in her mouth.

"Look." I was back at the bench, fussing motherly at Keturah's face with my handkerchief. "Look, we're going to be here for several more hours, anyway. If you have stuff to do, go do it. Leave me a phone number if you want and I'll bring him by when we leave. Or you can come for him. I'm stuck here with my brats anyway, and a third kid won't be any extra strain."

Finally she relented, looking nervously several ways out of the park and once into the trees. No, it wasn't nervousness. It was guilt. We looked like dealers in white slaves, maybe, exchanging victims for some old sodomite's Sunday matinee. I don't know. But she did write a number on the edge of the paper and tore it off for me, then she tucked the rest of the paper high under her arm. She threaded her other arm through bamboo handles of a submarine purse till it crouched close to her body under the elbow. She went over to Sam at the slide and said something. He looked at me and at Thomas, nodded twice, and went back to the ladder. She paused for a minute at the edge of the park, sort of waved with her elbow still dug into her waist over the purse, then set off across Sixty-first Street walking diagonally into the traffic.

I don't think I realized the depth of Basil's desperation about me until the night I told him about my new job. I had conspired with Joanne to say nothing till later, so when Basil first came home, tired and wound-up as he often was, he paced around watering the coleus and straightening the magazines the kids had desecrated.

"Any mail, Joanne?" he finally asked. "Goddamn IRS heard from?"

"No. Some letter bombs for Matt from the collection agencies, that's all. What do you do with them, anyway, Matt? What happens if you just ignore them?"

"I never ignore them long. Just long enough to earn a sigh of relief from the person assigned to me when I do answer—even though I'm just offering a new excuse. The unemployed have lots of time to erect eloquent excuses."

"What about the phone bill, Joanne? That come? I'm sweating that after last week's drunken night with Patrick."

Patrick tends to call old fraternity brothers, ten years gone, when he drinks enough to forget time. He's otherwise normal but at a certain cc level he succumbs to reflex and dials distant emotions with a frenzy. That night he had dialed California to carry on a desultory shouting match with a brother-in-the-bonds remarkable, apparently, for his ability in college to have a "think-off." "Never had to put hand to gland," slurred Patrick after he had finally hung up, giving Basil good cause to worry about the bill.

"Well, calm yourself about Ma Bell, Basil," I said. "This time I'll be able to appease her some."

"Oh, no, Matt. None of your campaigns here. I've got enough problems already without subjecting my credit rating to your tissues of lies."

"Basil, Basil. I'm not talking about tissues. I'm talking about the root of all evil, Mammon, the wages of sin. My paychecks. I fall upon the thorns of life et cetera. I got work—"

"What? Je-sus. I knew there was something in the air, you two so poker-faced when I came in. Who'd you snag, then? Better not be some swish woman's mag."

"No, but close. The euphemism for the new me is "researcher" and the wages are a hundred and sixty dollars. A hundred and sixty gross—with widow's benefits or whatever you call them. Just about enough to pay for day care, cab fare, super Pampers, and TV guide. A kind of heaven."

"And the place, Matt, the place?"

"I think I'd rather not go into that just now, in mixed company, you see. How shall I say?"

"Come off it. We're all whores here, no need for shame. I'd have sold my virginity for a hundred and sixty dollars—I have in fact long since—so ... is it *People*?"

"*People* pays, and they don't hire single mothers from academe. No, not *People*. *Harper's Weekly*—a kind of listener-sponsored item, where the readers write most of it and idiots like me check up on them."

"Hey. That's not bad. Decent money, decent mag. What'd you do to get hired, blow the guy through his Rolodex?"

"Almost. It was more of a hum-job, really—I bored him into submission."

Basil was transported with joy. The beginning of the end, I think he hoped. Yesterday day care, today a job, tomorrow maybe—dare he hope?—a sty of my own someplace else?

Keturah and Thomas had been staring at "Kojak," conned by the infinitely more professional acting coming from the screen, the modulated voices, the fine timing. Nothing in real life can compete. But something about Basil's little jig with the plastic watering can caught their attention. Maybe it was Basil's elaborate waltz around the coffee table or Joanne's relieved laughter at his mood, but Keturah began to peck her head up and down, like those weird mechanical birds in cars. She was excited. Something new was happening. Thomas had learned already the conservatism of the very young. New mostly meant bad, or at least dangerous, and he snatched his blanket from the couch and toddled over to my side, calling "Matt? Matt?" like some desolate lost soul.

Basil is always a master of rejuvenation. After fixing us big drinks, he started swimming though his closet shelves, reaching around for something hidden there. Finally he fished out a fat manilla envelope boney with plastic containers. "I've been stockpiling chemical warfare agents for just such an occasion," Basil said, and he cleared off the coffee table and selected a container of white powder.

What happened next is not recommended in child-care books but it became one of the best events of Keturah's and Thomas' truncated childhood.

We used up the coke quite fast, sniffing it like anteaters and becoming immortal, as one does. Whereupon it seemed only logical and Olympian to take some speed to sustain the heights. Basil didn't have any among his hoard but I had been guarding some white Desoxyn pills for the imagined deadlines I would encounter in my apprenticeship to Mother Journalism—or for some night I would have to stay up exhausted with terminally sick children. (That scene has haunted me since my first months with Thomas when he was sick for days on end, only quiet while I walked him. By the middle of the second night I found myself blinded by fatigue, thinking earnestly about knocking his head against the stone fireplace—just a little knock, mind you—to shut him up so I could sleep).

I had ten pills, so we each took one and I kept seven for the future. But already the kids were enjoying themselves. Never had they seen such rapt adult enthusiasm, such eager attention. We read them all their favorite tedious books time and time again, at breakneck speed. Thomas brought out his records—Davy Crockett, Christmas favorites, Disney World—and we sang frenzied choruses, repeated choruses, of "It's a Small World, After All" and "King of the Wild Frontier," Thomas and Keturah flailing around the rooms in delighted abandon. Joanne and Thomas danced to every song on "The Sound of Music"—a record she'd bought them that week—and I found myself whirling like a dervish, Keturah shreiking with terror and delight pressed against my chest. Finally Keturah dropped off to sleep, nodding off by the blasting record player.

But Thomas and the rest of us were inexhaustible. Thomas wanted another supper, so Basil wrecked the kitchen making sandwiches for him. He dragged me into his room to see forgotten masterpieces of his I'd probably ignored time and time before. Joanne got out a belly-dance record and did a spirited bump and grind to it, stripping down to her underwear. Thomas clapped and howled when Basil and I did but seemed confused, as if he were watching some mysterious foreign rite.

Across the street at a bicycle store the goddamn burgular alarm had gone off half an hour before and was still going,

Mother's Day

so we could hear it above the record player. Last time it didn't stop all night. We were scheming feverishly about a raid over there to short it out and about to fortify ourselves with more speed. Suddenly Thomas stopped dead in his tracks. He had been doing a kind of rain dance to a Sesame Street record when he stopped, looked queerly at each of us and then walked slowly over to me.

"Matt? I'm tired, Matt. Going to bed." He looked at me calmly, nodded his head and said, "School tomorrow." He was very dignified as he said it. Then he leaned against me, reached for his blanket behind me on the floor, and fell asleep.

I looked at Joanne and Basil, suddenly feeling foolish. They were looking elsewhere. Basil reached over and flicked off the record player. Joanne began reflexively to collect ashtrays and glasses scattered around her.

I lay awake between the kids a long time, feeling tired but disconnected and curiously at peace. On Second Avenue several large trucks blundered by below and I remember thinking that no one had said anything before bed about the shadows of the night.

You've seen them—just never thought anything of it, I bet. All those children in supermarkets called Shaddap. Mothers slapping infants around in public places. What do you suppose goes on in private, then?

This is some of what I was thinking yesterday evening as I sprinted for day care after work. I saw a woman striding toward me carrying some large bags. Behind her was a curious noise that even the evening traffic couldn't drown out. A kind of high-pitched buzz like a transformer. When she got closer I saw the noise—a three-year-old dressed in a filthy white jumpsuit. He was carrying a popsicle in one hand, a pack of opened gum in the other and the world on both shoulders. He was running to keep up with his mother, tripping in his awkwardness, howling with misery. Tears had run the candy smears around his mouth and he looked like a smudged watercolor. They'd come some distance, because the popsicle was almost gone. His mother was young but her face squinted with strain. She was in a hurry, exhausted with a bag of too many groceries. And she was late—that was clear. Just like me.

I have been late now almost every day since I got work. Day care closes at six to help make you always late, just as supermarkets in this city close just before you could possibly reach them after work.

I work from ten to six, Mrs. Knapp tells me. Mrs. Knapp is one of the harpies recast, hired by magazines to keep things high-strung. Creative tension. She is probably fifty but you couldn't graph it. Just a straight line, her life, without childhood or even a mid-life crisis. I see her less on a graph than a microdot, staring deadpan at the world. A TV set, I swear, has more expression.

Anyway, Mrs. Knapp (who I'm supposed to call Faith but can't yet because my tongue tip gets caught in my jaw clamp when I try it) says we work from ten to six here and some of us work much longer. I guess I am supposed to be stung how the "us" leaves me out—maybe I am at times—but come five in the evening I am in the starting block at the office door, pining to be let out. I watch like a rodent for the chance to dart out into the oil-can rush-hour air and the noise of little children everywhere, buzzing, that I can hear high over the claptrap and kettledrums of the evening traffic.

Those children I hear are buzzing because they are running too hard behind rushed parents, because they are abandoned tired and filthy at the doorways to their schools, milling like little windups (click-clack, click-clack), waiting for a parent someplace running pell-mell for a bus that will then jam solid in the traffic icefloe.

Actually, the first few evenings went all right. Mrs. Knapp took pity at my distraction *"I'll do the rest."* She'd smile at me, fiendish. "Takes a while to settle in, I know."

Mother's Day

I think of roadbeds settling, of Venice—then bolt for the bronzed elevator door that opens and closes piped dentist's music every floor to the ground.

But tonight things are not all right. The circadian rhythms of editors is the problem. Here is how an editor clocks. Start the day at eleven-something with coffee and mail in a black study. When you've revived enough to eat, then luncheon, preferably extended, andirons of drink at each end. You take one of the guys from work, or some delight whose tits you admire. Expense account, of course. Which makes it now around three. I am waiting for you. I am waiting for you since ten fucking A.M., probably earlier in fact, since I have more work than I can do from ten to six and I need to run for day care at five-thirty so I come early. You are sluggish from three to four, shaking off the alcohol that drones like mosquitoes behind sleep. Then, God damn it, we get cracking. Where's that goddamn edit, anyway Vole? And no, that caption won't do, of course, try again. And how many—exactly!—are there welfare-mother amputees in this city; that adds a nice touch to the story. Jesus, why are you people so slow with these things, what have you been *doing* all day? This is a weekly, or didn't you know? Not an annual.

Which makes me late. The editor thinks you are an ingrate because you want to leave by six. A stickler, you are, for the letter of your contract. You don't give a damn for what you do, just what we do for you. We know the sort. And Mrs. Knapp knows the sort, too.

At this remark Mrs. Knapp draws herself to her full five feet ten inches, a ramrod of a woman with preternaturally blond hair coiled like a clockspring at her jaw. I think of her as an iron maiden inside out, with spikes for body contours. She has a honeyed voice, I admit, but crystalline with menace so it grates.

I haven't been able to like Mrs. Knapp, as you can see. I haven't been able to like the editor, either. They lack latitude, like clerics, and I hear the swish of righteousness in everything they do. I don't think they like me, either, though there's no visible discrimination here: they hate us all equally. There are three other women in my position, young martyred women with sharpened pencils over their ears, whom Mrs. Knapp and Mr. Pomerantz cordially hate. But I am older than my fellow minions, urgent as they are not. I am preoccupied with other deadlines. Keturah, for instance, had a swelling on her left eye yesterday, some random blow or sudden malignancy. I felt it hot and thumping against my chest last night. I should have taken her someplace, some emergency room I guess, this morning. But I didn't. And also it is now 5:47 and I can hear a drone out there beyond the sealed glass windows, beyond the white noise of our fluorescent lights, beyond the ghostly stale breathing of the ventilator.

"No quick way to run that down, Mr. Pomerantz. The unidexters, I mean."

"Unidex? Oh, I see. S'pose not. Never is a quick way. D'ja try the Welfare Department?"

"Closed for the day. They close at five."

"Five! What the hell time is it now. God, this is slow going. Well, I guess we skip it. We just skip it. In fact we are expert at skipping things here all of a sudden. Jesus. Hand me that."

I hand him the copy. 5:51.

"Will that be all? I mean it's clean. Checked for errors. And I've got to split in a minute."

"Call of the wild, eh? Boy, I wish I was a researcher again. Some hours. Yeah—OK. Just give it a final once-over and try the major's office for that statistic—just in case."

5:54.

I am hurdling pedestrians on the corner of Forty-sixth and Park. Thank God for all the ethnics in this city. Every other person stunted by wartime malnutrition. But here comes a dilemma. Some crone with shopping bags like dewlaps at her sides. First the weight pulls her one way, then the other, like a pendulum. Sometimes her balance is off and one spins her almost entirely around. Which makes her stop. Do I squeeze for the wall and risk a cul de sac? Do I go for the road space that cab is also heading for? Trust the cabbie and bolt is the decision, one hand to my heart (to hold in my pocket pens), the other crooked around the bottom of my shoulder bag. Last week running, I left the bag free and it cleaned out an ancient gentleman on a corner. Caught him in the throat at arm's length from my side as I did my parachute roll for the subway entrance.

Two blocks east so far. Now the question is when was the last IRT fire and have we had our daily man-on-the-tracks? A thing like that could keep me down there all night, no telephone, while the children self-destruct. I'll stay on the surface. At least I can run to Sixty-sixth and First—if my heart doesn't give out.

Here comes a bus, glacial in traffic. No hope for that. Better to run up Third Avenue looking for a cab. Two dollars and fifty cents that will be, but if I hold him for the kids we can get to Seventy-seventh for another dollar. And no horrors. Monday I tried the bus with them after school. Lunch boxes, a plastic bag of Keturah's soiled clothes, a monstrous roll of fingerpaintings, two children. We stood, if that's the word for it, most of the way, Keturah jammed upright between my legs, Thomas holding my jacket. Then we got a seat with three blocks to go and sat while the children stared at me first in relief then in worry because I was hiding behind my exoskeleton of grownup calm. Keturah started to cry. Nothing shatters my calm more efficiently. Then she cried louder when I glowered at her.

I am holding Keturah in my right arm with the paintings and the clothes bag. Hook Thomas' hand in my pocket and grab for the lunch boxes and I lunge for the bus door at Seventy-seventh. The latch on lunch boxes is right under the handle, so every time you go to pick one up it tries to open. This time Thomas' flipped open midway down the bus corridor, spewing its insides. Two ragged halves of peanut-butter-and-jelly sandwiches, swollen and purple like bruises, a carrot, and some orange skins. My fellow passengers stared horrified, as if I'd dropped a load of eyeballs. We just kept going, down the stairs and out, people staring, the driver gaping in his mirror at this scattered compost on the ribbed black rubber matting by the back door.

"What was I going to do? Stop mid flight and scoop it up like dog shit? Put Keturah down? Who would hold her? Pick it back up into the lunchbox, miss my stop and have to carry two children two extra blocks, meanwhile basking the extra bus ride in the outrage of assholes?"

"I don't know, Matt. I guess I really don't know." Joanne looks troubled but unsympathetic.

"Don't worry about it." Basil is laughing. "Minute you left, some senior citizen riding the buses to keep out of the nursing home would scoop it over with the side of his foot, surreptitiously. Then wolf it, skin and all. More nourishment than he's had in weeks, probably."

"That's it. I always feel that about this city. Giant cockroaches poised to snatch anything left unattended. Every time you drive the freeways and see those violated cars. You know, someone breaks down and goes for help. Legions of roaches swarm from behind the guard rails, strip the thing bare in seconds. Gone the radio, tires, battery, lights, seats, doors. Moments later you look back at it and all you see is a skeleton—like those animals in Tarzan movies that fall into the wrong stream. Picked clean. I'm beginning to get jumpy about my kids like that. One day I'm going to get there late and there'll be just this pile of little bones, like lunch-box crusts, carefully swept into the corner by the custodian."

So I took cabs early in the paycheck and ran the rest of each week. One day when I was particularly nauseated from

Mother's Day 115

exhaustion I risked the bus. You have to change at the UN but that seemed better than vomiting on my only clothes for the week. Especially since there hadn't been time for lunch and it would be only green oily stuff coming out, midtown bile. Here in midtown mostly I get the dry heaves—a kind of exercise in futility as the CNS tells me things about my life I do not choose to hear. The dry heaves keep me from my lunch quite often, a kind of mourning sickness, but even when I can afford lunch I often skip it. Feeding myself under these conditions is inhospitable. I think it's the office overhead light, busy like trapped tiny flies, homing in on me. And the walls. We have intrusive walls here that seem to move in on you during the day. By two in the afternoon I am bumping into walls that at eight A.M. were arm's length away. I have to leave my office every few minutes to run copy to a person in a hurry who has been waiting for it and is angry with me, the bearer of bad tidings. But even that is better than being pressed flat by the moving walls. When I come back to my office each time usually all four lights on my telephone panel are blinking. All I can think of is an unanswered emergency. By three in the afternoon I hear my phone from floors away and rush back to find one more light blinking and no message with the operator. I am sure it is a child near death someplace. I've started calling the school when I find these lights. Just in case.

By the time my bus gets to the UN that day it is six-oh-seven. In my present condition I can't run from there to school by seven, so I transfer uptown. I try for a window seat and fail. I scheme from stop to stop just what I will do, step by step, when the rictus comes. I my friend's bee-sting kit—she's allergic and carries Adrenalin with her everywhere—instructions describe anaphylactic shock. A prominent symptom, it says, is "a sense of impending disaster." As soon as I am late anywhere these days—and I am late everywhere these days, a life without leeway—I get the symptom. Today it is fighting for supremacy with the rictus. I think I prefer the rictus, which doesn't constrict the heart, at least. I don't know what you call this but it is the opposite of sweat. Something is drawn inwards instead of squeezed out through the pores. You feel cold, and naked. Also there's someone breathing heavy hot breaths on the back of my neck, jammed up against me as I brace myself by the exit door. I wonder if the bell works back here. If I miss my stop and have to walk back I'm going to collapse. My knees are already hinged backwards.

It is half a block east from First Avenue to the Yorkville Co-operative Whatnot. I pass a school, empty now since this afternoon. The sidewalks are shiny with tin-foil wrappers and pieces of bright paper. Some of them have melted into the asphalt. I should have taken a cab but then I wouldn't have had the four dollars we agreed to pay the late teacher. So this way that teacher stays later. Usually there are one or two kids just sitting on the steps by the building, staring at their lunch boxes or looking up the street for a parent. I don't see anyone today.

I don't even see the doorman in his meticulous blue pants and cap, proper West Indian that he is. Can it be my watch is wrong and it is tomorrow or a weekend? There is a smelly corridor below ground in the back of the building that leads to the playground out back. The playground is locked all the time to prevent vandalism (otherwise known as use)—but maybe the kids are playing in the corridor. The fancy marble foyer floor turns to ribbed cement as soon as you turn the corner. The air smells latrine and cool the closer I get to the locked day-care rooms. The corridor is empty except for Keturah's bag of today's soiled clothes. So they were here sometime since school, the children, so there was school today and they should be in the hall with the doorman. Sometimes when I am particularly late for things my mind overloads and shuts down and I can't figure out why I am rushing and what it is I have forgotten.

Mother's Day

What it is I want to do now is run screaming from the door of the building, my arms out like a kid making a plane. If I had lights and a siren I would turn them on, screech around corners, looking.

Instead I try the elevators. It seems everyday in New York I read about kids dismembered in elevators. Should I ride each one to each floor? What if the kids are on one while I am on the other? Should I wait for both elevators to return to this floor? I press my ear against the metal doors to see if I can hear children somewhere deep inside the shaft. No children. Of course, if the elevator has beheaded them already, there wouldn't be any noise. In fact, why is it the elevators don't seem to be moving? Then one, then the other comes down empty and I am running now for the street. One hand on my pocket for the pens, one on my outrigger shoulder bag.

I've never been the last parent and I can't be now. There must be other children here. Maybe the doorman took them all someplace, or one of the parents with hers when she found my children left alone. There's the flintstone park at First Avenue, giant concrete everythings to thwart the vandals and goths. Maybe they are there, listening soberly in a circle to some parent reading a story.

Here's the doorman trotting from the building across the street. He doesn't look friendly this evening.

"Hello, ah—"

"Good evenin', Mista."

"My children—from the day care, you know?—I can't find them."

"All the children gone, sir, just a short time back."

"Where'd they—I mean, who'd they? How?"

"Teacher had to go herself this evenin'."

"Yes? And—"

"Children just playing in the lobby till they parents come."

"And all the children gone now?"

"Gone. Yes."

* * *

New Yorkers are much maligned. They are in fact among the most tolerant of people. So you see a two-and-a-half-year-old, alone, toying on the edge of the Second Avenue evening rush. Well, city kids. You know. Street wise. And anyway that's his business. He has a right to these streets as much as anyone else. Besides, confront him and he might be wired to explosives like those gook kids in Nam or something. Who knows.

Tolerance.

I found Thomas between First and Second, pushing a small yellow Tonka bulldozer he took to school with him. I'd argued with him about that. Everything he takes gets broken or lost, it seems, and anyway the teachers beg parents to keep toys home, since sharing with twenty others is tough on two-year-olds. The bulldozer was in the gutter by the curb, and Thomas was duck-walking behind it, making whirring noises, intent.

I think what made me most angry was how casual he acted. He mostly wanted to show me how he still had his bulldozer and I am jerking him from the gutter in a fury of precautions about passing cars, screaming about Keturah. Thomas' face dropped, then froze. "Keturah, Thomas, where's Keturah? Thomas!—"

She was back in the school building, he said, so we ran the two blocks. I had yanked Thomas so hard in my anger he'd turned weak all over. Couldn't walk fast enough, like those men you see in documentaries stumbling in fear towards their execution. So I was carrying him against my right side. He dropped the bulldozer and we left it there, because I am increasingly angry at him for some reason. I always used to sneer at those parents who'd bust their child because he'd strayed out into the road and almost been hit. No longer. I used to be incredulous that parents walked with the kid on the car side of them, dangerously close to the edge. No longer. Tonight I could hoist Thomas high over my

Mother's Day

head and throw him into Second Avenue traffic. I wouldn't even have to pretend to myself, like those other parents, that it was an accident.

I was sweet as treacle with Keturah when we found her. She was sitting on the lap, you see, of a middle-aged stony-faced thin woman in a menopause lime-green pantsuit who was dying to ask how I could be so irresponsible and uncaring as to leave a baby like this alone. She didn't ask, though. Just started to explain with her teeth stuck together that she'd found the child crawling in the foyer and its brother there had said Matt was coming later.

She was like an angry mother-in-law. She wanted to say something vicious about my character but instead she blurted something about this baby always crying for Matt.

"I work here in bookkeeping, next to the school. This cute little baby is always sitting by the door over there, crying for "Matt, Matt." I've talked to the teachers about it and we all think there is something seriously wrong with her, crying like that for Matt."

"I see. Would you think there was something seriously wrong if she was crying for her mother?"

"No. Of course not."

"Well, I *am* her mother—"

Another thing she didn't say was something about wanting to inform the authorities on why these kids didn't have a suitable-looking mother instead of me with a first name and all. She was sort of out of breath, this woman, and I suspect she had stayed late after work, waiting for someone named Matt whom she wanted to smite about the head with an umbrella.

So I smiled ever so sweetly at Keturah, pretending not to notice the spreading stain of wet on the woman's left pant leg, thanked her profusely with a stream of words I didn't interrupt until I was turned and out of the office door and clacking over the fancy marble paving toward the foyer entrance.

I forgot all about the soiled clothes in the hall I'd found earlier and I never saw them again. The roaches. That night I had to wash Keturah's clothes in the sink and dry them with Joanne's orange hair dryer. And Keturah went to bed with just a diaper. And Thomas cried himself to sleep about his abandoned Tonka bulldozer. I listened to him crying and felt parallel shivers of hate and satisfaction tingle along the edges of my clenched jaw.

Usually they go to bed fully dressed. Pajamas are a frill you dispense with in this business. First because they are just another torment at the laundromat. But also because you have to fight them on and off children who are either wet from a bath—the pajamas stick at the legs and arms—or involved in the decathalon while you do it. Fianlly, trying to dress two exhausted children in a hurry in the morning with a headache and a skeleton of bonemeal from lack of sleep doesn't recommend itself. I've found that clothes from the dryer bag are curiously wrinkled at night but by the morning sleep has nicely smoothed them out.

The children have a bath at night. That in itself is an act of sainthood. By seven at night muscles in my back and legs are turnbuckle tight, like rigging, and I feel steel cable as I stretch to bend down over the bath. Keturah always makes unexpected slides under the water and has to be rescued, coughing and surprised each time. Water has splashed everywhere already—children's water splashes more than ours—and either you hunker, tightening the wiring, or you kneel and wet your pants. If I have the energy I strip to my underwear so I don't have to scream so much in the bathroom, where the sound, confined, vibrates off the porcelain and ricochets booming back at you. Thomas always has to pee after he has gotten in the tub and I don't dare let him crawl out on his own after the first several catastrophic falls he took that way. Keturah just pisses in the bathwater, looking preoccupied. Not that she is uninterested in such processes. Now that she can stand braced against things she insists on assisting when I relieve myself. Several nights ago Joanne walked in on me peeing to see Keturah braced against my leg proudly directing the flow. I'm not sure what she made of the scene—she hasn't mentioned it—but my having to ponder it as a result makes me less sure now that it will continue.

This evening the children are just bathed and wrapped in towels. Thomas' hair sticks up in ratty points but he looks unnaturally pure somehow as he marches into the living room with a towel twisted awkwardly around him. Joanne made a towel turban for Keturah, who toddles in to show it off to Basil's friend, Francine, who is here to photograph children this evening. She begins to work her camera and the kids first stare in confusion. Keturah recovers first and stands suddenly to a kind of attention, her busbee on her head, like a palace guard. The camera makes a sizzling noise, then Keturah looks at me on the couch and trundles over to cling to my legs. While I am trying to dress them in their room for tomorrow, Francine's machine hisses in the background. Both kids are thrashing on their backs on the bed while I tickle and they shriek with pleasure.

At best now the kids are used to my fatigue and indifference in the evenings. Tonight they are glowing with the attention. Thomas wants a picture of himself holding a cardboard box he crayoned into a house. Then holding a prize candy bar Francine brought him. He holds the candy bar—a Baby Ruth—right up in front of his face and Francine tries not to giggle as she solemnly strategies her picture. Francine has long reddish hair and a slightly wolverine French jaw. I think her hair reminds the kids of Cindy, because they are soon crawling on her lap, fighting for snuggling space. Now it is her turn to look confused.

I don't think she's had much to do with children. She looks giddy and at the same time shoots looks at me as if I might be offended. I'm not, but the scene reminds me how efficient these kids have become at scrounging affection from adults. They're like those pathetic girl children whores you see in the Middle East who ape the seductive wiles of their grown sisterhood hoping for their share of the trade. My kids zero in on women, often driving them quickly away in panic, but whenever I visit a single mother friend with kids I am touched by the quick gifts her children want to give this stranger—a cherished stuffed animal, a miniature truck they keep in some special place. Parents may not think they need partners any longer, but children don't seem to have heard that yet.

Francine helps put the kids to bed, seduced into a sudden loneliness by them. She wants to read them a story and they almost swoon with pleasure, so simple are their needs.

She is reading a dopey book they love about a mother cat and her stereotyped litter—why do they crave such trash?—and from the living room, where I am unstrung with fatigue on the couch, I can hear Francine's frenchified pronunciations being repeatedly corrected. Basil is surreptitiously watching the news, his evening anodyne, and Joanne has retired to the spare room in collapse. Some of Francine's pictures were Polaroid, drying now on the loft shelf.

What these pictures make me think of is Cindy, for some reason. She will never see them—pictures of good moments with the kids I hoard, like icons—but if she could, how would she feel? Like I feel when I see pictures of my older sister as a child?—as if a strange amnesia had cheated me of a part of myself?

The children are quiet now. Francine is still reading, but uncorrected. How much simpler it would be to love them if they were someone else's children.

CHAPTER X

"Basil, I have something to tell you." We are alone at P.J. Clark's for lunch. Basil is taking me to celebrate my new job. The level of noise is so high we can chat in insulated privacy though we share a table with two beefy men in pin-stripes and regimental ties.

"No kidding. You've decided to resign from your job already?"

"Not exactly—but close. Our friendship I may have to resign from. This is ticklish but I can't stand the heat any longer."

"What could be ticklish after all these years? I thought we were down to bare granite, rock upon rock. You stole some loose change from my pants pocket, or what? Come off it, Vole. Cut the mystery."

"It's about Joanne—"

"She's newly with child?"

"Not exactly. But—"

"Jesus, Vole. She comes with the apartment, didn't I tell you that?"

"No, you didn't and she doesn't. But she *has*—or rather I have forced it."

"You flatter yourself. But go on. This is better than an appetizer. Vikes, God knows, I can use at this shrivelled stage of my life."

"I've been sleeping with Joanne, Basil. Like—"

"Like brother and sister, you were going to say?"

"Like brother and sister aren't supposed to. Worse. Like sister and sis—"

"—Order?" The waiter pokes his voice into our cocoon of private noise. We order almost impatiently. Basil is always unpredictable. He seemed energized by my paltry confession. Those guys at the next table were shouting about seaplanes.

"Well?" Basil was looking carefully noncommital.

"Well, it's not exactly incestuous. But it is distinctly unnatural. I think we're having a strange kind of extrasexual item, you see."

"Aw. You lied. You said there'd be vikes. Now all I'm going to get is some emotional claptrap? Jesus. And *I'm* buying, yetst."

"No, I don't make myself clear. I keep feeling I should be saying this like Peter Lorre, whining and thick Eastern Europe. But this is tricky, as I said."

"Must be for Christ's sake. Sure takes long enough to get to the point. Or isn't there any point? Maybe you're just setting me up, you prick? You wouldn't do that to a friend, would you? A friend who's picking up the tab? You set me up, you take me to lunch—that's the way they do it here in New York. Didn't you know?"

"OK. It's your lunch. Here goes."

"Finally something to sink the teeth into, I hope."

"Joanne and I are sleeping together—or have been, till I got work and had to swear off."

"I know. Thomas told me."

"Jesus. He did, that little prick? Kids these days have no discretion. I told him not to tell you—"

"That was nice—"

"Well, I wanted to tell you myself first."

"Sure took a long time, oh, bosom pal. Or were you waiting maybe to come one time more than once? I know you're getting old."

"Actually, I—I find myself between a rock and a hard place."

"That's what I said. Our naked friendship. Bedrock."

"No. This way: I know almost only women these days. Since I'm a mother. They're the ones I find more in myself—"

"Or you in them?"

"And me in them, you're right. But I'm no longer sure about rights and permissions. Do I come to ask permission for a woman who happens to be living with you but who offers herself, an independent party to a merger? You don't think of her as your property, I know that, and yet you are my primary friend, I keep thinking. And if there is a risk to this hanky-panky, I don't want the risk to be you. Your friendship. See what I am saying?"

"A mouthful is what you are saying. But I see. We're all up against it, these days, not only you. But it's all right about Joanne. OK? You didn't need my permission but you would have had it anyway. It was actually Joanne told me about you two, couple weeks ago. I blackmailed her into it by saying I was going to find out from you. You think I haven't noticed how newly softened up she's become?"

That was a long lunch. It turned out Basil was delighted with what he called Joanne's "progress." Women needed help with this leg of their liberation and concerned men should be willing to offer their expertise. We laughed about that. Basil talked about the sister of a friend who wanted help. So he found her work in a massage parlor on the East

Side, giving hand-jobs. "Until there's some equality of response, some equality of practice, I don't see how we can hope for any breakthroughs," he said. "I mean, I treat you as my equal. You give good hand-jobs—I assume. But can Joanne? She needs our help."

Basil said he had some Quaaludes, a new drug to me but coin of the realm in the city. A sedative that hypnotizes the inhibitions. And Joanne had been primed. After she told him about our relationship, Basil urged her to have us both together since she was having us both, anyway, apart. A necessary step, he told her, a breakthrough in liberation from her sex's timidity. *She* would be having us, not us her. It would be for her—a free-standing woman of parts, using them.

The medical term is *in vitro,* and there was something laboratory about the whole evening, two weeks later, when the deed was done.

First there were the fat white tablets. Quaaludes suspend disbelief—a virtue these days—and delay anxiety enough to make it obsolete. And that was a help. I felt like a kind of midwife, anyway, more than any sort of reckless voluptuary. I felt a kind of lesbian concern for Joanne's well-being. I was straining mostly to catch Joanne's rhythms, sense her needs, successfully bring forth this opportunity for her—like a mother at her daughter's first coming out.

All of which was made complex since it had been agreed I was to be the deflowerer. You will remember our conversation, Joanne's and mine, about the consequences of procreative sex, and my promise, untimely she had said, about an ancient, unnatural—and sterile—alternative. In bed together since then she had brought the subject up, theoretical she said, for sisterly advice.

"But that's *evil*, Matt. And probably dangerous as well. I mean, who does it except those kind of desperate men you see in gay movies? They look like they're going to tear—"

"Who *does* it? My God, Joanne. I see now a spiritual

Mother's Day

failure in your upbringing. It's this nasty Talmudic unimaginativeness. You lack a proper Catholic education, is what it is."

"Catholic! They don't even allow orgasms, I heard. Isn't that right?"

"Popes are too old for orgasms, perhaps. But any good Catholic girl in any wholesome Catholic country—any good Catholic girl knows that while you have to keep the hymen for Mr. Right, catechism classes say nothing about not taking it up the ass. In fact, one clear lesson of Catholic upbringing is that it is meek and just to take it up the ass. Most of the martyrs seem to have managed it, for instance."

"Matt, seriously. Does't it hurt, though. I mean—"

"I've never known a properly brought-up Catholic lass to utter a sound. No, not true. Maria, a girl I knew once, would always cry out. But it was never pain. Only a delicious debasement, she'd say. Mary Magdalene never had it so rough, she'd say, and cry out pushing back on me, redeemed."

"You are a rotten bastard, Matt, at times. I wonder what you are going to say about me. You men probably tell all, don't you. Always like that, too—brutal and cold-blooded."

"C'mon, Joanne. Who would I tell—Basil? Basil's friends? Sometimes I admit I take Thomas aside and whisper libidinous outrages into his tiny male ear, but otherwise—"

"Well, why are you so rotten about Maria, then?"

"I think you're right. I think it's habit. There are rules among men about how to talk dirty. You don't sweet-talk sex to men. It's embarrassing, for one. And anyone who does it, for another, turns out in my experience to be homosexual and after my virgin whatnot."

"As you are after mine."

"Oh, no. You misunderstand. I'm indifferent about it. I just offer my services. A favor. You don't have the equipment to do it yourself—right? And besides, there is this deep visceral—I almost said "Catholic"—submission about it, a kind of profound freedom and surrender, when you have someone do it for you. That's what all the pornographic and pious scriptures say, anyway."

Nothing came of these talks. I mean nothing immediate and carnal. Joanne brought up the subject several times, the last one on the afternoon she and Basil had decided we three would sleep together that night.

"Matt, I'm uptight about tonight."

"That could prove dangerous, you realize. Injure a friend, would you—"

"Basil says I should choose who, you know, takes me there. And I—"

"From what I remember about Basil and me—I mean stature—it's six of one, half dozen of the other. But for you now, it's a different matter. I'd choose on strict religious grounds, myself, if I were you. Where there's a tradition."

"Oh, Matt, don't be that way now. You're not talking for an audience of men. I'm trying to say something personal to you. What's happened to you the last couple of weeks? You're hard and nasty a lot. I hate it when you talk to me like that."

"I'm sorry. I guess I'm uptight, too. I've come to like being another woman to your woman. But I'm not thrilled about getting it on with Basil. For some reason men together creeps me out, while I become increasingly sweet on lesbianism. Not that Basil is remotely gay, but just this image of two men, engorged engines, maneuvering around one another to impale you—it just doesn't make me altogether serene."

"Well, what I was going to say is that I choose you. For tonight's thing. OK?"

"For you, my dear, even that—though of course I wouldn't do that for just anyone.... No, I'm sorry again. I didn't mean to be weird. You're sweet and I'm touched. In fact, just for a minute, there, was the first time I've felt anything erotic about the whole undertaking. And Joanne? Relax. That's essential. Then you'll like it. Two men at the same time ought to be every modern woman's dream, we're told. Three, if you're greedy."

In an eerie almost clinical embrace late that evening, Joanne did cry out, but all my sources tell me it was pleasure, Christian or otherwise. The quaaludes helped defuse us all, though they threatened my engine in ambushes most of the night. I'd lose track, lose concentration, and the machine would slink unnoticed into its lair. Joanne coaxed it back time and again, attentive and sisterly about it. Then sculpted it rigid for the work at hand.

Basil was on his back on the floor and Joanne settled herself down facing him on her knees and guided him into her. She was kneeling over his legs—suddenly there seemed far too many legs—and reaching back with one hand to pull me to her. I admire women their determination and aplomb. I thought I should be tentative and gentle but Joanne would have none of it. She was urging me into her. She was iron tight with determination, then suddenly she relaxed and pulled me partway into her. I felt her tense. Basil felt it too, inside her, and said something I couldn't quite hear. I started to pull out and she flinched, impatient. She crooked her arm behind her again and pulled hard with her hand against the small of my back as I knelt on the floor in back of her.

And that was it. Deep inside her Basil and I started shifting. She rocked forward on her knees against him, then back against me, and I mostly remember thinking how full she must be feeling and how little I was able to concentrate. Her pressure on me was intense and I kept wondering if I would be able to come even if I could concentrate enough to make that happen. Suddenly I was coming—had anyone else come?—and then we were all lying in a collapsed heap, like some monstrous arachnid gorged into prostration.

I have finally understood that work is not, as fathers have been taught to think, a means of nourishing children. Work—modern work—is designed to prevent children. Reduce population. It kills them off when they already exist. Or it kills off their potential in prospective parents. It used to be enough just to keep childbearing women from gainful employment—that way families just died of neglect, malnourishment, ignorance, poverty, and disease. Not enough of them, apparently. So now what we call work, the grinding stress of artificial pressures for incomprehensible goals, has been evolved to make the impulse for children in men, laughably once called sex, a furious kind of abusive mechanism. The agents, once vigorous monomaniac sperm, have become at best frenzied kamikaze tadpoles hurling themselves forward like death waves. Unreasonable stress produces the need for unreasonable gratifications.

You'll notice only the youngest teenage females procreate any longer. None older than fourteen. Millions of other women, theoretically childbearers, liberated into almost constant sex, produce nothing. They mostly use devices, I know, but I suspect they don't have to. There isn't enough repose, there isn't enough simple biology in sex anymore to allow conception. We are suffering from a kind of careerist ligation of the biologies, work induced.

End of diatribe. This has been brought on tonight for the thirty-ninth time in thirty-nine days of work. Both children were sick today, sick really since the day before yesterday, with fevers and a kind of thrush that looks suspiciously like early chicken pox. I took them to day care anyway—how else can I work to pay the place even what I owe for this month?—but yesterday I tried to discover what our magic insurance package, so lionized here by the employer, would do to help if this turns out to be chicken pox.

Already the kids' *after*-after-noon baby-sitter—the one I have to cab them to at six when my work spills over into what little time for them I have left—has said she cannot nurse them. She has an infant of her own and can't risk exposure. So I can hire a nurse to come to Basil and Joanne's—at forty dollars a day—or I can stay home with

Mother's Day

them myself, since Joanne is back at work, now that no one's home to play house with.

"Well, ah, Mr. Vole, our policies don't allow for either of those type options." The benefits officer is perplexed and has lapsed into Fortran. He is sympathetic by nature, earnest in his work, and stumped.

"Well, what has the company done in the past? I mean, you must have had hundreds of mothers before with the problem. Right?"

"As a matter of fact—not to my recollection."

"No children sick?"

"Not this type problem. I guess they took vacation time— we have generous policies about advancing unearned vacation, Mr. Vole. Or maybe hired someone to come in. Or get a relative ... Maybe the children's mother, Mr. Vole?"

"She works."

I have to get sick myself, it appears. Then I can be out on paid sick time. Never before has a mother thought to press the subject further. That may have been women's secret strength: no standards. If you have no expectations you do not grind your teeth every night after work, thirty-nine infinities in a row. And you don't bring up touchy subjects with your employer. Like VD or hemorrhoids, or certain unsavory sexual preferences. Hardly the thing you demand your employer's benefits pay for.

I was about to get the pox myself when the kids' fevers abated late tonight, just before bed. So maybe they won't have chicken pox. The redness of the skin is gone. God knows it could be anything—pellagra, beriberi, Bilharzia, I don't know. Once already they've caught a social disease from me. Scabies, via Frances that cold outdoor night, I suppose, burrowing in me for warmth. Scabies get active at bedtime, itching like ants, and it was only because the damn kids wouldn't sleep that I finally took them to our local pediatric clinic. The nurse practitioner looked them over, then balefully at me. We all three had to coat our entire body twice a day with an evil-smelling white lotion, which I suspect is not so much to suffocate the scabies as to make you an unwelcome partner in any pending contagions. Anyway, this is not scabies. But it could be anything miasmal from that cesspit of a school they go to. The fumes there alone would asphyxiate anyone insufficiently numbed by city life, neglect, or ignorance. Children also have no standards—why else could they continue to love you after all those injustices you hand out daily? Children at the Yorkville Co-Operative Whatnot don't know the world should smell any different. The teachers might have once, but they are so zombied by the demands made of them, their circuit-breakers switched long ago. They just maneuver autonomic through the chaos of children, sewage and debris. Poleaxed as I am when I encounter that school each day, I find myself holding my breath and fleeing it as soon as I can.

I got sidetracked. I wanted to tell you about sex and liberation. As the weeks pass, Basil and Joanne and I again sleeping together, I begin to understand the implacable logic of liberation.

Joanne began to act queerly at times, peevish and demanding of new stimulus, contrary and mono-syllabic. Basil became puzzled and sometimes angry with her. She was supposed to be exhilarated by her new freedoms, he chided, not regressed into adolescence. I mostly packed my equipment and left quietly. I was unsure what I felt, sensing a sympathy I didn't quite understand.

Basil began to work later at nights again, so Joanne and I spent more time in bed alone. We were almost embarrassed the first time Basil returned and found us in bed already, but he was merely pleased. Joanne was ready for him instantly this way, slippery like graphite from an hour of languid play. Basil stripped and buried himself in her while I looked on, gentling her nipples. I knew Basil's pleasure that night, the simple regressive pleasure of morning sex when you are less separated from your urgencies, less the technician, and you come, as Basil did, early and helpless.

Since day care the children had begun to sleep evenings without me, exhausted into privacy by the stresses of their own new lives. Sometimes still they would demand I lie down with them, and I would, but Joanne would come and wake me once the kids had slipped into sleep.

All of which probably sounds satisfactory to you—surreptitious without risk, an intoxication of freedoms. Sexuality expanded closer to contemporary needs. Well, an expansion had taken place. And it was intoxicating. But mostly, like other intoxicants, it turned out to be more of a nice idea than a nice thing.

Like being a single parent. After Cindy left last spring I told myself time and again what a relief it was she was gone. How much better it was—how much better *anything* was— than the nasty subterranean toxins of a failed marriage. You grow into something more than you were before, you expand, you become freer. And that was right. I did. But at a cost. Every step I took was new for me, but someone—in this case Thomas and Keturah—has to pay. Then, weeks later, I began to pay, too. After that, *any* parent, any marginal helpmeet would have been welcome.

Parenthood requires training, rigorous training, like mountain climbing. Deep knee-bends, wind sprints, sit-ups. Otherwise you feel, as I do these days, as if you were running the 220 hurdles in a Denver Boot. Or else you crave, as I do more and more these days, the dignity of death—a final solution to the agonies of being alone with little children.

Basil saw the sexual liberation of Joanne as a clean and angular idea, a kind of stainless-steel structure gleaming with enlightenment. Joanne had resisted him at first, thinking what she wanted was love and security. At least this is what she told me evenings while we toyed with one another, feeling out new intimacies like someone blind in a new home. In one way any sex with Basil had been exploration for Joanne, who had never lived with a man before. Before him sex was strange stiffnesses and private spasms. She had lived with Basil now for almost eight months, a lifetime of sex she felt, and it was only after I moved in that she had begun to consider some of the more elaborate things Basil had suggested to her.

But sex among friends is overrated. We ask it to carry too much freight. That is what Joanne says she sensed with me. Now the categories seemed looser and the urgencies diffused. If I could be so womanly with children then perhaps whatever she gave in sex to me would not be giving in. I kept no score, she said, and she felt she could try things without risk.

What I am trying to say is that we call things sex which are not sex. I wish I could say that becoming a mother freed me from those lurid, makeshift fantasies about women that people tell us is sex. I wish I could say that out of the woman I have become I am a born-again man, saved from the miseries men are prey to.

But I can't. Joanne's intimacies with me were different from those I had felt for any other woman. Her response to me gave me pleasure in her that was free from the block-and-tackle mechanisms of men's fantasy needs. But the tenitis of male eroticism, the head noise of my gender never fully disappeared.

That's where the freight I was talking about comes in. I am beginning to suspect that much of that hardware we call sex, isn't. Someone somewhere for probably stopgap reasons had called it that and we have ever since misunderstood what we are about. Sometimes the gentle easing of pleasure I felt with Joanne, the considerate, tender engines of intimacy—that might have been sex, a kind of love in motion. But other times what I felt when she proffered new risks was nothing of love, nothing much even of friendship. More a furious curiosity. I felt determined and mischievous, like playing doctor when you pinched too hard, or kept pushing till someone cried out.

When Joanne became sullen and withdrawn with me, or demanding, I'd have Bosch-like fantasies about her, intricate and wanton and cruel. Those I'd never tell her, though, and during work the next day I'd catch brief re-runs at bad moments and wonder what kind of madman I was becoming.

I told myself it was city life. It makes for craven, masturbatory needs. City sex becomes masturbatory; city entertainment becomes masturbatory; city eating becomes masturbatory. All forms of gratification seemed to become anti-social.

But what it was was liberation, the loosing of the dogs of possibility. Becoming woman to my children had freed me from the inbred restraints on intimacy with which society has protected the sexes from one another.

And it was freeing Joanne from the bonds that held her to Basil. All this talk of sexual freedom has meant different things for men and women—though nobody told us that. Basil thought that freedom was being able to talk about secret geometries of possibility and being able, perhaps, to loose a woman into acting them out with him. And so he was satisfied they would be equally satisfying for her. But they weren't. The possibility of intimacy with men, a true forbidden fruit, seemed connected to her willingness to forgo monogamy. She misinterpreted intimacy, thinking it physical.

"Matt, I think I'm losing my grip sometimes." We were walking one cool September afternoon with the children through our neighborhood toward Gracie Park on the East River. The children seemed less demonic today, and Thomas tagged happily alongside me, a large sticky lollypop in hand.

Joanne had been carrying Keturah on her shoulders and now Keturah's head was drooping as she began to fall asleep.

We passed the Hungarian butchery on Second Avenue, decorated inside with animal unmentionables strung up in leathery intestines. The air smelled of paprika and gasoline.

"I don't know what I feel about anything anymore. I mean I wanted to *marry* Basil, I knew that from the beginning, and now I think at times nothing could be worse. I feel like I don't need him. Lots of other men have working parts. You know. He seems to think we have something profound—he keeps saying that after he's come—and I am feeling nothing now compared to what I felt when I first moved in. And then there's you—"

"I'm spoken for. I'm a child bride. I have hostages to fortune—or nature's revenge—whatever you want to call it."

"No, Matt, I mean it. I don't know what to make of this. You're like my mother, somehow—"

"Your midwife, I like to think—"

"My mother and my sister and my best girl friend. I don't know how to feel about you at all. I love you, I know that."

"I don't know nothing about love, Joanne. I am learning about friendships, give and take—with lots of take. But love maybe doesn't exist except for one's children. And then it is a terrifying, volcanic thing no one would wish upon a friend. Ever."

A burly red-headed man without a shirt is selling trinkets and cheap imported toys. His display tray rests on a folding canvas stool and Thomas snatches at a wooden snake dangling from a painted stick. The snake is red and black beads of wood, connected like vertebrae, that arch and coil with the movement of the wind.

"I want the snake, Matt. Snake."

"No snakes, Thomas. That's what started it all."

Joanne smiles faintly at the remark and tucks an arm around my waist.

"I want the snake. I want snake." Thomas is gearing up for battle, pulling now against the flow, digging in his heels like a fisherman pulling a net.

"Why not, Matt?" Joanne has a quiet placating way with the kids I resent. She wasn't that way when she had to cope all day.

"Christ, Joanne. It's just going to break between here and the river. A dollar fifty gone. More tears. God damn it, Thomas, stop pulling. What you want a rotten snake for anyway? You got a lollypop just a block or two ago—"

Thomas says nothing, just mimes a desperate grab for the man's tray. The man is watching us deadpan, secure in his stock in trade.

"Here Matt, let's do it this way. Thomas? Thomas! Look. Matt is going to buy the snake but you keep it in the bag till we get to the park. You can play with it later, OK?"

"I don't like snakes I get to play with later"—and he cranks out his lower lip like a drawbridge and begins to cry.

Most of the afternoon was halcyon, though. Thomas played with his snake and broke it happily. Keturah dribbled her rainbow ice over Joanne and me equally. Then she played quietly in the dirt by the park bench while we watched the crowds, lazy in the summer afternoon. Keturah timed her bowels right and Joanne was able to change her in the dank ladies room at the park. I tried the men's room but it was lurid with splashed purple vomit and sworls of caked shit, hand-painted on the walls and sinks. Ladies, apparently, don't do that. At least not in Gracie Park.

It was about four in the afternoon as we made our way back to Seventy-seventh Street. The wind had disappeared somewhere to the west, taking most of the sounds with it. Seventy-eighth Street seemed peaceful and slow, full of old people on stoops, sunning themselves like turtles. I was carrying Thomas on my shoulders but here he wanted to get down and play with a caricature of a dog chained to the handbag of a dozing old woman on a doorstep. Thomas' chattering woke her along with several elderly neighbors, and their turtle necks stretched in antique lines as they craned to see the child. No one else in New York notices children—except to complain, or administer a secretive kick when you're not looking. But I noticed the old woman as she slowly focused giant gray eyes on Keturah and Thomas. Her face relaxed out of its squint, the lines disappeared, and she looked like an ancient photograph of herself young, smiling shy but secretive at something we would never know.

The hardware store was still open and Joanne went in for the nails Basil had asked for. She took Keturah in with her. From my shoulders again Thomas pulled at my hair, or ears, according to which part of the display window he wanted to see. He was animated by the logic of machinery in the window. He asked to get down from my shoulders, then begged to go in the store. The cool wooden smell of hardware stores. Soon we found Joanne and Keturah inspecting locks and keys—shiny brass rows of them. Joanne and I moved to the vats full of nails, which were spiked and gleaming like pirate treasure in the gloom.

We ran our hands through the different sizes, figuring Basil's needs against our sudden childlike wants. Until the attendant came to help I didn't notice Thomas was gone. One lapse and he slides from sight.

"You do the nails, Joanne. I'm going for Thomas. Meet you outside."

"OK. Where'd he go?"

He'd gone back to the window we'd seen from the outside. What had caught his eye was plumbing supplies. At first I didn't see him it was so dark in the store, then out in the display window I saw a movement. There were people stopping by that part of the window outside. As I clambered up onto the window shelf I found what they were watching: a small blond boy carefully peeing into a turquoise display toilet.

I made like I never saw them out there. I took a quick look back into the bowels of the store but no one there had seen me. I reached for Thomas silently and jerked him sideways toward me. His pants were at his knees and he was still spraying when he collapsed at my feet. I could feel the eyes at the window from outside but I just lifted him by the pants so they slid up in place and stepped off the window to the floor inside. I moved quickly behind the paint racks, cupped Thomas's scream of incomprehension with one hand and held him immobile with the other. We stood there maybe a full minute, me holding my breath and Thomas staring wide-eyed at me. My pulse was hiccuping, adrenalin was squirting around inside, and I was fighting a modern survival impulse—my flight-or-flight response.

I put my finger to my lips trying to look conspiratorial, waited another couple of seconds, then marched quickly to the front door. The attached bell rattled me but I turned sharply as we got out and walked stiffly down the street, not daring to notice any bystanders.

In an alcove by the shoe store at the corner I realized I was grinning crazily, wanting to scream. I looked at Thomas, trying to be stern, but he was grinning, too, having seen mine. We backed out onto the street and I was hugging Thomas to me, crying crazy tears. Then Joanne came up to us looking puzzled, only to start hooting herself when I told her. Keturah caught it too and we sat on the stoop nearby, howling. The children stared at these transformed adults, astonished at their good fortune.

I think that was the first and last nice afternoon with children I had in New York. Certainly it was the last one shared with other adults. Work warps time, so I'm not sure it all happened this fast, but sometime soon after that day Basil came to me with an announcement.

"Matt, I think we're going to have to regroup."

"Oh-oh. I was afraid something was brewing."

"Sex is still fine with her but I just feel Joanne falling away from me."

"*Post coitum omne animal triste,* Basil. You know that. Anyway, you admit she's still good at anything she puts her hands to—"

"You're incorrigible. I mean it, I think things need re-negotiating. I'm losing her."

"And?"

"And I don't want that."

"You think I should go, huh?"

"No. I don't think anyone should go. That's not what I'm saying. I think you should stay and Joanne should stay and the kids should stay—"

"The kids!"

"The kids. Times I would like to kill them. Lots of times. And most of the rest of the time I feel them make me walk on eggshells around here. But I don't want them to leave. You, on the other hand—you can go anytime. You cuckolder, you cad and child abuser. But leave them be."

As we talked that night, Basil surprised me with his plea for family. The children had gotten to him. Breaking and entering.

What was I to say to him? That he'd been outgrown, used up? That we'd eaten him like preying mantises, Joanne and I, in our implacable female needs—and now he was dispensable? I don't think that mantises negotiate, but we tried it, Basil and I, that evening.

I went first. "You think I should lay off Joanne, as it were? Would that help?"

"I don't think so, Matt. Your unnatural relationship with her doesn't compete with me—at least I should hope not."

"Ah, the Virtuous Basil, straight as a slide rule."

"You know what I mean. Right now I think I need you to hold her here. That much I think I've understood. And the kids, too. She seems so hard and shiny when I try to talk about us."

"Innocence lost, I would say. Cosmic bitterness. Nothing personal. And anyway, you and I contributed—remember? Liberating her and all. You wouldn't deny a person a chance at disillusion, would you?"

"Why'd she go back to work? We said we'd support her—"

"Got me. I'm beginning to think work is a child of the Hyena. Lately I stare at that light humming above my desk and I think I see the Hyena, purring up there with his thumbs hooked in his suspenders. He seems to be saying something about wanting to wipe out fatherhood in my lifetime."

"Well, now that you bring it up, Matt, I wanted to speak to you about your Hyena or whatever you call it. One thing has got to change here if the family is going to survive and prosper."

"Only one?"

"I can't deal with the desperation. Anything I want changed—anything I need, even—I look at you and feel I can't ask it. You're spread too thin already. I can't justify putting new burdens on you. So I am just guilty and pissed-off most of the time. Joanne feels it, too."

"Who, me? Desperate? I'm thriving, haven't you noticed? Budding career. Day care for the kids. Hot and cold running sodomy. ... Heaven, not desperation."

"I admire your bravado, Matt. I really do. But I think sometimes it keeps you reckless with us all. We've got to cool down the mixture. The way it is you are so martyred you are one up on us all the time."

"Two up, not one. But I'll compromise. I'll give you one and we'll be equal. Actually, I guess I don't have to do a thing. They've burrowed in anyway—haven't they? Got you by the balls or whatever it is leads to a man's heart. The avuncular fallacy is that it gives you an out. It doesn't. It's worse than parenthood. At least parents are protected from the little perpetrators by all the hatred they feel for them, the almost constant fatigue and bad blood. You avoid too much of that in your role—and it suckers you into an artificial, rose-colored trap."

"Look, Matt. I don't know what the hell you're talking about. The Hyena has rotted your brain. All I'm saying—it's very simple—is that without some semblance of order here we can't survive, Joanne and me. Neither can you and the kids."

"So what you're saying is what I said you were saying: we should get out. In reality that is what others always wish about children—out of sight. It used to be they could be seen, at least, if not heard. Now no one wants them even seen. Not bus drivers, bosses, teachers, friends. You know, there is something loathsome about the pettiness of a childless person, something small and orderly. He has the soul of a philatelist."

We got nowhere, as you can see. Joanne tried gently to say some of the same things. They were right, of course. Children *are* a pain in the ass—I'm the first to declare it. But children are not a choice for me, as they are to Joanne and Basil. An option to exercise. For me they are part of my life, autonomic, and everything else seems trivial alongside.

Like overtime. It should be spelled Overtime, with the big O, if my colleagues at work are to be believed. I've been taken into the inner sanctum, I guess, because I am invited now to stay late, work shoulder to shoulder with the titans.

My mistake. After the first few days I internalized anxieties about being late for day care. So as far as my bosses are concerned the problem is solved. I'm one of the boys. True, I don't go drinking lunch with the rest of them—me and the secretaries brown-bag it furtively at our desks—but the bosses chalk that up to dedication, I guess, because come the next deadline crisis and I'm invited, as I say, to remain late.

This is how that works. At five-forty-seven I bolt for day care by cab. Hold the meter, I tell him when we get there, for a buck extra will you hold the meter and wait for my passengers so we can continue uptown? OK? The driver's been had and he resents it, but he waits. Can't find Keturah's lunch box, both kids are screaming for me to stop and see what they've done today, but I'm almost knocking them down as I scurry about for their scattered things. I'm early today and the aide tries to smile, but she's so tired it comes

Mother's Day

out a drunken leer. She swallows, embarrassed. The cabbie has my shoulder bag—collateral—but if I don't get back there fast he'll just take off, I know. Everything I own is in there. I've got a nattering child in each arm when I get to the cab and the driver is grousing about how long he's had to wait, it's rush hour and he could be making money. He stares out his window at me while I try to open the cap door. I put a kid down, shift the lunch boxes, clothes bag, three paintings, and an egg-box model Thomas made. The driver revvs the engine. Thomas crawls in and sits on the near side so I have to hipcheck him across the seat to get in quick. He starts screaming—I've jammed his arm under me—and the driver can't hear me shout where we're going. He jerks the car forward in fury.

I'd found the ad in my laundromat on Second Avenue. She sits for kids anytime, the ad says, responsible adult. Responsible *single* adult, it turns out, with a wide-eyed sickly infant by a father since decamped. If you're home anyway, she tells me, you might as well get paid for it.

Tonight she's taking in two children who look like refugees from war. There is a fine saffron-and-plum bruise on Keturah's left cheekbone, new today, and her clothes seem to have been used to sweep out under the radiators. They have diagonal streaks of dark, wet dirt. Thomas' T-shirt is torn at the left armpit and his knee is bleeding, he says, from falling in the playground. What playground? I wonder what stay-at-home Lucia is thinking as I shovel the kids through her door at 6:17. Her kid is naked but clean, sucking its thumb and holding Lucia's leg at about the knee. What do I care? Maybe for her $2.50-an-hour fee Lucia doesn't have to get any of the usual embarrassed disclaimers about the kids' appearance. Especially since for $2.50 an hour I have to walk four floors with two kids each way. With Basil's stairs and these in any one day I feel like Tenzing.

Lucia lives on Ninety-fourth so it's a reasonable sprint for the subway at Ninety-sixth. I've got to save cab fare for the dead children later tonight. No way you can take two sleeping children on a bus in their pajamas (which Lucia insists they must have).

All this—plus the reflex tedium of daywork, extended like chewing gum beyond its flavor—is overtime. Totals for the occasion: Cabs, $7.75. Subways, $1.00. Sitter, $10.00. Dinner—optional (read "skipped," because I ran out of tuna in the morning and there was only enough for the kids and me for lunch). I've enjoyed several bouts of overtime so far, each more expensive than the last.

I think there is a basic difference between men mothers and women mothers. Men mothers have standards. They don't know any better. They haven't spent years ingesting with their mother's milk the wisdom of the Hyena. And this mother at least, shreds of testosterone still intact, won't pay the price.

CHAPTER XI

A peculiar gentleness comes over me at such times. First a vast calm lowers itself over my agitation, like the start of a summer storm. Synapses still crackle inside, the body scurrying with distress signals. My heart speeds up and I am sweating cold like citrus. But as the pain concentrates high in the stomach all the other agitation seems to be happening prophylactically elsewhere, in an envelope.

I should say if I haven't already that as the children began to grow in me, I have developed ulcers. Remember ulcers? Men have given them up of late, for women to have their turn—along with lethal smoking, violent crime, and obscene phone calls. But for me they arrived with Thomas and Keturah. Labor pains, perhaps, for mothers of my gender.

Anyway, tonight my ulcers are seething in the acid of my days, and my stomach is being pulled tighter by a large metal clamp inside. Crude, but nothing subtler will get the message across. Corporal punishment. Ignore conventional distress signals and the body takes it upon itself to create relief.

It is a curious kind of relief, I admit, such intense concentrating pain. But it focuses me inward, forcibly separating me from the children. They hover confused at my distraction but the pain has made them periphery and I hardly notice.

What has happened is that Basil has taken Joanne away for a few days' vacation. She was suffering from prostration and Basil had taken her to wherever it is he retreats from us these days. Obviously things had been bad, but I hadn't noticed anything unusual myself. A few tantrums more per minute, maybe, more symphonies of self-pitying harangue from me. And there had been the doorbell imbroglio, Thomas playing the black buttons by the mailboxes like an accordion.

He had dragged himself from the store with me one afternoon after school. And dragged at me one corner too many. Keturah I was anyway carrying, along with the groceries. It is always a trade-off: more trips up and down with the kids or a Sisyphian load of groceries each time. This time I thought I had opted for Sisyphus.

Thomas had pleaded to be picked up as soon as he had milked the gum machine he came down for. I couldn't carry him, I patiently explained—there were people watching—then ushered him out to the street where he promptly tripped and lay sprawled on the hardened phlegm, vomit, and blood pavement in front of the bar next to the deli. I kept walking toward the corner by our apartment. First he bawled, then heaved himself miraculously to his feet only to catch me up and sprawl again on the pavement, this time among the gum studs, candy ants, and petrified cigarette filters in front of the tobacconist.

The pear-shaped rabbi from next door happened by then, stared with his infinite capacity for outrage, then snorted and hurried off. Thomas looked at me vindicated, then began methodically to bang his head on the pavement.

So I carried him, too. What would you have done? I put Keturah on my shoulders, the groceries in my left arm,

Mother's Day

stooped low to curl my right arm about the back of Thomas' knees and hoisted him up. Still, I couldn't hold him beyond the stoop of our place. I put him down. He bawled again. I jammed the door open with my key and held it, waiting, while Thomas refused to budge.

When I let the door lock shut he was still sitting on the stoop, miming abandonment. I think Keturah, the groceries and I had reached the third-floor landing when I knew something was wrong. People in their apartments started howling like trapped coyotes. Buzzers agitated everywhere. Doors were hurled open and people peered down the stairwell, their jaundiced city faces a magically healthy native-American red.

That was last week sometime. Then yesterday I came home forever from overtime and the 5:50 day-care high-hurdles. I can no longer afford the cost. I came home to find Basil and Joanne packing like chipmunks.

"Packing? You getting a divorce?"

"Vacation, Vole. We told you last week. Remember?" Basil sounded as if his jaw were wired.

I didn't remember. These days I forget a lot, but I don't think this time I had anything to forget.

So tonight I am alone with Thomas and Keturah and my duodenum. The pain comes in waves, a graceful walking charge like ancient battles. Between, there are moments of frightful calm. Organizing calm.

First I tried Cindy. That made sense. She's been calling lately, asking after the kids as if they had once been hers. She understands nothing of our needs, even commonplaces, but some stray atavism could still feel for her tonight and make her help. At work they said she'd call back. She never did. A further organizing calm.

Tomorrow I will not work. Plan A, Part I. Tonight I don't go to my friendly local emergency room, because what do I do with the children? Plan A, Part II. Anyway, last time I went there they were suspicious, as if my pain were a moral lapse. It's one of those nice Hyena touches. You have control because you know in your heart there are others there in worse pain. You have control where others don't so you are not really sick. If you're not really sick, why all the grayness about the gills, this stiff-man-syndrome look about you? Immoral, obviously, or faking for some controlled substance. Only an outright immoralist would lie for downs.

I was cool and didn't tell them too much about my illness. If you do that you are really suspect. Common folk aren't supposed to know the Hippocratic mysteries. But still the doctor decided against treatment. So I just lay there writhing on the cold folding bed in the green-tiled corridor and the idiot intern talking solicitously about antacid and the bland diet. That shit went out ten years ago and he doesn't know it. Finally they tired of my blubbering and judged it better to knock me out with Demerol than risk expelling me for noise, then being sued when I collapse and bleed to death on the corner.

But that was when I had Basil with money—you pay as you go in this place—and Joanne to cope with the kids. Tonight they are on vacation. So Part III: stun the pain with home remedy and promise myself a life change. I've had four ulcer attacks since I came to New York three months ago. Before that I had two a year. Nowadays they don't respond to pills so well as they used to, but I will try.

"Thomas, don't go to sleep yet. Here watch the movie—good movie tonight, Thomas. Good movie."

"I'm tired, Matt."

"Thomas, listen. Matt is sick, you understand? Sick. You have to help. Keturah is too small to help. You have to." Do almost-three-year-olds track like us? Do they live with us in the same continuum? I am talking to Thomas bent over from the pain, squeezing out the words almost without air. That's novel and interests him. He studies me carefully as I teach him the drill.

First the clock. I draw a clock face at nine—no mistaking that, I think. It's eight-thirty now tonight and I must keep him up till nine so I can set the alarm for nine tomorrow morning.

Now we are working the phone, Thomas practicing. If I don't wake when the alarm goes he is to dial the operator and read her numbers. Does he really know the numbers? He reads them now but did he just remember from me reading them? I hope my office will know where we are. Thomas has trouble saying "emergency" for the operator but his rendition will have to do.

By nine tonight I am moaning with each breath out, sweating and rolling on the bed between the children. I set the alarm. Now I swallow the phenobarbs, six of them tonight. If I take too few and wake before the pain is gone I'll never be able to get under it again. I know that from bitter experience.

Keturah is cuddled naked to my stomach, which feels like iron to me now but softens to her warmth. She is asleep in only her diaper so I can get the warmth. Thomas is on the other side asking me weird questions, trying to domesticate his fears.

"Is work sick, too, Matt? Who is the operator—work's friend? Now is nine o'clock, too? Matt is sick: will Matt die?" I am answering in monosyllables between groans. It hurts to breathe, let alone talk, but luckily Thomas seems to be slipping rapidly astern.

I have three options. The pain will pass and the alarm will wake me. The pain is this time an appendix which will burst because I have masked its urgencies. Or this time the ulcer will uncork, like a drain, and I will bleed. When they wake me I'll be dead. What do children do alone when you are dead? Crawl around the corpse till they get hungry and eat off pieces? Keturah doesn't even have serviceable teeth.

I'm suffering from mettle fatigue. The children become increasingly litigious. They sense victory but seem to take little pleasure in it.

Keturah is today a year old. Majority. Since early morning

she'd done her adversary best to finish off my failing will. Children these days must be skillful. With parents of today's ilk they have to be ruthless but precise to live to the ripe age of one. She's watching me with a cool, trained eye.

I saw that look once on a beach in the Carribbean. A mangy stray dog was dying on a deserted beach, surrounded in a solemn circle by vultures. They peered from a respectful distance, professional and patient, conferring in quiet asides. As the dog's movements became feebler they would take a step forward. I tried to chase them away and they only looked indignant. Just doing our job, buddy.

That's the look Keturah has now as I dither about breakfast. Breakfast is all I can handle at the moment. Not that we have any up here in the apartment. We're out of everything since Basil and Joanne left. I need to decide whether I leave the kids here alone, lock them in, as I creak down six flights and back for raw materials. I know I can't haul both kids down there and back. Maybe it would be better just to settle in quietly and die here with dignity. No heroic measures.

Actually, dying seems to have passed me by. Another option gone. I kept waiting while the phenobarbs took effect that night, half hoping for an out-of-body experience. It didn't come—and even if it had I know I would have heard that voice survivors report, scolding me back to my responsibilities. Instead I just woke the next morning—yesterday morning—to a deep mortal quietude. My stomach seemed to have been disconnected and I felt a kind of atavistic relief— one less organ heard from—as I imagine I would feel to be relieved somehow of my children.

Times I find myself wishing for a visit from the body snatchers. That way I wouldn't be responsible for them gone but would still be free. I suspect that's what happened when you read about children who fall from windows, electrocute themselves, run under delivery vans. The burden has become so great the parent has secretly—unconsciously—looked the other way.

Mother's Day

Yesterday morning I never raised my voice. I never cared enough to have to. Maybe that's what "relaxed" means: too gone to care. I walked quietly about like a shock victim, separated from the stress, protected. I never even bothered to call work and they didn't call me. We had macaroni for breakfast, with parmesan from the shelf on the refrigerator door. That was all there was. Keturah got the only milk. She consumes very little else so sometimes I sneak an egg into it, or some of those phony polyvinylchloride vitamins they sell for kids.

But this morning there is nothing even for her bottle. We all ate some soggy graham crackers earlier. The children grinned happy at the feast, and at the fact I seem not to have shouted at them for almost two days. I'm not sure happy is the right word. Glad is maybe better. They are glad to be free of the hassle, but, as I said, Keturah is struggling to do her job now. That's where the adversary part comes in, Keturah doing her job.

Two scenes from my past bear on this. I am in a hard-shell Baptist church in the Tennessee mountains. The preacher has for an hour had my hair standing up on the back of my neck. Supplicants have been galvanized from their seats to his lectern, rushing to be saved. Several are writhing on the floor making sounds suspiciously like orgasm. Which doesn't help settle the neck hairs much, since several of them are those bullet-eyed Tennessee wenches who look at you and turn the air to cordite. The preacher is now leaping back and forth over his lectern, moved by the spirit of the Lord, and pointing at those of us left in our seats, calling us forward to surrender. Soon I am one of only a handful left and he comes down the aisle at me, his huge soup-bone hand grabbing mine. He's not pulling, mind you—you have to surrender yourself—but he is urging like hell. I feel like I will either fuse into solid bone myself or run screaming down the aisle with him.

That's one scene. The other takes place about a year after

Thomas is born. He is sitting on the bottom step of our house in a shambles of scattered clean laundry I'd just piled there moments before. I had been sweeping the hall madly because guests were coming. I was about to haul the laundry when he reached up and deliberately tumbled the pile off the step. To see what would happen. And he was looking queerly at me, the way you eye weather clouds. Till that moment I had never once shouted at him, never lost my control, never surrendered.

Suddenly some cog slipped and I was watching this grown adult slamming the metal dustpan time and time again against the banister, jumping up and down in one place and apparently shouting something in Serbo-Croatian. Then this adult had hurled the dustpan against the glass front door and snatched up the child, who was being shaken by both arms high above the man's face.

When I found out who was doing this to Thomas, I remember putting him down without looking at him and staring horrified at the wallpaper—constipated roses, grinning in pink and white. When I finally looked at Thomas, expecting to find him traumatized for life, deformed by this assaultive rage, I found to my astonishment a look of visible relief on his round, perfectly smooth and now beautiful face.

He felt relief. Stage I of his job done. I was now just as out of control as he was, I was human like him again, something he could understand. The preacher I just told you about never got me that day, because he was asking a further stage of surrender, the one that Keturah is working on now.

Maybe it's just spending too much time with children, but I begin to see things in crude images. Parenthood looks to me like a quickly narrowing passage. Increasing unknown forces push you further and further in. You shed things as you go, just to fit. The stress increases. There are rhythms, muffled circular constrictions at each stage. You shed more.

Keturah is working on a crucial stage, I can tell, because I am not even feeling much constriction today yet she goes about her work like someone close to the end of a consuming labor. Maybe they are paying us back, our children, for the still vivid miseries of birth. If they went through them it means we forgot enough to wish that upon them, so they are reminding us again. If so, I am somewhere at the tight end of the womb, between contractions, and gone are almost all my insulated amniotic assumptions.

At my most philosophic I tell myself all this must be for a reason. Probably unfinished childhood business of my own. But I wish there were some other way of completing it.

The third day I missed work they called. The kids and I were watching Mr. Rogers and I pined for Joanne's play-by-play. But vaguely, because although I had run out of phenobarbs I'd found Basil's pharmacopoeia back behind his sweater shelf. We bring you today, folks, a genteel calm, courtesy of Rorer & Rorer, Pharmacists. Large sedate white tablets' worth of calm. Even the children have slacked off, sensing a plateau, perhaps. For the third day in a row I don't care what they break or spill or eat—but I've been contemplating the rat poison myself, so they don't get any of that. The rat poison looks like cocaine a bit more every time I contemplate it. But meantime we are all calm and that is something.

What I told work was I had an ulcer attack and was recovering. I like that expression for ulcers—"recovering," the way an oyster coats its irritating pearl. Fine fat downs like these Rorers must be good for resurfacing the pearl because I can't even imagine brewing any gastric acid today.

By the fifth day they were sounding angry at work so I told them I was being reabsorbed into Manpower, Inc., my parent company. The way a nervous pregnant rabbit reabsorbs its young. Mrs. Knapp was distinctly confused.

"Manpower? You were Permanent Temp, as I remember?"

"Summer Int., I believe, Mrs. Knapp. Intern for the solstice, which has re-turned into fall. I really can't explain it now but I think I shall not be coming back, thank you very much. Please have them send my check—plus overtime—to the following address?"

Not much has been clear since then, but since each genus of pills has only been enough for one day I can keep track that way. If it's Tofranil this must be Thursday. That was a little joke. Ha, ha. I've been constipated for some time now and I guess it is the side-effects—though not eating may have contributed, do you think? Keturah has had no trouble with her bowels. I've started to re-use disposable diapers by re-lining the plastic coat with Kleenex. Works OK in the privacy of your income-terminated sixth floor walk-up

Where are Basil and Joanne? No one has called since those shiny green-and-beige capsules. I can't seem to get it together to call anyone myself. I did get to the deli one day sometime and bought the rest of my money in milk and tuna and Oreos and Pampers. Which are running out. Oreos beat graham crackers for breakfast and I find we can all sleep through lunch, so we've got at least another couple of days. I would like to clean up this place for Basil and Joanne, but when I begin to think where I could begin I seem to lose track and I'm too tired to start again for a long time.

Then when I talked to them on the phone—Basil was with Joanne, because he yanked into the conversation halfway—when I talked to them I began choking up. They were back, they said, and had decided some things.

"No sweat," I said. "I have, too. I bet we decided the very same things. Or thing."

"Matt, how come you're not at work? It's Tuesday."

"Terminated. Pulled the plug."

"Jesus."

She said "Jesus," then Basil came on the line and said it, too. Then I made a short dignified speech.

"I've decided to terminate, too. When my check with its invaluable overtime comes, we go. Thieves in the night.

Meantime, I suggest you stay elsewhere if you can till I can fumigate the place. Maybe I could just set fire to it and you collect on the insurance. What about that?"

They didn't stay someplace else, of course. In fact they seemed in a big hurry to get home and came crowding in the door out of breath for some reason. The kids and I retreated to the back bedroom and I read them first an Easter coloring book, then a Christmas one. Twice. Joanne came in once in between to try to talk but her face was set so hard in lines she couldn't move her jaws right and sounded sick. She shined with suntan and smelled of coconut.

This time before we left on the train for Connecticut, I made damn sure that Thomas peed at home.

CHAPTER XII

"Now how am I ever going to get to see them?

"Cindy, you saw them exactly twice the whole time we were in New York—"

"You're doing this deliberately. I know it. You—"

"Cindy. Cindy. I'm not doing this for convenience. I don't see—"

"You don't see. You don't see anything you don't want to—"

"I don't see any other way. I'm not sure I even see *this* way. I was at the end of my rope."

"Big deal. You don't *enjoy* your job so you quit. The rest of us work, too, you know. We don't enjoy *our* jobs, either. But we don't quit."

"And the rest of you have only your puny selves to look out for. Only yourselves to haul each night up six flights of stairs. Only yourselves to sleep for, cook for, wash laundry for, commute for. Only yourselves to carry on your back every minute of the day."

"Shit, Matthew. Shit."

"Shit is right, Cindy. Look: want to switch? Gather your pieces together. Take over here. I'll go back to New York and work. I'll support you all, for Christ's sake, on what it cost me just to put them in that sewer of a school."

"You know I can't do that. I couldn't leave. I'd have to start all over again. I'm just getting myself settled in my job now."

"Job. Job. Job. This is life-life-life I'm talking about. Human children and a once-human parent or two."

"You always have to moralize, don't you? Parents versus jobs. It used to be freedom versus fascism, you remember? You never change."

"This is useless. Worse than useless. I'm tired. You are welcome any time to see them—as you have always been. You're welcome to *have* them, in fact. I am *not* kidnapping them. What maniac would kidnap a pair of millstones? They've got *me* captive. And so have you. I'm the one with no choices, not them or you."

"I'm going to see a lawyer and—"

"Skip the lawyer. Go straight to a fucking judge, why don't you, and see how far that gets you. You'll get slapped with abandonment and have to pay us support as well. Judges don't take kindly to parents who skip out on their children, Cindy, or have you forgotten that?"

This conversation took place less than a week after we'd returned to the run-down farm house in this backwater of Connecticut. The house has been fixed up since we left last spring but my side still looks like those pictures you've seen of Appalachia. Outside, abandoned equipment and cars. My Ford seems to have grown into the tall grass. It won't start. Inside the neighbors cleaned up after we left, but it's difficult to tell the difference unless you were intimate with each earlier depradation. And the kids—today I looked at them and it's hard to see how anyone could have gotten so dirty in just three years.

These phone calls are particularly charming because they

take place at the neighbors'. The phone company cut me off for life, I think, when I welched on my paltry bill before we left. The wires are there but the machine is gone, leaving a shocking clean rectangle on the kitchen wall. Elsewhere the wall is furry with grease.

So I am summoned from next door to speak through clenched teeth to Cindy in New York, who feels I've done her wrong.

Some things have been settled, though. With what remains of my last paycheck I have exactly a week to find work, get the kids taken care of, and get my car fixed so I can effect the above. I was feeling remarkably sanguine about all this until that call from Cindy. I even had pastoral visions of her returning here, us settled into the huge chlorophyll quiet of this place, the family walking hand-in-hand into the high blue horizons of these splendid fall days.

I suppose that was a form of withdrawal, that soft-mindedness. The accumulated effects of all those anti-depressants I took the last few weeks in New York. Anti-depressants. Interesting idea, that. You can apparently be induced by them to ignore the facts that pull your shoulders closer and closer together in front of you, a traction on the spirit. And somehow you are thought otherwise unaffected and can make judgments, reasonable judgments, concerning the survival of this existential family gnawing away at your innards.

Really how they work, those anti-depressants, seems more like marriage. You stop taking it and you feel euphoric for a while. Then, as I just noticed from this call from Cindy, you get a terminal case of the Realities.

When I get back from the call Thomas is nowhere to be seen. I tried to take him with me when the neighbor came for me but he dodged the other way in fear, thinking I'd conjured up some cause to punish him. Maybe now he's gone for good. Wherever the wild things are. I haven't much self-respect left but I know enough to stopper instantly the relief that thought gives me. I could feel the muscles holding my shoulders give a little. I am learning something about danger signals and that is an escalation.

In times like these you must walk slowly. Above all else. I can see the Hyena grinning up there, knowing, waiting for me to begin screaming and stampeding in all directions at lunatic speed, like those high-speed chases in silent films. So I'm *strolling* now from room to room in my side of the house, Keturah under my arm squirming. I'm talking to her in Adult.

"Where's Thomas, Keturah? Where do you suppose he is, that Thomas? Maybe here, in the broom closet, Keturah? Ah, no, of course not. Tricky little devil, eh? Now I got it. Upstairs. Of course. Sheer brilliance, don't you think? Under the crib? Let's see. No. Well, my bedroom most likely. I've waited this room till last—just to give him his fun—see, Keturah? His fun is now over, though, because he's got to be in this closet. Right—here!"

But he wasn't. Now I'm really going to have to go slow. This is critical. He bolted to the kitchen as I rushed for the phone, didn't he? How long was I on with Cindy? How long did she talk? No, rave. How long did Cindy rave? Fifteen minutes? The Hyena is nodding vigorously. Fifteen minutes it is.

I checked the bathroom before but did I check behind the shower curtain?

"Brace yourself, Keturah. We've outfoxed him and he's going to squeal with delight when we find him, scaring you but leaving me unruffled, one way or the other. Unruffled."

I'm relieved he's not behind the shower curtain, because on the steps down here I began to see it splashed with blood and Thomas curled up by the drain with his wrists pumping all over the enamel. Child suicide is on the rise. That's what *Women's Day* says. I can believe it. But I expect children get some assistance, you know? I see parents handing out materials. This morning, boys and girls, we're doing Suicide. Each person gets one kit to start. Just one, please. Here's your lye, dear. No, dear, you had the blades last week. Johnny's turn today. Now we don't have much time this morning, so watch carefully, children. . . .

What were once stately lawns surround the house. Couple of large trees which are marmalade orange today in the sunlight. The lawn is uncut on my side of the house and it's cowlicked with cold grass from the dew. Running in that, a kid would leave a trail, maybe. A little trail of wet prints padding off toward the treeline, maybe, or to some hiding place in the lilac border just in front of that. I hope the neighbors can't see me as I lope like this in my bathrobe toward the trees down there. We're only just back in the vicinity and they need to build up their tolerance a bit. Maybe they won't notice. The grass shines icy blue in the morning cold, the color of my bathrobe close enough.

I haven't once thought of it since we went to New York but there's of course the well. Of course.

Now, children, today we do the well. We only have one well so we *all* have to share today. Won't that be fun? Now who'd we start with last week, do you remember anyone? Jason, that's right. So this morning we begin with—yes, that's right. Thomas. Tho-mas! Please pay attention, because we don't have much time this morning. Thomas, are you paying attention?

Keturah is cold, I can tell. Or is it me? Someone is shivering. A minute ago we almost stumbled on some overgrown tuft of wet grass and Keturah giggled. But she's got on only her Pamper and it's cold enough this morning to snap the apples we're passing on these timeworn, unpruned apple trees behind the lilac hedge. Some apples are down and they'd make tricky going if you were naive enough to be running at a time like this. I caught myself back there, as I said, in a couple of what can only be called lopes, but now I am casual, stepping through the old orchard toward the

Mother's Day 161

wellhouse in the corner down there by those giant pines.

What ideas they had back then. This ornate place with windows and a door, like a kid's playhouse, but very low to the ground and the door mostly below ground at the bottom of stone steps. There are pine needles underfoot and drifted against the wellhouse like dunes. The door is open this morning but then maybe it hasn't been closed in a generation, I don't remember. There's a nice stone floor, too, around the black opening in the center. Cold to bare feet but not icy like the autumn grass out there. Pipes drop down the other side of the hole, I see, but this side is nicely clear. I can feel those twitches in my right arm holding Keturah. I've felt them before. I guess I'm holding her too tight, that's all, and the muscles are just protesting. That must be it. Now the real moment of style. This makes it or breaks it with the Hyena. Whatever else all morning now you've got to be impeccable. One false move and he's got you forever. That kind of disgrace you never overcome. You know mothers you see so slatternly and fat and even their pink curlers on shoddy? Like that. Not a shred of respect left. Surrendered.

The hole is large enough for a person but it's pitch black down there where I'm looking. Keturah and I are lying on the rock and just my head is over the edge of the hole. I can't see a thing and it's hard to concentrate because Keturah is thrashing and wiggling with impatience. There's no noise below. I just sneezed because of all the dust in here and my sneeze echoed deep into this blackness. Then I decided to drop a pebble, but it seemed to hit water almost as soon as it got out of sight. So if he's down there I ought to be able to see him. Kids float—right? Like adults? He had on bright-green pajamas.

Keturah almost squirmed out of my grip a second ago so we're back at the door. Thomas is not down there, I'm pretty sure. I don't have a flashlight but maybe the neighbors do. That's the kind of thing they'd have. In case of nuclear attack.

Thomas wasn't in the well. I didn't tell them why I needed the flashlight, because I fear those judgments other parents make so quickly. What if I came to you at eight in the morning and asked to borrow a flashlight in case my son was in the well?

"Just bring it back," was all the neighbor lady said. Didn't I *say* "borrow"?

The well is shallow, it turns out, and with the light you can see pebbles at the bottom. Keturah is now crying, disappointed maybe but probably just cold from our second trip to the wellhouse. I hope she hasn't memorized the route. It would take some time to totter there, or crawl, but one good phone call might be just long enough.

Now we have five hundred acres to search on the other side of the house. Soft rolling hills separated by mean stone walls and occasional decorative copses. The fields are brown this time of year, which helps, since when last seen Thomas had on bright-green Dr. Dentons. Lime green, with flapping white plastic feet.

Keturah is already several times heavier than when we started out. Specific gravity increases with time, I guess. So does surface tension. But don't let the Hyena notice. You could run screaming through these fields and be undone forever after.

The first field took about half an hour and yielded nothing lime green. We are now at the top of the second field looking down acres of shattered corn casings toward what looks like a stream. At least there is a line of trees and shrubs meandering along the bottom of the hill. Down is easier than up or around, so that's the way we're going. I wish I'd worn shoes. I wish I had that pack carrier I used to use with Thomas on other kinds of hikes. He used to sleep I remember, bumping gently against my back.

It is a stream. Someone has built a rustic wooden bridge across it, I can see now, and the water is about two feet deep under the bridge, purring over green stones. Keturah is pointing at the water and leaning far over my arm toward it. If my arm weren't so stiff I might just let her fall I'm so tired, but there are no signals running south of the shoulder, which aches.

The sun is warmer down here and the grass is dry along the banks as we walk downstream. No point in going upstream—right? Even Thomas is not that contrary. The stream bends out from under the trees into the sun in places, and the sediment sparkles as the water ripples over it. What I would really like to do is sit here on this warm bank in the long grass, dangle my feet maybe in the water. I am sweating in my bathrobe for some reason. It's beautifully quiet here in the autumn sun, even the water is discreet as it shoulders its way around the rocks and old wood.

I guess first I heard a splash, then what might have been an excited bird downstream from us. I'd been sitting by the stream sluggish with sun, but I dragged myself up, hoisted Keturah to my shoulder and headed for the noise. It had come from around a bend in the trees that followed the stream. I noticed several here were turning purple and the sun was shining off the leaves. First I saw the dog, a large black Labrador wagging his tail at something. He was facing away from me and wagging so hard his whole hindquarters were shifting from side to side. He was shoulder deep in a pool formed by the stream. A step closer and I saw Thomas naked next to him, pulling on his collar. Thomas was talking at him in high-pitched syllables that sounded like me giving orders in a hurry. When I got close enough for Thomas to see me, he let go of the dog's collar and squinted at me into the sun. His body was ivory and seemed splendidly made. The splashes of water on it caught colors from the trees and winked like gold. He seemed to be standing very straight as the water pushed against his thighs and he looked more beautiful and clean even than the incorruptible blue fall sky holding up the trees around us. We just sat on the edge of the pool, Keturah and I, and I held her by her hands and she squealed and kicked her toes in the water. The dog sniffed at her once or twice, then went back to Thomas and nudged him in the chest with his nose.

In the most recent conversation with Cindy I began to scream about money. Didn't she care that her children were dying here for lack of it? I couldn't put them in school and if I couldn't put them in school I couldn't work and I wouldn't be able to work till I got the car fixed and she should give us money since she was there living high in New York, a swinging single, and I was the one here slowly going under for the second time.

That at least cut the phone conversation short. She hung up. Which means there is no one to help me. Used to be grandparents but they don't make them like they used to. Till recently you could sucker anyone over fifty with children, but no more. Grandparents barely have time enough for their own problems, let alone yours. And anyway, who has grandparents? Who even has parents around anymore? And if you do have parents, you are so concerned about their own needs you don't want to add burdens to them. They're barely surviving themselves, having crack-ups, divorces, elaborate kinds of therapy.

I tried to get back my old job at the bank. Teller Matthew. I'd worked there for a while after Thomas was born. But the ante has gone up. Now you need several advanced degrees.

Any job more sophisticated is automatically out. With children bumbling between the keys it would take me more than my week just to type out a résumé, for God's sake. And what would the résumé say? I can thread a safety pin in the dark with one hand on a moving child without sticking him in the belly? I'm faster than a speeding toddler? I can leap staircases in a single bound? I can roll giant boulders forever uphill?

* * *

Montville hunkers with abandoned factories, but one of the still-working ones down by the river has a sign out today: "Hiring Strander Operators." I'm not sure what those are, exactly, but if a single parent has skills in any department it is stranding and operating.

This mill must have once been the pride of Northeastern Connecticut, a fine old brick building several stories high, squatting astride the river. These days the river runs thick and volatile with effluent. And late at night when the mill dumps its waste, the river froths up like a gigantic bubble bath. Drunken late-night drivers on the bridge downstream screech to a stop at the sight of a giant moving wall of dirty soapsuds. Montville-sur-Merde.

Montville is home of the Beethoven Cable & Wire Co. Bee-THO-ven is how you say it, I find out, when I call for an appointment.

"Appointment? Nah. Just come by durin' first shift. Ask for me, like I say, in the mornin'. Rennie."

I've got to watch myself, I realize. If there's one thing they're not going to want to hire it is some asshole asking for an appointment—like walking in there in white kid gloves to my elbows.

"River? What was that?" We're standing between two SJ 434s, giant shiny tubes the size of canoes which spin at several times the speed of light, it looks like, impeding small talk.

"What's the name of the river?" I am shouting in what I take to be casual blue-collar fashion. I am also wishing I hadn't said anything to start with. What asshole cares about the name of a river? Especially Rennie, whose name is clearly René. He's one of this area's resident low-rents, a Kanuck.

René has an elaborately broken nose and two milky-green eyes, like winter water. He squints them as he tries to lip-read what I'm saying. He's foreman and he's supposed to be showing me around but we can only occasionally hear each other speak.

"*Four-thirty-four over there. Some machine.*" Rene is smart, you can see, and he's sizing me up, trying to figure out what this Waspy looking asshole with short sandy hair and freckles is doing here in the first place. I wore my oldest clothes today, tried to make them look as if they were my best by washing and ironing them, but I don't think he's fooled. There's clearly something wrong about my asshole questions, my desperation, the five-year hiatus in my work life. I couldn't tell him I'd spent that time in graduate school, so I tried to tell him first thing that I'd goofed off all that time after I flunked out of community college. Smoking dope and taking odd jobs. But I said "taking" instead of "takin' " and I saw him squint those eyes a little more.

But at least I can read and it is clear I'm genuinely impressed with the noise of the machinery, the concrete floor that shakes like linoleum. I am careful not to ask too many other dumb questions. This is only a job, right? But as we pass them I fondle the machines with what I take to be the proper mixture of familiarity and contempt. That seems to do it. He's going to risk me, I can tell. He's given up the squinting. So now I try the question. I'm going to have to start tomorrow and there isn't time to do this any other way.

I'm the first mother ever to apply for a job there, I guess. No women working there now, I noticed. His eyes almost closed entirely when I asked him about child care. I carefully said "Kids. Takin' care of kids" but still he was dumbfounded. He looked like he was trying to shake water out of his ears the way he kept cocking his head and nodding it at the same time. Squinting at me silently. Finally he decided I was not putting him on. No, he didn't know anything about it. He didn't even live in this town, himself.

"What about the old lady?"

"She took off."

"Her folks, then—or yours?"

"Out of state."

"Jeez. That's a pisser. Why work? Whyn'tja go on welfare?"

"I don't think they give men with children welfare."

"Yeah, probably don't. Every lazy nigger and long-hair in the place'd be on welfare if they did. Right? Just knock up the first snatch comes along. —Sorry, no offense. OK? Look, try asking Joseph over on the Four-thirty-fours. He's got kids, lives right over there in the town."

Joseph told me he was fifty and had six children and no idea about who took care of kids if it wasn't the wife. By now this was becoming embarrassing and I began to worry René might have second thoughts about me.

"No sweat," I am saying to René as we close away the shop noise with his thick metal office door. "I'll fix it up. I'll show up for work day after tomorrow. Or as soon as you want." I was walking out the door before René shouted after me.

"Hey! What shift you want?"

I wasn't sure what he was talking about. I stared at him stupidly, thinking what to say.

"How're you gonna know what woman you want for your kids if you don't know what shift? Look, I'll put you on first. OK? To start out."

"Thanks. Thanks, René. Oh yeah, what's the hours?"

He looked at me hard again. "Eight to four-thirty. Half hour for lunch."

"Right. See you Wednesday. Do I bring anything?"

"Just your ass. And a sling to hang it in if you're late." He grinned a fine set of stained and broken teeth—pickup-hockey teeth—and headed back out into the insulating roar of the shop.

Sitting babies is a cottage industry in these parts. I found someone for my kids before I was halfway home. Most of this area is in ruins, abandoned mills and collapsed farms. The other parts seem to be clusters of ancient tenements erected by the mills in better times. Rows of wooden two-story houses, green-and-gray-tarpaper shingles, cars so old they're almost dignified with their toothless grills and sagging frames. It was a '53 Plymouth, in fact, that got me my baby-sitter.

My father had owned one like that when I was too young to drive, and I still think of it as something magic and unattainable. Playing by this car, which was up on blocks in deep grass, were far too many kids for anyone not living in a shoe. The neighboring houses looked deserted, so the other kids couldn't be just neighbors. I braked my Mustang (this will be a classic itself in a couple of years) and left it running since I still had no battery.

In charge was Marlene, a woman of unfathomable age and bulk. She was ironing just inside the front door where she could keep an eye on the kids, she said. Yeah, she took in first-shift kids, she said. She had to stay home anyway to look after Teddy since she'd been laid off. Her mother worked first shift at the shoe mill in Webster.

There was a TV in one corner of the parlor guarded by three infants in a crib. Teddie and the three other ambulatory children were in the yard, so that's why the TV was so low, she said. So she could hear the kids—right?

"How old are they, your kids?" she sounded genuinely interested in their ages but I was concentrating on not staring at her, looking for some neutral part of her body. She didn't have one. Her face was puffed like those tree frogs you see pictures of in the *National Geographic*. Her glasses dug channels in the flesh at the sides of her face. If there was a neck it was hidden by dewlaps which shook with the effort it took her to breathe. Her arms were crossed somehow just below huge breasts that stretched the black turtleneck she was wearing so that between each fiber shone the pink nylon of her brassiere. I realized I hadn't answered her.

"One and two-and-a-half. The infant's a girl, he's a boy—the larger ... ah ... one."

Mother's Day

I've gotten to her knees, which are squeezed into tight black slacks that peg in painfully at the ankles. I haven't dared to look at her hips and stuff, not directly, but the overall effect is heightened, I notice, by the conical shape her head takes under the scarf where tiers of pink curlers stack to a point. I settle for staring at her eyes, which are beautiful soft green, like a streambed, and seem trapped in the wrong body. She smiles with them and they quicken with reflected color from the doorway.

Marlene wants me to bring Pampers, a box of them to start, and two changes of clothes each. She'll feed them, she says, and I fight back an image of my children imprisoned in cages like pâté geese, Marlene cranking food through funnels shoved down their gullets. I instantly feel guilty at the thought. I've seen the supermarkets around here, they sell only the most poisonous processed foods. Marlene probably eats nothing. All that fat is water to dilute toxins. Two parts water, one part polyvinyl chloride.

Twenty dollars a week for both kids, Marlene is saying as I write her my neighbor's phone number. I say I'll be there at seven-thirty Wednesday. I almost cannot hear myself write because Marlene has begun bellowing like a water buffalo at Teddy and his pals. They have upset her laundry basket as they ran in the door. They seem to pay no attention to her bellows—that's a good sign I am thinking—but they do get out quickly after looking me over. Equal parts of hostility and indifference. Not all that different from the look I'm sure I'll receive from my neighbor when I get back today. She took my kids when I left this morning. She took my kids, I think, because she was too stunned and constricted of throat to say no. I think she's afraid they'll contaminate her house with anarchy.

"Good cable, see, is like a good woman. It lays flat on its back like this and doesn't move around. Now this here, off that two-ten-M, is bad cable. See the difference? Won't sit still."

We're in the storeroom, René and I, and he's issuing me tools and cautions. This is a tin shed behind the mill, fiercely padlocked at all times.

"Now we're not an uptight shop here but we don't want no expensive accidents, either. So keep your sleeves up above the elbows. Those machines suck one in and you've lost any more need for sleeves. And don't look straight at the turning drum. There's wire in there whipping around and chips fly off the die like shit through a tin horn. Things are always going wrong with this kind of cable, the feed wires are so thin."

For two weeks I've been here cocooned in the thunder of machines. The first week I worked 210's, simple, almost medieval machines that make heavy cable. They are easier to run, the 210's, and René apprenticed me here to a freak named Shadow. He'll show me the ropes. He's a veteran, Shadow tells me. He's been here already three months, longer than most people stay.

Shadow would be tall if he hadn't bent himself so out of shape with softening agents. As it is, his six-foot frame is languidly curved and seems weighted down by black hair that hangs to his shoulders in ropes. He's bitter, he says, because they put him on first shift. Now he has to take pills all day. Third shift, from eleven at night, you could smoke dope because the foreman slept most of the time. Pills are getting more expensive by the week, he says, and he doesn't know how much longer he'll be able to stay on here.

As you can see Shadow has said a mouthful for two weeks. Our machines are down so much of the time we can hear each other talk over here in the eastern corner of the building. When the machines are running we drift like drowned bodies in the crushing vibrations, leaning against the walls of noise. The rest of the time we walk about looking busy.

Mother's Day

"First thing, man, you gotta know is about tools. Never go noplace without a tool. Ya dig it? That way you look like you're working all the time but you don't hurt the quotas."

I've received such help from others here, as well. My second day I made the mistake of heading for the punch-clock when it was my turn to quit for lunch. Joseph was somehow at my side before I got there.

"Hey, bud? Ya wash up *before* ya punch out for lunch. Got it? *Before*. We don't need no trouble here from the likes of you—OK?"

And René explained about losing tools. You get to lose one each of your first set during your three-month trial period. After that you get to lose tools according to how much cable you produce.

Life is very simple here.

The new working class. I notice that workers here seem to have only two ages, young and very old. Joseph is the only middle-aged man here and that's probably because an antique sense of work keeps him tinkering with his machine, honing his production, day after day till everyone here finds him a pain in the ass.

The cynicism here is tonic. No one pretends any motivation. No one pretends this work has any value other than the pay it produces on Thursdays. For me that is $100 a week, gross. Take-home about $85. Two weeks' take-home pays my rent. One week pays baby-sitting for the month. The last week for the rest. Yet I am almost happy here, content at times for uninterrupted hours on end, drifting with the rhythms of my machines.

This week I am moved to the 434's I did so well with Shadow. All I did there as far as I can tell is develop an ear for the change in sound the machine makes when it breaks a strand as it twists wires through a die to make cable. Shadow has long ago lost such subtlety of ear, either through the buzz of his daily dose of downs or because, as I am beginning to suspect this week, the machines kill off such hearing. Anyway, now I am in the major leagues and I look almost enviously at Shadow mooning around in the shafts of dusty morning light. The oil covering his machines glows a soft yellow that looks gentle and otherworldly among the marine-gray paint and steely fluorescent light of the rest of the shop.

I work this machine alone and most of my thinking is absorbed these days in the intricate threading of fine wire through the insides of the spinner drum. The drum looks like a fat missile about twelve feet long. It is hollow with large square openings through which I reach my hands to thread the wires along its insides. I feel like a blind surgeon working deep inside warm intestines suturing with wire so fine I can barely feel it between the fingers.

Several times an hour a wire snaps inside the spinning drum and I kill the engine, wait for the drum to stop and probe around inside to find the break. I've come to ache for the numbing roar of the machine and the obliterating peace of mind it induces.

When I feel the need to sit and rest, I reach for a wrench and set out with a frown on my face to some distant part of the floor. From there I can circle to the bathroom, where, I've found, you hold your cock with the wrench to keep from burning it with grease from the hands. First time I saw a man doing this I thought he had some kind of prosthesis and looked away embarrassed. But when I tried unsuccessfully at home one night to remove rings of dark grease from my cock I realized what was going on.

I wish I could say my attention to my oil-stained cock had been preparatory or cosmetic but I cannot. I am fatigued beyond private parts. I am fatigued almost beyond myself. I have the soul of a bivalve. Open for sustenance, close for sleep. Only there are these children crowding my territory, rattling against my shell. Do bivalves eat their own young, you think?

Mother's Day

* * *

Skies are gray today. Skies are mostly gray. It's been raining now for a month, a cold metal November rain. Marlene doesn't seem to notice. She soft-shoes round her kitchen every morning when I get there, chortling to the kids as if this were just life we are all living. No bivalve she. Last night, for God's sake, as I lurch in after work for my kids, she is singing! And she is ironing underpants. Socks and underpants and towels and other things most people don't even wash. It has been raining, as I said, and children are sprawled all over her parlor. There must be ten of them. Half look passed-out, the rest feverish. Everyone is coughing. One thin crew-cut boy of five sounds like a black-lung victim. He hacks as if his lungs were made of orange crates. Thomas is blissfully silent but scarlet with fever as I feel his head. Not the first time. One or the other of them has been sick since we got here but the fever feels high enough I know tonight I won't sleep.

"What's wrong, Matthew? You look wiped out." Marlene is merry, almost, as she asks. Adversity rings like music in her ears. Last week she smiled as she told me about her sisters. They were just toddlers when she last saw them.

"My father run off with them after he split from Ma. Haven't seen them now for five years. That's why we don't let Teddy go to school. I stay here with him in case the old man gets any ideas, the old bastard." She smiled again at the recollection, absently patting Teddy's head. She'd been spoon-feeding him SpagettiO's but stopped for a moment and her hand started twirling a cut glass saltshaker on the black formica table. In the corner of the kitchen I heard the washing machine click as it changed cycle. The humming made me ache for the numbing simplicity of my 434's.

CHAPTER XIII

I think constantly of Joanne.

Sex is the last vestige of connecting tissue when all else is gone. It is the life force reduced. Sex is supposed to be in the high brain centers but it is really more like those plants that only flower when denied adequate sustenance. They flower desperate to prove life by reproducing—not in joy or loving gratitude.

Anyway, I think of Joanne more as time passes. It is dark now when I go to work and when I come back. The house is cold, because I can't afford to keep it warm. The kids and I sleep in our clothes. We eat whatever we can eat that takes less than ten minutes to prepare—frozen foods, mostly, that I have to buy from my local country store at inflated prices. Frozen pizza, macaroni and cheese, tuna casserole. Thomas and I will one day wake up looking like Marlene. Keturah still eats nothing, just drinks quantities of milk from her bottle. I suppose it is the bottle she needs, not the milk. Another bivalve.

Mother's Day

And I suspect my thoughts of Joanne are not much elevated from that. It's not a sisterly Joanne I encounter in those rare idle moments of the brain. I think of her amplitude, her breasts stacked high like thunderheads, the now unthinkable abandon of her buttocks. Hardly sisterly thoughts.

Sometimes I awake late at night from terrible grinding dreams, sure something terminal has happened to a child. Sometimes I can't move I'm so frightened. But when I do move and find Thomas and Keturah sleeping utterly relaxed and innocent I am stricken with love for them that unsettles me and prevents my usual dive back into sleep.

Last night I had been dreaming the children were sitting in a small boat tied to me by a rope. Also tied to me was a gigantic barge loaded with crushed rock. I would push the children out in their boat, smiling, then the barge would lurch toward them at terrifying speed, threatening to crush them against the pier like a Dixie cup. Each time the barge barely missed. Each time I sent them out again.

I've had that same dream several times these last weeks. Sometimes it takes place in utter silence, some underground chamber. Other times the barge thunders toward them sounding like my 434's. The water vibrates like the floors at Beethoven on first shift.

Last night the noise was still in my ears as I prowled the nursery studying the sleeping kids for any signs they might have been in the same dream. Keturah was sleeping on her knees, her head tucked into the mattress like an ostrich. Her back was exposed because her shirt has come untucked from her jeans. I ran my hand up under her shirt and waited to feel the shoulders expand with her breathing.

Thomas stirred across the room in his crib, then settled quiet on his side. It was so cold in there I'd lost feeling in my feet.

I put coats on top of each child. Then the squeaky board in the hall put me in mind of Karen that night several lifetimes ago. I had begun to fantasize about Joanne while I was with the kids but it was Karen I was remembering now, Karen anchored to me by desperation that night, Karen attached to me by an umbilicus.

I have tried Karen twice in the last weeks but she doesn't answer her phone. If it's still her phone. There must be other Karens someplace.

Joanne faded out of my fantasies after that. To be accurate, only Joanne's face and personality faded out. Her jeweler's hands remained, as did her buttocks swaying as she rests there on her knees. Basil is not there with us in the fantasy and I see her soft brown hair tossed over her head and splayed over the pillow where she's buried her face.

A mother of invention, what I did was advertise. The contemporary way, now that fantasy is no longer enough.

The December 9 issue of the Montville *Courant* carried it under discreet black caps: WANTED—MOTHER. And the phone began ringing minutes after I pulled into the driveway from work. Thomas was still crying in the car because I'd refused to carry him even though he said he felt sick. And Keturah was screaming for her baba. And I was already on the phone with the first of five available mothers so desperate that they would move in with me, as my ad suggested, to care for this motherless family. The first two were elderly—grandmothers, really. Mrs. Kropowlski of Montville and Mrs. Crespaux of Rogers. No, they didn't have small children of their own and yes they were free to live in during the working week. Not what I had in mind at all but I took their numbers.

Suzanne called around nine when I had fallen asleep trying to read the kids a story. I was a bit abrupt on the phone with her. She was enthusiastic, then coy, on the phone.

"Two grandmothers have called already," I said.

"Well, I'm not a grandmother, if that's what you wanted."

"I tried to make it clear in the ad—"

Mother's Day

"I think you did—"

"—just what I needed. This is no picnic, you realize."

"Mr. Vole. I read your ad. I am an experienced mother, as you said, and I'm willing to trade room and board and a small monthly fee—"

"Ah. Perhaps we could meet, Mrs.—?"

"Suzanne Dolbier. Yes. Sure."

The Suzanne I had imagined that night as I lay awake scheming was not the Suzanne I met two days later in a scrupulously clean, sad apartment several rows of tenements behind Marlene's.

This Suzanne is pale, though she blushed from time to time in our conversation. Marlene is watching the kids tonight—I told her I had a date—so I have as much time with Suzanne as I have money for Marlene. Suzanne has blond hair, fake blond hair, stuffed into a blue bandana that is tied at the top of her head like Aunt Jemima's. There are definitely breasts beneath the man's denim work shirt that hangs down over the top of her jeans, but nothing exceptional, nothing like Joanne's, which had kept swimming up at me during the two nights I have planned this meeting. Suzanne keeps getting up from the tiny round kitchen table to adjust things in this one downstairs room, to fiddle with the tea she keeps making, to listen for her kids, who she says are upstairs. They are about Keturah's and Thomas' ages, she said, but I was not concentrating the first time she said this, because she was climbing the stairs and her jeans moved hypnotically as she did.

Why am I now so fascinated with asses? I wasn't this way before. At least not since I was sixteen, playing slap and tickle with Patricia Murphy in her parents' living room while they watched TV in the den. Then I had been consumed with ass, Patricia's pert, sassy ass she kept offering me in lieu of her unassailable virginity. I don't think the subject even came up with Cindy, though she had one certainly.

Now it comes up again and again as Suzanne moves

around. We are mothers talking about children and I am thinking sudden regressed thoughts about the solemn, provocative swing of her hips as she ushers it around in her nervous forays.

There is a cardboard box in the corner full of broken toys. Suzanne went there to show me a new toy she'd bought for her oldest boy. I'd seen that play school before, I told her, and I told her how it ambushed me with Karen. She laughed and widened her eyes at me, then suddenly looked shy and fiddled with her tea bag.

"What's the situation with this apartment, Suzanne? If you, ah, were to work for me, there? What I mean is who—"

"This is paid up till January. Two months. The last we're going to hear from their old man." She's pointing at the ceiling when she says that, where the children sleep. She talks about him as if he belonged only to the kids. "After that I don't know. I can't stay on here, anyways. My caseworker says it costs too much."

"Jesus. Where do they expect you to live with two small children? In an igloo?"

"They don't expect anything. I only just got them to cough up money for little Joey. He's been sick for three weeks and now the neighbor says it looks like pneumonia. Tomorrow I can take him to the doctor, the caseworker says. They don't expect anything and I don't think they can ever afford to care."

I'm paying her $60 a month with room and board. She looked like she wanted to protest the $60, then she just looked at me suddenly bold and smiled some kind of secret smile. She has beautiful teeth which you never see because she puts her fingers over her mouth almost every time she smiles. This time she didn't, and she didn't stare shyly at the floor, either, as she did every time before.

Nor was she shy about my helping her to move in. Her car is uninsured—she can't afford it—and besides little Joey is barking with a scary cough and she could hardly be expected to leave him in my charge. But still there was something almost challenging in the way she kept adding one more trip for some forgotten—some unnecessarily forgotten—item.

The other kid is Jonathan. He's about three and intensely skinny. Neglect was my first thought—that reflex parent righteousness about another parent. But now I think it's the result of his unceasing energizing. He spins like a bobbin, that kid, bumps into walls when he's not running. And he is almost never not running. If you give him crayons he will scatter them in minutes. He's in some sort of constant seizure, it looks like. He doesn't sleep nights till hours after he should, and he is up at five making busy noises like a giant rodent in the walls.

Already I resent him and Suzanne can see that. He wants to kiss me goodnight and I find myself almost gagging. No reason, because he is a bright-eyed enthusiastic-looking kid who seems full of genuine smiles. But somehow his energy seems morbid to me and I don't want to touch him.

Suzanne is weird about Jonathan. She is exhausted one moment, unable even to move to prevent him from some mindless depredation. The next moment she is screeching at him, grabbing him by his Dachau arms and hurling him out of the room for crossing her. He is always crossing her. He seems to say no by reflex. Then, having said it, to dig in and defend his position till physically overpowered. I've watched this so many times already Suzanne must sense my confusion, because after three days here she begins to make peculiar roundabout statements.

"What he needs is a man, Matt. That's all he needs." If Jonathan's behavior hadn't been uppermost in my mind I wouldn't have known what she was talking about. The kids—even Jonathan—have been asleep for more than an hour already and Suzanne and I have been scurrying around washing dishes, sweeping up, and clearing fire lanes through the toys and kid paraphernalia that now sprout quadrupled in any freestanding space available.

"What he needs, Matt, is someone to keep him in line. Man's work. His father could never do it right."

"What do you mean, 'man's work'? Is this stuff I'm doing woman's work—laundry, cooking, babies?"

"Of course. You shouldn't be doing any of this. I should be doing it."

"And the man just sits on his ass? Reading his paper and calling for his slippers?"

"Look, Matt. You work hard all day—right? I mean real work. Not sitting at a desk talking on a phone. Hard dangerous work. You come home and you expect some peace. Some peace and order. I need help with the peace and order. The rest I can do myself. I know you don't like this idea but a house needs discipline. That's men's work at home, not this other stuff."

"Discipline? Jesus, Suzanne. That's not discipline. That's tyranny. The worst kind. Look around you where you live. Women working sixteen hours a day at home and men out drinking with the boys.

"That's not what I see around me. I see almost no men at all. And the only ones who act it sometimes only do that when they've been drinking. So there. I need help with Jonathan. I can't make him mind me. He's flying around all the time. He needs someone to keep him in line. So does Thomas—only you don't see that. We all need that sometimes."

"Nobody needs that, Suzanne. Nobody."

"Matt, you're lying to yourself. I saw you last night with Thomas when he wouldn't go to sleep. He was asking for a lickin' and you pretended you weren't pissed off when you were. You wanted to bust that kid, just the way you want to bust Jonathan. Just the way I want to bust them raising hell all day. That's what a father's for, and you're not doing it."

Mother's Day

* * *

All that was philosophical inquiry. Prolegomena, really, to the substantive matters that began about a week later when Suzanne presented herself in my room at bedtime.

She'd been acting obscure all evening. I had come home to find the house in impeccable order. Thomas and Jonathan were upstairs with her, building with blocks in the nursery. The babies were already asleep. Suzanne was involved with the boys' game and hardly spoke when I came in except to say supper would be ready at seven if I wanted to get cleaned up. Keturah wasn't totally asleep and she smiled at me around the nipple of her bottle when I leaned over the crib side to nuzzle her. And Thomas merely said "Hi, Matt, got any candy?" and went on with the blocks.

Something was up. The combination of such order and quietude unnerved me. I have come to steel myself for reentry after work these days. The children are howling or hurtling down the hall after me. The babies are in the kitchen splashed in their food or crawling over the filth on the kitchen floor. Suzanne in her bandana and rolled-up sleeves is running everywhere in amputated, schizophrenic motions, never finishing anything she starts out to do. The place looks worse than it ever has when I was alone.

But not tonight. I realize I am unsettled as I languish uninterrupted in the shower, then put on clean clothes that are piled orderly on the bed. This is the first time in weeks I haven't had to paw around in the basket for clothes I tossed there in a daze from the dryer some evening after work.

"Good stew, Suzanne. Use that recipe I clipped?"
"No. My mother-in-law's. 'Frog stew,' my husband used to call it. You like it, huh?"
"Umm." I'm rapidly becoming monosyllabic. I haven't the energy to hoist myself up on words tonight. Relaxation is insidious. I fear it since Basil told me about a kid he'd taught

in elementary school. The kid was tough, from the ghetto, and independent. He lived under filthy conditions alone with an alcoholic mother. Then one day going home he was hit by a car. His mother sobered up and for a week in the hospital lavished attention and love upon him. He was never the same after that. A broken kid, Basil said, who'd discovered what he'd been missing.

I fear this feeling. Letting down my guard. Does Suzanne know what she's up to? What is she up to? She geishas me like tonight—like her first nights here—then provokes me to fury at her with deliberate lapses. Why? What convoluted mummeries are these? What arcane strategies does Suzanne think she's bound to?

We watched TV and I was nodding off before half the movie was over. Lots of good lines, I kept telling myself, but it's as if they weren't really coming all the way through. I was dozing in the armchair and Suzanne was sewing a patch—sewing a patch!—on some kid's pants. She was sitting on a ratty caned Calvinist chair by the door, keeping an ear cocked for the kids.

She'd gone upstairs once or twice before I had heard anything, and returned looking innocent when I shot her quizzical looks. I dozed again, because the TV was off when I awoke and Suzanne was standing over me in a green nightgown. She'd had a shower and her head was wrapped in a yellow towel turban.

"Matt? Matt. It's late. You'd better go up to bed. OK? You awake now?"

"Yeah. Thanks. What time is it?"

"Ten-thirty or so—I left my watch in the bathroom."

"It's cold, Suzanne. Aren't you cold like that? You got enough blankets on your bed in there? I worry about that some nights and forget to ask you later."

"Fine. No problem. You going up now? It's not so warm I plan to stand here all night like your mother and be sure you get to bed."

Mother's Day

"Right. Thanks, Suzanne. And, ah, thanks for everything tonight. So peaceful—you know?"

"Woman's work, Matt...."

Much of the gloss of civilization has been honed away this generation. Two weeks is plenty for adulterous decisions. I can't say I hadn't had fantasies about Suzanne when there was space enough between waking and sleeping. And she'd certainly been speaking some subterranean language the night of our interview. But for several nights running recently things had been such chaos when I came home that my fantasies were never wholly successful. I'd begin conjuring up that slim pale figure I imagined under those denims and then I would be boiling with rage about the disaster underfoot. The figure would slink quickly away. Anger and sex don't mix. We know that. So most of my thinking—the fantasies were reduced thus quickly to mere thinking—was about whether I'd be better off alone, after all.

And I was thinking that again tonight, balancing it with the unholy order and virtual collapse of my guard tonight, when Suzanne walked into my room.

When I went up there I had undressed and slipped into bed and willed myself a womb of body heat to fend off the cold of my bedding. I hadn't turned off the light because that meant moving my arm out from inside the womb. Then Suzanne was standing there with her hairbrush in her hand and her head at an angle so she could brush the bleached yellow hair that now hung straight to her shoulder.

"Can I sit a minute?"

"Sure. Cold as hell up here, isn't it?"

"Yeah, I guess."

There was a silence while Suzanne scraped at the hair with her brush and looked at me out of the sides of her wide green eyes. I realized she had on some kind of eyelash stuff because it sparkled oddly in the light.

"It's about that sixty dollars, Matt."

"Oh, yeah. Well, I don't see what I can do right now—"

"No. You're not understanding me."

"I'm not?"

"I'm here to earn the rest of that sixty dollars. I've been waiting for you to demand your money's worth but you just don't see, do you? That *was* part of the deal, wasn't it? What you advertised for? Woman's work, Matt? This is woman's work...."

Man's work left something to be desired that night. Or maybe nothing to be desired. Whatever else Suzanne is, she is no dynamo in bed, so I don't feel so bad about it as I might.

No, that's not right. I feel good about it. That's what I am saying. I don't feel bad at all. I'm learning, Suzanne would say.

First we had a little dance about the light. She'd stood up from the side of the bed where she'd been sitting and had put her brush down on the headboard. Then she'd stood there a moment looking at me again with that half-cocked dimple smile on each cheek I saw when we first talked.

"You reach the light, Suzanne?"

"You want it off?"

"I don't care. What about you?"

"Matt—you want it on or off? Which?" She seemed to have flushed and her cheekbones had high dots of red. "Don't you know anything you want?"

"I want it off. No, I want it on."

A triumph. I did want it on. I wanted to see her finally out from under all those sloppy men's shirts. Her hair looked nicer loose like this than under that bandana.

She crossed her arms and grabbed the nightgown at about her hips. She looked once more at me, smiled to herself, then pulled it smoothly over her head, turned around and bent slightly to put it on the chair with my clothes. Then she stood by the bed looking at me again. Her intent look unnerved me.

"Come on in, Suzanne. Get in, for Christ's sake. You'll turn to a pillar of salt or something."

"Pillar of salt?" She is working her legs down alongside me and they are cold and electric at the same time. "Pillar of salt? Matt, you are very weird, have I told you that?"

"You are very delicious, Suzanne. Have I told you that? As well as weirder by far than I could ever be."

She was typically female—all business. She had reached for my cock, which was already critical from all this pantomime. She began stroking it while I was still dawdling with my fingers on her shoulder blades—or some such place. I can remember being surprised and confused and wondering if we'd somehow skipped a stage. I was still puzzling that one out when she let go of my cock and with both hands started tickling me violently by the sides of my ribs. I jumped and grabbed her hands and wrestled them off me. She was panting and I was outraged at the failure of decorum.

"Cut that out, Suzanne. This is not a slumber party."

"OK, Matt. I'll cut it out. I promise."

But the minute I let her hands go, she grabbed for my sides again, tickling in a kind of desperation. This time my outrage turned into a kind of panic. I slammed my hands down on her forearms and yanked them apart, falling off balance onto her in the process. I started to say something as she kept struggling to free her arms, then her mouth rubbed against mine in the fray and I found myself kissing her hard, forcing my tongue into her mouth like a crazed teenager at a drive-in.

She kissed back hard but underneath me she crossed her legs, roughing up my privates in the process. Then she bit my ear quite hard and squirmed harder to turn over. I found myself genuinely angry and trying to flatten her out on her back with the weight of my body over hers and working my left knee down to uncross her legs.

This is not my style, as you know, and I was off balance, trying to think hard and being interrupted regularly by some neat gesture of hers that made it less and less possible to think.

Her arms went limp and she whispered something that sounded like "OK, OK" so I let them go. She threaded them gently under my arms, nary a tickle, and across my back. That's more like it. I'm beginning to slow up in relief and I hold my head back to look at her below me. She makes a face at me, wrinkles her nose and presses her lower lip out. Then she pinches me hard in the middle of my back.

"Suzanne! What the hell. You little bitch—" and I grab her arms again and try to pin them under her sides on the bed. "Cut it out, Suzanne. Or you'll be sorry."

I sound like I used to wrestling with my girl cousins when I was seven.

So does she. "Make me. Make me—you wouldn't know how." And she flips herself on her side again and pulls her knees to her chest.

I let her go and she just lies there, curled up, her jaw set and her mouth flat and defiant.

This is every man's dream, right? Take a defiant woman by force? John Wayne would know what to do.

But not me. This makes me nervous and I'm feeling a little sick. Does she want me or not? And if she does, why all this struggle? You don't force a woman, I know that. Don't I?

She stares at me, smiles a little smile and rolls on her back, her knees still to her chest. Very deliberately she reaches out one foot against my chest as I'm kneeling there feeling stupid. Then the other foot. Then another smile, this time widening her eyes, then a swift kick almost knocks me off the bed. Now she's rolled over on her stomach, tensed again. I can see the tension because her buttocks are now high curved spheres.

"God damn it, Suzanne." The tone is almost whining and I am kneeling on the bed again looking at her back. I reach for her shoulders in what I think of as a soothing gesture. She flings her elbows back and shakes my hands off with a twitch of her shoulders. Then she hooks a foot around to kick me in the side.

"Ow. You bitch. What *is* this?" and without thinking I land a hard slap on her buttocks, the way you would an annoying child. She kicks me again and I slap her buttocks again, harder this time, so it stings. She has pushed away from the wall and has shoved herself up against me now. She's on her side and reaching between her legs and pulling my cock towards her vagina. It slips around for a moment—the whole area feels like hot ball bearings in grease, like the inside of my 434—then I am pulling her hips toward me as I get into her. I want to come already, only this time I'm not worrying about my partner's needs as I pound myself against her buttocks, pulling on her hips to get in deeper and trying to remember to look down between us to see since the light is still on.

I have come, come hard, before I can work that out and she is pulling at me underneath as if that would make more come.

I don't think we said a single word, just fell asleep my lying on top of her back. I dimly remember her reaching down to pull up the blankets and my wishing I could even imagine having the wherewithal to come like that again.

Early December, about two weeks after my first bedroom encounter with Suzanne, René ordered me to second shift. Four-thirty to midnight.

I see the imprint of the Hyena in this. Suzanne unnerves me. She had been coming to my bed, then two nights she didn't come at first and I had to coax her. It's the coaxing frightens me. I've come to like it. Without my new working hours I might still have escaped this. But nobody around takes second-shift kids—I asked Marlene yesterday—and now I cannot send Suzanne away.

The 434's whirl and thunder at night just as they did during the day, but now I am constantly fighting sleep. The noise funnels around me like surf and I begin to doze, wanting just to loose myself into its breaking swells. It's still dark when I get to work and come home, just as it was during the day, but now my body craves food almost hourly, as if I had some terrible worm. I bring two lunchboxes this shift, like the rest of them, and stand by my machines wolfing sandwiches until my lunch break at nine. You hold the sandwich by its plastic bag so as not to smear it with grease.

Only two of us break for lunch around nine and the other guy, I don't know his name, is already asleep against the back wall when I get to the office where we eat. It's so quiet there, only the fluorescent lights ticking, that I eat my second lunch as quickly as I can, then tuck my head into my elbow on the table and doze until I'm due back out on the floor. My shirt smells of oil from the machines and I dream of hot summer roads and a plane droning lazily somewhere high above.

Mostly, though, I dream dark satanic dreams of Suzanne. For three nights Suzanne has showed up at my bed like some genie from a bottle, almost before I realized I wanted her. For three days the house remained faultless, the children almost invisible. Sometimes I wonder how she makes all this happen, what unimaginable powers she holds over the kids. I think of frightful folk tales. Some night I will return from work and find the children carefully cut up for stew, mewing quietly among the carrots, onions, and neatly quartered potatoes. Probably it's doses of belladonna. Maybe she's found my ancient ulcer pills and feeds them, numbing the children.

The fourth night Suzanne asked me after I stumbled home if I wanted her to come with me to bed.

"Of course, Suzanne—I mean, if you want to, of course."

"So you don't care."

"Not true. I care a lot. I need you there."

"Well, I can't. Not tonight."

"Wha—? Well, sure. You OK? Something the matter?"

"You wouldn't understand—"

"Try me. A woman's problem. After all this mothering I'm a woman myself."

"You know? Sometimes, Matthew, you amaze me."

"Only sometimes?"

"Oh, forget it."

"C'mon now Suzanne. I was just kidding."

"I wish you were. But I wonder about you. You really think that about women, don't you?"

"Yeah. I don't only think that. I know it. There's nothing a woman with children goes through I don't go through, too. I've been alone with babies. I've picked up after kids for sixteen hours straight, then had to stay up all night with one of them sick. I've had no one to help me, only people bitching that the place is a mess, I look like shit, and how come they can't get any peace around here. I've gone privately crazy like the rest of you."

"You understand nothing. That's no sweat, all that stuff, for a woman. You think we shouldn't have to do that, I know, but you're wrong. It's the other stuff drives women crazy, not this. And anyway, first you get Marlene, now me to do it for you—"

"That's not fair—"

"Anyway, look at these other women. Look at Cindy. You told me yourself she is quickly cutting herself off from her kids—"

"'Cauterizing' is what I said. Stanching the flow so she doesn't bleed to death with guilt."

"Whatever you want to call it, she's sick as far as I'm concerned. No woman leaves her kids like that unless she's sick. Then calls like she did yesterday, you told me, and cries about the kids for two minutes and talks about her job for an hour. You told me that. Her *job*! She can have her jobs. Where's that get you? Now there're judges saying men don't have to support us, don't have to support the kids, because we got equal rights. My husband—their *father*—

paying nothing for Jon and Joey and no one will do anything about it. If I hadn't found you—"

She looked at me suddenly to see if I'd seen. I looked blank. This is the longest conversation we've had after work, it's after midnight and I don't have to feign blankness. I feel as motivated as an artichoke. I could believe I was an artichoke if it weren't for these spasms of annoyance I feel for Suzanne. Annoyance stitched with weird irritations of the groin, like fine electric flashes. Pinpricks at the very edges of my mind.

We're sitting in the kitchen. The floor in here is so clean tonight it reflects the overhead ring of fluorescent light and hurts my eyes. I've never seen it do that before. It makes me tired just to think of it. And it makes me unaccountably angry. I wish I could just haul myself up to bed and rest, but something inside me itches.

"I've had it tonight, Suzanne. I'm going up."

"Alone?"

"You're the one'll have to answer that, I guess. I'm going."

I was already asleep when Suzanne began getting under the covers. She'd crawled over me next to the wall. She had on her bra and panties and she rolled away from me when I reached sleepily for her.

That woke me up. I hitched up on one elbow and looked at her back. In the dark the bra strap gleamed dull white like bone. She didn't move. I shifted next to her and reached over to cup a breast. She shook me off and rolled on her stomach.

"Suzanne?"

"I don't want to talk about it."

"Would you like me to sleep somewhere else, maybe?"

"Suit yourself. Just don't *talk* about it."

I lay there a while silent, unable now to sleep, becoming angry. I grabbed for her shoulder to turn her over facing me.

"Suzanne, God damn it. What the hell—?"

Even in the dark I could see the disgust on her face. Her

neck muscles were standing out and her face pinched as if in pain.

" 'Suzanne, God damn it' what, Matt. Can't you ever say what you want without all this crap? So now you're horny, huh? All this talk about liberated women and now you want me to put out for you on demand. So OK, I'll get you your rocks off. No big thing."

She flipped off the covers even though it was cold up here. Almost angrily she knelt up, pushed me on my back and slid her mouth over my cock. I could feel the teeth graze its sides as she moved down on it. I started to reach for her and she shoved my hand away, then reached back for her bra and unhooked it, pushing herself further down on my cock till she started to gag. She reached for my hand and pushed it roughly against her breast and then began pushing down hard again on my cock.

This time she really gagged and I could feel her chest spasm in a rictus, like a dry heave. She was breathing labored through her nose.

"Suzanne?"

She didn't stop to answer, just made an annoyed noise and pushed my hand harder to her breast.

By now her working on the cock had triggered my need and I began to thrust up at her face. This time she buried herself on my groin and I thought I felt my cock slide against the back of her throat. A spasm had started again in her chest but this time she kept me back there while it repeated itself two or three times. I thought she was going to be sick but the muscles in my thighs and toes were jumping and I wanted desperately for her not to stop. She pulled back gently, relaxing, and began to put pressure on the head of the cock, forcing her teeth down on it, then releasing them just as they began to hurt. Now she was sliding down and back its full length again, pumping, and I involuntarily reached for her head to keep it there, deep on me. I was trying not to come and moving her down on me so I'd have to. She took a deep breath through her nose. Something released in her throat and she forced me deeper back in her mouth just as I started to pump semen in convulsive bursts. Her spasms continued, three or four of them, till I had stopped coming, then she slowly slid her mouth back to the end of my cock. Very deliberately she set her teeth into it till I winced and yanked it out of her mouth.

She straightened up, hooked her thumbs in the elastic of her panties and slipped them off. She affected a look of wounded innocence—chin raised in profile and her mouth slightly opened in surprise—when I shot her a quizzical look.

"Yes, Matthew?"

"No. Nothing. Never mind. Just more of my talk."

Then she smiled, a little smugly I thought, and cozied down next to me in the bed.

"It's cold," I said. "Isn't it? Don't we need covers?"

"You get them, Matt. You get them."

CHAPTER XIV

Children multiply in geometric progression. Four children now in my house is four times as many as two children, and all sixteen of them seem to be tripping underfoot now that I am home days.

I am quickly forgetting what it was like when I had to coolie the three of us forth and back. I am quickly forgetting what it was like those endless weeks impelling myself foward every moment to fall anyway increasingly behind on everything that had to be done. I am forgetting all that because Suzanne monopolizes my craw.

Somehow what was once chaos is now holocaust. Apocalypse. Food and feces underfoot, Joey and Keturah getting and spending for four. Suspicious puddles anywhere nonporous, especially the kitchen floor, whose white linoleum smoulders with filth like lignite. At night walking through it on bottle missions for the babies I can hear it heave with the exertions of transplanted New York cockroaches. A million frenzied crinkles—and blunt snappings underfoot for the ones who didn't get away.

I am screaming now at nights when I deadhead through the door like an empty midnight bus to find abandoned diapers, shipwrecked bottles, toys and graham crackers crowding me for walking space in the hall. Last night the boys were still awake, cawing like jays in their room.

"One fucking o'clock, Suzanne. Jesus!"

"I'm sorry. I fell asleep." She had been curled up on her bed in the room adjoining the nursery when I shook her awake in a fury.

"Fell asleep? I know about falling asleep, Suzanne. I'm asleep now, too, but what about these—" I am pointing my fist at two suddenly silent three-year-olds, frozen in their cribs. "What about *these*? Now they'll *never* be able to get to sleep tonight. *Never*."

She looks up at me from her bed and hangs her head.

"ASLEEP! You hear, you rotten kids? ASLEEP. RIGHT NOW!" I rushed at them like a pteradactyl and caught one each by the hair in my claws. Thomas instantly began to cry, infuriating me, so I shook him deep by the roots. Now he's really crying, howling like some gothic ghost. Jonathan began to bawl for his mother and I clipped him one upside his ear. Boy, that felt good. I looked at Suzanne to see what she was thinking now about discipline. She looks only interested, like some eager patron at a play.

Thomas is changing key now and it grates on what remains of my ears after eight hours of the 434's. The beds are catercornered to one another so I drop Jonathan, who is dumbstruck silent, and grab Thomas with both hands at the shoulders. I know already I want to hurt him, that little snivelling shit, and I know also to keep my hand away from his throat. Once after a phone call from Cindy last week, I squeezed him so hard at the throat that my dishpan hands oozed blood from the cracks.

I push him down hard on his back in the bed. "SLEEP, THOMAS. This is where people SLEEP, Thomas. You may not know it yet but you WILL. People SLEEP at one fucking o'clock in the morning. SLEEP! SLEEP! SLEEP!" Those were crashes, those last three shouts, and Thomas is pounded deeper into his mattress each time. His head is jerking back when I lift him and he is trying to make noise but doesn't seem able to.

Suzanne got up from her bed and came over to Jonathan. She covered him with a blanket. Then she turned to me.

"Enough, Matt."

"Stay out of this. I warn you."

"Matt, enough. It's my fault."

"Yes, God damn it, it *is* your fault. All this is your fault. Shit in the hallway is your fault. Debris everywhere is your fault. You have kids policing each corner, stomping food into cracks in the floor. That's your fault. This place stinks! It's like some prison camp only there isn't even a solitary I can escape to. Or one for you. God damn it, Suzanne, if you weren't—"

"If I weren't what, Matt?"

"Forget it. Just shut up."

"No, I won't forget it, Matt. And I won't shut up. If I weren't what is what I want to know. If I weren't *what!*"

"God damn it, Suzanne. Shut up."

"Oh, so now the almighty Matthew is threatening me. I thought you had just learned how to beat up kids. Finally. Big deal. I have nothing to fear from you, you asshole. I know your type. I told you that already a thousand times."

Suzanne was turning to go back into her room when I grabbed her elbow and pulled her around to face me. She looked at me deadpan, then smiled that tiny tight smile she has.

"Yes, Matthew. *Mother* Matthew? What're you going to do, take me over your knee? You wouldn't *dare.*" Suzanne looked hard at me then rocked her head back on her shoulders and spat at me, closing her eyes and aiming the tip of her tongue between tight lips.

I slapped her so hard across that weasel face I thought I

heard something break. She didn't move. Jonathan was calling "Mama, Mama" and I saw that both kids were staring up at us, stunned. We must have looked like dinosaurs blocking the skies in mortal combat.

Suzanne spat once more before I had time to think, then I was pulling her by the shirtfront and the hair out of the nursery, scattering metal cars and wooden blocks from underfoot. I really don't know what I had in mind but I was strangely buoyed by that look of awe on the kids' faces. Suzanne was trying to bite my hand on her shirt and I just yanked harder on her hair till she fell on the landing by my bedroom.

"Get up, God damn it. Get up or I'll kick you up. You can't pull this shit on me forever, Suzanne. You can't pull this shit forever—you ought to have known that."

"You're a pussy-whipped asshole. Pussy-whip." She was spitting the words out as she hauled herself to her feet and into my room.

"Stop it, Suzanne. Stop it. I warn you, goddamit. I'm losing it tonight. You better stop."

"Oh. Poor Matthew's losing it. What happens if poor Matthew loses it, huh? What happens to naughty Suzanne?" She was talking in baby talk, her voice an octave higher than usual. "You asshole, Matt. Nothing happens to Suzanne—right? More goddam talk. TALK!"

"Shut up. If you go and wake the other two now, Suzanne—"

"Oh, there he goes again, whine whine whine. That's what happens to Suzanne—right? Whine. You just don't make it, Matt. You just don't make—"

"What happens to Suzanne? Jesus, you're a bitch. I'd bust you so easily tonight. I'd belt the shit out of you—"

"Oh, Matthew's going to go for his belt? Like the boys at the mill. Wow. We have to see this. Matthew doesn't even have a belt, remember? Remember when I said you needed one for the boys?"

"Oh yes, I do have a belt, Suzanne. Don't—"

"And he wouldn't use it anyways, would he, Matthew? That's fascism and Matthew is no fascist, not our pussy-whip Matthew. Maybe Cindy will call up now and put you in your place again. How about that?"

Suzanne was now white in the face and breathing hard through her nose with anger.

"There. Look at that, Matthew. See that?" Suzanne had unsnapped her jeans and was pushing them over her hips. She was pointing now with her index finger at her white nylon panties. "See that? There"—and her pants were now at her knees—"see that? That's what a man speaks to, Matthew. Not a whiner, though, not a pussy-whip like Matthew—but what you'll never be. See? I knew it. I didn't have anything to fear in the first place."

All of a sudden my bones ached. I could feel my breathing come in stutters and I was sweating so hard my hair began to walk on my scalp.

"You're a cunt, Suzanne, just like the rest of them. A common cunt. I'm really tempted. I really am. For once in my life I am really tempted. You'll be sorry you provoked me if you don't get that ass of yours out of my room right now. Get *out!*"

Instead Suzanne reached back and slipped down her panties to her knees. Slowly she bent over. She reached behind with both hands, took a cheek in each and slowly pulled them apart. "Kiss my asshole, Matt. Kiss it."

I remember that I pushed her to the floor on her back and slapped her face several times. She was fighting me, trying to kick with her pants at her knees. She got herself up and I must have pushed her down again this time across the bed because I was kneeling on her back and punching her in the shoulders. Then I was slapping her buttocks, hard, and she was crying out for the first time. I liked that crying and I kept slapping harder.

Somehow she was on her knees now, crying out and

cursing me, and the more she cried out the more enraged I became. There were weals on her back where I'd punched her and her buttocks were almost scarlet and hot to the touch. I kept slapping at them till my hands began to hurt.

On the wall by the bed there's a hook when I hang my work clothes. Now there's only a naked metal coat hanger there. I am thinking about my hand hurting and the thought only makes me more angry, so I push Suzanne down on her stomach and reach across her for the hanger. The first slash from the hanger leaves a livid white line across her. She howls and stuffs a pillow against her face. I slash at her buttocks once or twice more, then her legs and back. She moves back on her knees, tucking her legs close under her and shielding the back of her thighs with a hand.

Something about that movement makes we want to fuck her hard, to hurt her more.

"Don't move, you cunt, or I'll slash you again. Don't move."

She says nothing but turns her head to watch me pull off my pants. My cock has already worked itself hard out the fly of my underwear and I have to crouch to unhook myself from it.

"What are you looking at?"—and I slash her again across the buttocks which contracted with the pain. She gasped and buried her face in the pillow.

She started to spread her knees as I knelt up behind her and I pushed myself into her as far as I could. She was slippery and wet and she didn't make a sound as I pumped. I pulled out suddenly furious at her silence and pushed the head against the cleft between her hot cheeks. She uttered a low kind of wail from the pillow but seemed to relax entirely at the same moment so the head popped in almost without effort. In a reflex she tried to pull away off it but I held her back against me by the hips. I pushed harder and slid deeper into her. Now she shouted something into the pillow then began to cry convulsively as I pumped as hard

Mother's Day

as I could against her. I came almost immediately, too soon, and felt no relief. Only more rage for being spent. Suzanne pressed her head deeper into the pillow and groaned as I began flailing her shoulders and back with open slaps from my hands. Then I was punching her, still pushing in her to give her pain from behind, and pounding the back of her head.

She stopped making any noise, just occasional whimpers, and I realized all at once that I was supremely tired. I fell against her from behind and we collapsed onto the bed. I remember I was soothing the hair on the back of her head, caressing her the way I do a crying child, and feeling a great growing stiffness in my arms.

Cindy called again. I told her she should send the money to the kids instead of wasting it on the phone. Which wasn't helpful, I know, but I don't find myself much inclined toward cooperation. Why bother, when as far as I can see I am a burden to everyone to whom I am not an outright danger.

Cindy wants to know how the kids are. What do I tell her? They're fine? I've populated the house with alligators and giant vampire bats? Wolves run slavering outside their windows at night? In the basement, I could whisper earnestly to her, the urine monster makes ominous peeping sounds as it hunkers at the bottom of the staircase.

I could tell her the reason for the horrors is they baby-sit for me night and day. Monsters do not sleep. I know she'll think me crazy but I was never more sane. Now that Suzanne isn't here to make most everything beside the point, I've got to do something.

"Suzanne is gone? Couldn't take it, I suppose." Cindy sounds tired to hear this.

"Oh, yeah. She could take it all right. I couldn't. She drove me wild, that woman. She was a demon."

"Demon. Of course. Always the woman. Before it was

fascist Cindy's fault, then immature Joanne's—remember Joanne?—and now that evil calculating demon Suzanne. You're sick, Matt. The more I meet people here, the more I'm alone with my life, the sicker I think you are."

"Thanks. These calls are a great help. By the way, why do I get these calls—to help me along with the children?"

"I just want to know about them. I don't give a damn about your problems. If I had any way to do it—"

"You'd wave your fairy wand and turn them into porcelain miniatures—fit for today's smart career girl's mantelpiece?"

"Oh, shit. I'm so tired of listening to you bitch. Someday you'll be sorry, Matt, when I get them away from you—"

"*Some* day? I'm sorry now. There's nothing to take from me I haven't already taken from myself."

So Suzanne is gone and the monsters regroup. I suppose Suzanne was only doing her job, like the kids—like those vultures on the beach—but some things, perhaps, are better left undone.

Tonight the tumult of the machines keeps me floating above all this, a hawk riding thermals over traffic. My machines haven't gone down once tonight, so I am mercifully indifferent to all this loathing far below. My aerie.

That morning seems particularly distant. I woke in bed to find Suzanne gone. It was just after nine. The house was unnaturally quiet. I felt sick with loathing but curiously energized. Then I heard Suzanne's voice, and those of the kids, chattering as they clattered across the front porch. What were they doing outside on a December morning? Everyone sounded animated and I wondered if after last night they were plotting to axe-murder me in my sleep.

The front door opened downstairs and I could hear lots of hushings and what sounded like Suzanne setting something heavy on the floor. Everyone trooped into a side room and then it was quiet. I suppose I dozed off again, exhilarating half-dreams of clear blue snow days, I remember, blurred around the edges as if troubled by static. Then a vacuum cleaner started and I could hear Suzanne humming as she worked it around the downstairs hall. We don't have a vacuum cleaner. I slept again dreaming of my 434's propped up and whirring on a long tidal sandbar. They are surrounded with powderpaint blue seas.

I woke up when Suzanne began on the stairs. The hall echoed with the bumps and crashes as she worked the machine into the edges. The machine stopped. I could hear Suzanne in the kitchen down there. Where were the kids, so quiet?

Suzanne appeared in my room carrying a glass of orange juice.

"Morning, Matt." She sounded energetic and businesslike, the morning nurse. "Sleep well?" She was smiling and her hair smelled of shampoo when she leaned over me to hand me the glass.

"How're the kids?" I said. I was thinking of the dinosaur war last night and what they must have heard, perhaps seen, after that.

"They're *fine*, Matt. Easy this morning. I think it was good for them—"

"Not good for you—or me."

"You don't feel well?" She sat on the bed next to me and ran her hands across my chest.

"You. You feel peachy keen after that?" I looked at her and she was gazing at me innocent again, as if no answer were needed. "I've never done *anything*—"

"Matt, please don't talk about it. OK? I feel fine. Don't ruin the day. Besides, I've got the kids' rooms to vacuum before I can even begin what I've got planned—I borrowed it from Janice and she's coming later for coffee. I took the kids for a ride to Montville to get it." She was standing up, and seemed to be brushing something off her sleeves with both hands. "You stay here in bed awhile," and she leaned over and nuzzled me, then walked quickly out of the room. How could anyone fit themselves into jeans so tight after last night? I kept looking at her back, as if anything might show through the clothes.

Janice arrived for coffee about an hour later and came up with Suzanne to say hello. Suzanne was smiling and Janice looked amused.

"I hear the little lady got a whuppin' last night, Matt. High time, I'd say. She's been asking for it, I bet. She's a mean one, Suzanne. But today she's a pussycat, I'm thinking."

I didn't know what to say so I smiled back, trying to look as satisfied with myself as they did.

After that we had several days of paralyzed quiet. If I wasn't dead silent I was monosyllabic. Suzanne mistook this for forcefulness, I suppose, as she probably did my unwillingness to argue about anything. I just said what I wanted, because I couldn't stand to hear my own voice more than that. The children looked at me with big wide eyes and kept their distance. I wonder what Suzanne has told *them*?

She was asleep in my bed when I got home from work the next few nights but I slept alone in hers. I'm afraid to touch her. Each night I've gone instead into the kids' room and picked up Keturah and Thomas, one at a time, and sat with them by the window, rocking. Keturah woke up once but just smiled and went back to sleep. Thomas never woke. He seemed unnaturally subdued and I kept looking at him during the day to see if I could discover what he was thinking. Nothing showed. He began to come regularly to sit on my lap when I was trying to read or just unwind before work. Saturday morning I was working on my car and Thomas got himself dressed in his winter clothes and came out announcing he was going to help. He busied himself mimicking anything I did, looking dead serious, frowning from time to time. Probably because I looked that way. How is it that kids are so *willing*? They just don't give up. Each time I have shouted at him or pushed him away, grumpy, when I'm tired, he just looks at me and goes away, only to try again later as if nothing has happened. Don't they ever learn?

I plotted Suzanne's exit, those days, while I watched the house decay around me. Suzanne seemed so secure her choreography became rough-edged. She thought she had me and she almost did.

For about a week I tried to rationalize. It was an isolated incident. Both of us were overwrought. I've been working too hard. Anyone would break under the circumstances.

Why was I afraid to touch her, then? Why was it at nights by the machines I found myself thinking dark thoughts I couldn't even acknowledge and had to busy myself with some chore to chase away? All along I knew she would have to go, and all along I plotted her exit.

A week passed and I was getting desperate. I called Marlene again. No one she knew took second shift but she would ask. Janice came by again with her baby and I almost thought of asking her to take Suzanne's place until I remembered her satisfied smile that morning. I'm going to have to give Suzanne money when she goes. That means I don't pay the oil bill again. But she's got to have money back at her apartment and already Joey is crouping at nights, waking me from her bedroom where I continue to sleep alone.

Only once did Suzanne say anything about my doing this. The day after Janice's visit, Friday, I guess, Suzanne came into her room in the morning. She was wearing her nightgown and sat for a minute on the bed.

"Matthew? It's late and I have to go to Welfare today. My caseworker. You'll watch the kids? I'll be back by lunch."

She walked to her closet and pulled out a dress. She held it in front of her at arm's length, then turned to me.

"Matt? I want you to see something." She lay the dress on the bed and began hauling her nightgown over her head.

"Hey! Suzanne! No. Wait a second. I don't—" I was out of

bed and out of her door before she had the nightgown over her head.

"But Matt," I heard her call from the other room, "I just wanted you to see— Oh, it doesn't matter."

Minutes later she came into my room in her dress. "I'm not mad, you know. I like having a man. I know you don't want me now—that's why you sleep there—but I want you to know that when you do I'll be good to you again. I don't see why you're so spooky about it. But that's your business."

Then she showed up at two-thirty one afternoon on foot. She'd had a flat tire on the back road and abandoned the car. She doesn't know how to change a flat, she said, and hung her head. All that day I had been cracking up with the kids, who were by then screaming in unison in their rooms. Could Suzanne have planned this? Does she know what she is doing? I wanted to slug her. Hold her up against the front door and punch her face. She saw that. She knows.

I left the house five minutes later and hitchhiked to work. I tried to sleep during lunch that night but Suzanne kept swimming into focus. I fought back visions of hurting her, of her crying out and burying her face in the pillow.

So she is gone. She cried horribly when I told her. She was utterly confused, scared. She kept saying hadn't she been trying, Matt, and hadn't things gotten a lot better, and if I was angry that was OK, OK. She needed me, she said.

She needed *me*? She was standing in my bedroom with Joey on her hip and sobbing while she mechanically smoothed the back of his head. He was looking on interested, then confused, then he began to bawl and I shouted at her to get him out of there so I could have some peace.

So now she's gone. I gave her a paycheck and all the groceries we had to help pay for the food stamps we'd used. She said she was hoping to get her car on the road and she'd like to visit sometimes.

"I'll miss the kids, Matt. And I'll miss you. I wish you understood."

"I understand too much already. But sure, come and visit anytime. We'll be here. We're not going anywhere."

Janice found me someone for the afternoons. That's all I can afford. I told the neighbors it would be for just awhile, till I can find someone permanent, and they agreed. What could they say—no? Pat comes at three-thirty and stays till seven-thirty when the kids go to bed. Somehow in that time she manages to sweep and clean the place, even do the dishes. I think I love her for that. She's an elderly twisted woman of indeterminate age. She's considerably bent over, which gives her the appearance of great determination and speed, like a motorcyclist in rain.

After Pat leaves, the neighbors open the adjoining upstairs door and listen for the kids. I worked for three days to clean the upstairs after Suzanne left. I hope the neighbors don't venture downstairs. One look at the cockroaches after dark and we'd be out of here in a minute. If there's one thing tidy couples hate it's cockroaches. Why is that?

When I come home at night now the house is dark and quiet as death. Just the upstairs bathroom light is left on. Sometimes, though, there are other lights and I wonder if Thomas has been up after the neighbors are asleep, prowling the house, turning on lights he can reach. Sometimes at night above the machines I think I can hear children screaming, alone in the house, and I have to bite the insides of my mouth to stop the noise.

My Christmas present to myself was to call Joanne. I collected all the change I could find and called her from the pay phone at the laundromat.

"I'm not into sex these days, Matt. I've had it with men" is what she said when I asked her to come up for a weekend. "I split up with Basil because I got tired of that movie. I realized the other day," she continued, "that my father was a tyrant and manipulated me. And all the rest, too. No, not all the rest. Not you. You were no tyrant—but you used me, too.

I'm tired of being used and I don't think I can handle that for a while."

"I wasn't inviting you up for sex, Joanne." I don't know if that was a lie or not. "I just need someone to talk to. These people up here are crazier even than people in New York."

"I need to talk to you, too. But not yet. I really do need to see you, Matt. I've been thinking about you a lot. But not right now. Maybe if Cindy does come there for Christmas, you could get Basil to put you up. We could meet for lunch and talk—OK? Call me if you come down."

Cindy arrived for Christmas armed with presents and a fierce new determination. She had thrown over work three days early and planned to stay five.

We weathered a day there together, since I had to work Thursday to pick up a paycheck. Cindy set to cleaning within an hour of her arrival. She bustled so hard she unnerved the children. They spent extra time hanging on to me everywhere I went in the house to escape the fuss. She cleaned more in that morning than I can in a month. I could see she hates me for my paralysis.

That afternoon she read to the children and won them over. I never seem to read to them. I watched from the doorway as Cindy sat with them on Suzanne's bed. Thomas curled up next to her, leaning his head on her side and holding on to her arm. Keturah sat between Cindy and the book on her lap. It had begun snowing and I could see the dark specks of snow crowding the window by the bed. For some reason all the relief I expected to feel at being free of the children had turned to melancholy. I kept seeing the scene as I would years later, when there would only be regret and the children would have long since grown away from me.

The money I had hoarded for Christmas presents for the kids I spent on gasoline to New York. Basil had said he would be away but I was welcome to stay there. I had a key, right? I had a key. Cindy very gently told me she'd give them presents from me.

I left Friday morning while Cindy had the kids at the supermarket. I couldn't face the tears I knew there'd be. I still can't leave for work without both children grabbing at my sleeves and weeping as if I were never coming back. Each day I end up having to come back up to the front door for yet another kiss and another kiss till I end up howling at them, cursing them for making me late. This time I went in silence.

Mettle fatigue.

Basil's apartment is quiet as a vacuum. It's in unfamiliar order but everywhere there are ambushes. Bright wooden beads still lodged under radiators. A drawer full of marbles I'd hidden long ago from Keturah's windpipe. In what is now the spare room is a pile of shredded magazines, abandoned drawings and coloring books. Crayon doesn't fade and the pile looks bright and out of place against the empty gray of the windows. How could someone single and childless not have had time to throw this out? How could it still be here from another life? Some people haven't even lived one life.

My first night here I lay with Joanne's ghost in Basil's loft. Free finally to sleep uninterrupted, I floated awake trying to induce her. She appeared when I eased demands but balked at urgencies I'd saved for her. Finally I got her to sit crosslegged on the loft the way she did mornings, brushing wet hair away from the back of her neck. I could smell the creme rinse. She let me caress her neck and I fell asleep doing that, overcome with gentleness.

Soon after, I was awake, though, wanting her hard, then wanting anyone. The loft rumbled with the traffic and I dozed thinking of my machines, then thinking of Suzanne. She caught me unprepared for her and I succumbed, but there was no magic. Only that muffled crying out and my most rudimentary sleight of hand. I came fast alone—one does—then slept uneasy through the night.

I remember waking in a fright, as if I'd missed something. It was light outside and Second Avenue clattered in the clear winter air. I could hear the gear teeth of the trucks shifting down. I dozed to the noise and dreamt that I was shouting through it to the street below. Someone was down there with Thomas, holding him tightly by the hand. They had forgotten his clothes. I kept asking why I should cooperate but they couldn't hear. Then I was at the windowsill in the spare room, my hair waving in the wind, leaning way out over the pavement to drop his belongings. They were neatly zipped in a blue shoulder bag which spun silently onto the street where they were standing. Someone else was with Keturah, I believe, up there with me, but they had left before I came back from the room.

I am reduced to monk's needs. Simple completed necessities are all the luxury I need. Five uninterrupted minutes in the shower, free of distant screams or dreadful crashes. My first complete daytime evacuation of the bowels. After breakfast a fulsome toilet of the teeth, floss extra, courtesy of Basil's medicine cabinet.

Then what? What do people do with time? I watered the plants. I eased the bowels again. The noises of the city died away. They became a large fly, nuzzling a windowpane. The glass rattled back.

I have walked now for almost twelve hours. I walked movies first, last afternoon, browsing the pictures under glass and the velvet sidewalk chains. Then the shops. Tormented people, inexplicably trapped, pacing. There were stores apparently for children, though everything there was white and only dead children in antique photographs wear white. I had a beer and a sandwich which ended costing me

Mother's Day

a week's electricity bill. The bar smelled of kitty litter and leather polish. People posed on stools.

Since then I have walked airlines and camera shops and diamonds. Then there were no longer any people, only the bleaker light of night, and tumbling newspapers. Blocks now of shuttered shops and cardboard garbage. It's so cold now the sides of buildings creak. I don't see a person for blocks and when I do they seem unimpressed.

Only the prostitutes seem interested. For seconds as I pass, each is animated against the cold. She will stamp her foot or hug herself and want to talk. At first I didn't talk back, trying to look worldly and unflappable. But now it is late and they are bolder and more urgent.

"Hey. Want to go out?" She is tall and black with a tiny short skirt in this cold, and a patchy rabbit fur jacket. "Hey, Mister!"

"Thanks, but I don't think I have the money." That has shut them up tonight before, but not this one. She has beautiful skin, like molasses, which shines warmly in the cold light of the city.

"How much you want to pay?" She looks solicitous more than anything else, and her eyes are friendly the way they crinkle at the edges when she smiles. No one else has smiled at me since I began walking.

"I don't know—what do things cost? No, it doesn't matter. I can't."

"You cop or what?"

"I look like a cop?"

"You look a little strange. You OK? You strange? See my sister over there? See Sheryl in the red pants? Want to party with her and me? A party and you can have anything strange you want, you know? I can't risk nothing strange by myself. You hear me?"

"Strange? No. But I really am broke."

"OK, Mister. Any way you want it. But don't be patting

your jacket pocket like that every few steps if you're broke. People might think you got something there, you hear?"

"Thanks. I wish I did have something there because I like you."

"Name's Charlene. I'm here every night from nine to three, on this corner—" She hadn't finished the sentence before she'd turned and scampered back into the lee of a subway entrance where her friend had been standing.

That was just below Port Authority on Eighth, I think. Forty-second Street was full of ugly men and police. No women. You couldn't sin there even if you could afford to. The bookstores were warm and I stopped in two for a few moments on my walk east. The second one had peep-show booths behind a curtain at the back. I spent two quarters and watched a young moon-faced redhead with freckles deep-throat a flabby long-hair who was pushing a skin-colored vibrator into her vagina each time she went down on him. I could see her gag and remembered Suzanne. I didn't have enough quarters to see the rest of the show but the last part isn't my favorite, anyway. They always come all over her face or hair or breasts—to show the coming is real, I guess—and she is supposed to smile at that and rub it in, or lick it from her fingers.

Park Avenue was bitter cold and clean. No baffles for the wind, which polished sides of buildings as it nosed downtown. It shoved roughly at my back as I walked, faster now. It's after two and I can't even think of sleeping. My legs are numb. Every few blocks I notice that my feet are hurting but it seems important to walk more, and then my feet stop hurting again.

Two girls were crouched behind the subway entrance, smoking, when I ducked behind to escape the wind for a moment. They were both white, and young, it looked like. One had blond hair and a long brown sheepskin coat. I couldn't see her face very well. The other was in high white go-go boots and a white miniskirt. Her pea jacket was open

Mother's Day 211

in the front and I could see large pointed breasts under a low-cut white body stocking. Her hair was teased high on her head like a country singer.

"Cold, huh?" she said. She looked tired and had dark rings under her eyes but still her face looked open.

"Freezing. How do you stand it out here on nights like this?"

"You just stand it. Want to go out?"

"No. I guess not. I'm just walking."

"Look, it beats walking, let me tell you. We've got a place just down the street if you want."

"I don't have the money, thanks anyway."

"Wait. What can you spend? It's freezing out here. It's late. I've got to go anyway in a minute."

"Yeah. You do?"

"Look. I need one more for the night. Doesn't have to be much. Jesus, it's freezing all of a sudden. Look, I can take it, you understand? A lot of them can't but I can. Whatever you got in mind—except walking." She smiled and hooked her arm through mine. "C'mon. Janet?" She turned back to her friend. "You coming in soon? OK. See you then."

We walked two or three blocks. I started again to protest that I had no money but she just laughed.

"You gotta have *some* money. Nobody doesn't have *no* money. I bet you got plenty. Look, you need cab fare after? I'll leave you cab fare. The rest is mine, OK?"

"There isn't much rest. Believe me."

"I believe you. But I need it and I can't stay out here any more. You're nice. What's your name?"

"Matthew. Matthew—"

"I'm Gina. You from around here?"

"No, Connecticut."

"I'm from Tennessee. Ever been there?"

"No."

"One mean place." She smiled a broad smile. "That's how I can take it."

We went down a side street where we stopped by a small iron gate. She led me down some steps to a basement apartment. There was a light on inside, and I could hear music.

"Who's in there?" I was suddenly scared.

"No one. Just my kid. I leave the music on when I'm on the street."

"Oh."

The apartment was warm and bright, clean. Gina went into a room off the hall to check on her kid. Then she came out and hung her jacket on the back of a chair in the living room at the end of the hall. I sat on a red corduroy couch jammed into a corner. There were small low tables everywhere, shiny in the light, but empty of any clutter. Not even ashtrays. And under a radiator in the hall I could see a small red toy truck.

"You have a toddler, huh?"

She looked at me strangely and stopped pushing her hair straight in the mirror.

"Who told you that? Aw, don't tell me I hooked a cop. You look a little strange maybe, but not a cop. Are you?"

"No, not a cop. A mother. I've got toddlers myself. That's why I noticed. The empty tables."

"Yeah. You are strange. Look, in case you got any ideas, Janet'll be here any minute. OK?" But she smiled nonetheless and collapsed on an armchair across from the couch.

"You in a hurry? If you are we can go in there right away." She was pointing toward an open door that led into a room next to the child's. There was a soft light in there and I could see a bureau with some tubes and jars on it.

"Hey. You got a wife to go with your kids?"

"No. We're split."

"So who helps with the kids?"

"No one helps you with kids."

"Me too. Her old man's been gone almost a year. But it ain't right like this. I mean I make good money sometimes

Mother's Day

and we have a decent place here, me and the baby, but still it almost kills me, this kid, with no old man around." She was leaning back in her chair, staring at the ceiling. Something she was thinking amused her because she smiled, then sat up straight and looked me over.

" 'Matthew,' huh? You big?"

"Five foot seven—"

She laughed. "You *are* strange. I mean your prick—is it big?"

"No. At least no one ever said anything about it."

"OK. Just checking. Here I offer you anything and then I'm thinking you're so strange you might be big, you know?"

She got up from the chair and walked over to the room she'd pointed to. I heard some water running, a bureau drawer opening. In a minute she came out and walked over to the couch.

"So, we going to do some business?"

I felt for my jacket pocket, trying to remember exactly how much I had in there. The few minutes of rest in here, the warmth, had left me addled with exhaustion and the last thing I thought I wanted was to crank myself up now for sex. Still, some part of the brain was exhorting me onward. I pictured smoldering overheated electrodes in there, smelling like burning plastic.

"I don't know about doing any business. I think I'm too far gone tonight. Maybe tomorrow—or is it the next day?—after I sleep."

Gina had been standing in front of me toying with the hook on the side of her skirt. She was twisted round working on it with both hands when I spoke, and the skirt was pulled tight against her hips and one cheek of her ass. The skirt was so short I could see the cleft of skin where that cheek joined the back of her leg. She must have taken off her panties in the room. Everything in my body that had been signaling about fatigue went quiet as the cold fanatical eroticism of the mind intervened.

"Well—but anyway I don't have the money."

"God damn it. What's wrong with you? Look I need that money. I need it tonight. Now. I'm trying to be cool about it but I need it—understand? I don't care how much—I want it. What're you holding out for? Too uptight to say it? Look, I'm giving you the works. I *know* you, I can see you in there. This mother shit don't change nothin in a man."

Just then Janet let herself in. Gina went over to her at the door and whispered something. Janet looked surprised, then shrugged. Gina came back across the room to the couch as Janet dropped her coat across the armchair. Gina seated herself next to me on the couch and started working at my fly zipper.

"Let's see it. Jeez, I thought you was tired and here's the thing riding up under your belt. Yeah. OK. You're not that big." She had pulled my cock out and now turned to Janet.

"I'm going to show him a good time but I want you there with us. I'm taking no chances." She turned to me. "You like to take a woman up the ass? I bet you do. I can take all you got. And how about whuppin'? You like to whup a woman good? You can, for what you got in that pocket. I need that money but I'm no fucking thief. C'mon."

Gina got up and unhooked the skirt, stepping out of it. I was standing up, trying to tuck my cock back into the pants.

"Never mind that," she said. "I got plans for it right quick." She turned and began an elaborate swing of her ass as she walked to the bedroom door. Her walk seemed self-conscious. She was trying to be sexy but her urgency a moment ago made her suddenly pathetic.

Janet came into the room lighting a cigarette and settled easily in a wicker chair in the corner. Over the bed was a hook with a pale green douche bag hanging from it. The bag was full and the hose hung straight down, bulging slightly at the clip. The hose ended in a black curved nozzle.

Gina saw me staring at the douche bag. She looked at

Mother's Day

Janet and laughed quietly. She was folding a blue towel and laying it on the edge of the bed nearest the nozzle. Just beyond the bed was a window with the shades pulled. The room was neat and orderly and a small light burned on the bureau. Gina was pointing near the light.

"Get me that tube there, will you?"

I was reaching for it as Gina came over and worked my belt and opened my pants. Janet smoked her cigarette and began casually to talk, like someone sharing a train compartment.

"Where you from—out of town?"

"He's from Connecticut," said Gina. "He's strange but he's not a cop. He's a mother. Mother Matthew—" and she giggled as if she were suddenly stoned while she worked off the top on the tube. I stepped out of my pants, first having to undo my shoes, which I'd forgotten about. My feet smelled hot and I was embarrassed. "Here," she said, handing me the open tube, "put some in me. With your finger."

I squeezed some out and she was bending over the bed where she'd spread the towel. Her skin looked suddenly dark and shiny in the half-light.

"He's from Connecticut and his old lady's split and he's got little kids." She was talking almost nervously, I thought. Not as experienced as she was pretending. "He's got toddlers—ahh. Hey! This mother knows his business, Janet. That's right, Matthew. That feels good, real good— He's got toddlers who pull stuff off tables, Janet."

I put the tube back on the bureau and looked at Janet. She was looking for something in a drawer by her chair. She got up and handed me what turned out to be a wide black leather strap attached to a wood handle with shiny metal studs. The strap was about a foot long and as wide as a hand.

"You know how to do her?" Janet said sounding bored.

"No. I mean yes. But I don't think—"

"What?" Gina had turned her head from where she was leaning over the bed. "What? Matthew farting around again. I thought we'd settled that stuff, Matthew—"

"No, it's not that. You don't understand. It's not you. I like you. I want you—I really want you now. It's just— Oh, I don't know."

I was tired again, dead on my feet. I handed the strap back to Janet and my hand shook. I felt stone tired and jingly as if from too much coffee.

"Wait. Don't get upset. Here's the money." I reached for my shirt pocket where I'd stashed the money. I pulled it out in a wad. "I'll walk back. You can have it all."

Janet had dropped the strap in the drawer and now looked at Gina, annoyed. Gina had straightened up and was sitting on the edge of the bed. I couldn't tell what she felt but she looked hurt. She wasn't smiling anymore. I reached for my pants at the foot of the bed. Gina just sat there holding her elbows out at each side and her hands pushing in on her breasts. Her shoulders were hunched over and she looked cold. I was trying to hand her the wad of singles I'd fished from the pocket.

"Wait, Matthew." Her face seemed to brighten at a new idea. "Look—ever take a woman up the ass? It feels good. It hurts her a little but you feel good. You'd like it. Forget the other thing. I just thought you'd want that, you know? I wanted to make you feel like a man." She looked at me earnestly. "I liked the way you did that with the jelly. You're a good man. But I bet you never took a woman up the ass—am I right?"

"Yeah. You're right. I would have liked to. But ..."

But what? I was still hard. I was standing by the bed holding my pants in my hand then I thought I wanted her worse than before. I wanted to hear her crying out into the pillow. I wanted to force myself into her. I wanted to see her crying out with Janet watching her. And all this wanting made me scared, badly scared.

Mother's Day

I pulled on my pants quickly and picked up my shoes from the floor. Janet was now sitting on the other side of the bed, stabbing out her cigarette on an ashtray she held in her hand. Gina was still sitting as before, pushing her breasts harder against one another. The money crackled as it unfolded on the bed.

I put on my shoes by the couch in the living room and grabbed my jacket from the armchair.

"I'll let myself out, OK?" There was no answer. As I walked passed the baby's room I had a sudden urge to see it sleeping. It seemed ages since I'd seen a kid sleeping.

CHAPTER XV

I have walked one more night and one more day. I don't remember which was which. One of them was Christmas. There were people celebrating something on the streets. I went to Rockefeller Center for the trees and all there were were lights.

Unthinking once I reached to pat a small child on the head. His mother yanked him closer to her and glared bright-colored lights at me.

Joanne is either not home or not answering her phone.

I called Cindy twice to find out how things were.

"How do you mean 'how things are'? Things are *fine*, Matt. That satisfy you?"

"I just wanted to check—in case you'd tried to get me—"

"You mean in case I'd tried to get them. In case I have them locked in fascist solitary for infractions? Listen carefully, Matt, and you can hear them howling in their dungeons. Merry Christmas." We are so skilled by now at hurting one another. There was a pause while Cindy blew her nose. "Why can't you leave me alone, even for a day?" Then she hung up.

The second call, the neighbors said she couldn't come to the phone.

Cindy and I overlapped in Connecticut by half a day, just enough time. Cindy looked hollow-eyed but quiet. The children seemed happy. The house seemed larger it was so clean. The extreme order everywhere showed Cindy's outrage at its squalor.

"I can't keep it any other way, Cindy. You'd never understand how hard this is."

"Oh, yes I do, I understand perfectly. You hate this and you hate them because they are mine. They remind you of me."

"Only when they make me want to kill, when they break me down like you did. Otherwise they not only don't resemble you, they barely *remember* you. You keep conveniently forgetting: *I'm* their mother, not you. You are a visiting spinster aunt. They know my steady pokes better than they know you."

By midmorning we came to blows. I'd been screaming at her about money and she'd been screaming at me about the children's lack of care. The children were clinging again to me, looking alert and absurd at the same time, like sparrows. They kept stealing looks at me, then Cindy, then holding on harder, crying to be picked up, falling down. Thomas began to cry so loud we couldn't hear ourselves hate.

I reached for him, lifting him from the floor with one hand to his shirtfront and shaking him like a scatter rug. Keturah too began screeching and I shoved her off my pantleg so she fell on the hall floor. That was when Cindy hit me. I don't remember ever being hit so hard, but I think surprise anaesthetized me. All I felt was a high breaking rage, like surf, and Cindy was thrown against the front door. She didn't cry, which made me mad, and I tried to punch her hard someplace in the middle. I hit her arm and bounced into a breast.

"You pig! I always knew you were a pig!" She started to kick at my legs as I held her against the door with both hands on the front of her dress. Now she began crying loud, which started the kids again. I hadn't heard from them for a while. I whirled on them where they stood by the stairs.

"Don't you *touch* them. Matt, don't you goddam *touch* them." She had grabbed me from behind by my arm and was pulling hard, again and again. I broke loose and grabbed a child in each hand, starting up the stairs.

"I'm calling the police, Matt. I'm calling the police. You're crazy and I'm going to get you put away, you hear?" Cindy was already running for next door as I stumbled up the stairs.

Somewhere in the nursery I happened upon enough furniture and toys to heave around that the children were ignored. I was screaming about laundromats and baby-sitters and bed wetters and sleepless nights and heaving things against the wall by the changing table when I heard the door slam downstairs and Cindy running hard up the stairs. She stopped by the nursery door, saw the children sitting wide-eyed in their cribs. "There," she said. "I've done it. I called them. Now you've had it once and for all. You hear me, Matthew? The police are coming."

I stopped heaving things and sat in the middle of the floor. I don't think I said anything. Cindy started toward the kids, then changed her mind and rushed into the room where she'd slept. I heard her snap her suitcase shut, then she was running with it out the door and downstairs. Minutes later I heard her car start on the driveway.

The children were whimpering and it was lunchtime. I left them in their cribs and went downstairs to fix a bottle. Then I brought them down, very quietly, and we were sitting in the kitchen eating when the State Police showed up.

"You Vole, Matthew Vole?"

Mother's Day

"Yeah. C'mon in."

"Where's Mrs. Vole?"

"She's gone back to New York. Took off—as usual."

"She called us—"

"I know. We had our annual Christmas fight."

"These all the kids."

"Yeah. Two. Times they seem like *twenty*-two." I smiled at the older of the officers and patted each kid affectionately on the head. Keturah smiled, too, a kind of relief at the quiet. Thomas looked scared, but it was the police he was scared of.

I offered the men coffee and they sat down. The younger one was filling out a report and needed lots of neutral facts. I rattled them off between crisp, efficient kitchen moves for the children's food. The kitchen was spotless, thanks to Cindy, and I felt a giant bogus kind of house pride that the police had come at such a tidy time.

I made some jokes about Today's Woman. I said she'd left us months ago, soon as Keturah was born. I shrugged my shoulders and looked at the officers. They looked mostly bored. "If you'd gotten here earlier, you could have arrested her for desertion." The young one smiled at that. "I'm sorry you had to come. She gets hysterical every time she comes here. Guilt, I guess. I don't know why I put up with it, but then I think a kid should know his mother, you know?" Now the older one nodded.

"She said you were abusing the children, assaulting her."

"She said that? I did slap the kids upside the head—they were driving me crazy with their crying. But mostly I was just trying to get loose of her to get them in another room away from her foul mouth. Women today have no *idea* how to talk, anymore. You know?"

They seemed to know.

I have become ingrown, unhinged. I am disconnected, out of touch, feeling nothing, yet something somewhere is not right.

I have been tending my machines, who are undemanding. Cindy has called three times in the last six weeks. This week she called twice. She wants to plan. What's to plan? My life is monotone, I tell her, I am sleepwalking through a winter and there are no plans around. Twice I have fantasized about fucking Cindy, if you want to call that plans. I would invite her up to see the kids then make her pay for that in bed. Grandiose plans for February. Mostly, though, I ride the noise of my machines. And mostly, though, I hear the children crying through the noise.

I measure time by excess.

Twice when I've come home at nights, I've found matches on the floor in the kitchen. Lights were on that shouldn't have been. I couldn't ask the neighbors, because they'd put us out for sure if they knew. Piles of burnt matches neatly tucked under a corner of the stove.

Last week I woke to find Thomas peeing in my shoes in the hall by the front door. I chased him naked through the rain into the yard where I stood shaking him and screaming incredulities at him until I saw the neighbors peering from the window. Later that day my neighbor paid a call. He was polite, of course, even solicitous. What he wondered was if every little thing was quite all right. He wondered, frankly, if there might not be some other way. What he meant, he said, was, well, if I should get some help. It's hard to see a man like that, carrying on, you know. Of course. I didn't tell him this, but last week I saw his widdle wife ululating in the supermarket at her widdle kid. She was jamming the shopping cart back and forth, her face an inch from widdle kid's, and screaming at him about mommy's hurry. But then that's all right, because she's just a mother, and mothers have been doing that for years.

Since then the neighbors haven't paid me any visits, but that will come. You see, I burned the crib. I think you need a permit for that here, a variance.

Mother's Day

Increasingly I have had to stay at work beyond my shift. The 434's are acting up. Only I can soothe them. No one on third shift doesn't smoke dope. They are addled when they get there at midnight and the machines have too much down time as a result. René is worried about production and he's asking me to stay for pay and bring the ratings up.

I stayed till three last week, coaxing the machines. High above their roar the children screamed and screamed. I have been sure of late I'll find them drenched in blood when I come home. Here is how it will go. The kids are fast asleep and I am miles away feeling the floors shake under me at Beethoven Wire & Cable. Someone watching in the lilac hedge finds them there alone and one by one removes their toes. They screech, of course, but mostly all I hear is the machines. He uses stainless steel, this man, or pruning shears, and hacks them surgically if slowly. It takes him all the time till midnight just for the extremities. At one he gouges out the eyes. By two he's nearly done, toying with the jumping pipes he's looped out from the gut. He cleans his tools on Keturah's moronic quilt.

I was home by four one night. He'd missed the kids somehow. I put my lunch boxes in the kitchen sink and left my workboots by the front door. It was so late I was no longer tired. I made a bottle for Keturah and woke her up to feed it to her. She snuggled next to me on the rocking chair and I wrapped her in the quilt. She kept falling asleep and smiling mysterious smiles, so I put her back to bed.

Thomas woke up the instant I touched him. He opened his eyes wide in the half-light from the hall and looked at me. I picked him up and he reached back for his blanket. I was telling him how I'd worked almost the whole night, how my 434's hummed and shook and made drums of new shiny cable. We were sitting on the rocking chair by the window looking at the mist close to the snow on this damp March night. We talked about what he'd done after I went to work, what Pat had fixed for supper. She read them the fire-engine book, he said. I began to tell him what we would do when the spring came and we could go for walks in the fields, maybe swim in the stream where I'd found him that day with the big black dog. As I talked Thomas reached for his blanket and slowly stuffed a corner into his mouth. We must have rocked and I must've talked for fifteen or twenty minutes longer, and when I noticed I'd heard nothing from him I peered over his head and found he was fast asleep leaning against my shoulder with his blanket gently in his half-open mouth.

It was now five and the snow light from the windows had brightened but the nursery seemed dark and obscure, printed from coarse grainy film. It was several lives ago I last had a soft moment with Thomas or Keturah. So little joy. What conspires against us?

Thomas was still asleep against my shoulder, his closed eyes mute and anguished as medieval statues. Keturah had bunched herself into the bottom corner of her crib as if fleeing something. What becomes of wounded fragile children. Will they forget all this and be whole? Can you ever make it up, this waste?

Late next morning I became aware of noises from the nursery. Bird noises, orderly happy bird noises and sudden tattoos of feet across the floor. Could I have gotten up already once to feed them and now forgotten? No, that I don't forget. The sun was high and bright off the snow. I could see it frying on the ceiling. I had a dull metallic headache, my brain packed in aluminum foil.

When I moved in bed all noises in the nursery stopped suddenly. I heard one last scurrying, then more silence. No childhood silence is benign, I know, but I was unimaginative enough, too dulled by sleep, to steel myself for what I found.

In the nursery Thomas was nowhere to be seen. Keturah was standing in her crib, smiling broadly. The room reeked so strong it stung the nostrils. Each and every slat, each and every wooden surface of her crib was smeared with excrement and zinc-oxide paste. She was naked and her Pamper was lying in a corner of the mattress, next to the blue jar of zinc oxide. Keturah had shit smears on her arms and face, shit in her hair wherever there was room among the white smarmy patches of paste.

"Thomas! Thomas!"

No answer.

"Thomas, get your ass out here right now or I'll break you in little pieces."

No answer. Then, from under his bed I heard something being dragged across the floorboards. He pulled himself out from under the bed and put both hands over his face and head as he stood up.

I broke the crib before I burned it. I broke it in about twenty disparate pieces. The kids stood by awed, watching me render it small enough to clatter through the upstairs window into the yard below. That took about fifteen minutes of concentrated venom, during which I cursed the kids for ever being born, I cursed their mother for ever leaving us, I cursed the smug innocence of my middle-class upbringing, I cursed Suzanne for driving me over the brink.

Keturah was too horrible to touch, even, so apart from flinging her out of the crib I left her alone. Thomas became the culprit. He was cleaner and smelled only of zinc oxide, so I hit him. I slapped him hard to make him cry, then slapped him repeatedly to make him stop crying. When I was tired I ran them a bath and tried to scrub them both off as painfully as possible. It gave me solid satisfaction, that morning, to see them burn their eyes with shampoo. I first tried to prevent the soap in their eyes, then surrendered to my spleen and let it happen. Sometime before they were clean I remember shrieking at them again about my woes, punctuating each woe with violent smashes of a wet washcloth against the bathroom walls.

Later that afternoon Thomas and Keturah stood solemnly by while I doused the shattered crib pieces with gasoline and set it afire in the back-yard snow. I don't think the neighbors saw the crib go. But just at evening I saw the wife, all too casual, happen around the back of the house and peer at the blackened remains like a hieromancer.

The omens could not have been good, for tonight the children are sick. It's been two nights and two days since Keturah started. At first you tell they're sick because they're so easy. Quiet and tractable—as other people's children are said to be. If Thomas and Keturah are like that it means they are very sick. Only a little sick means constant whine and gnash. Now Keturah is vomiting yet again, this time on my jacket. It seems she was saving it for me. She and Thomas have vomited almost everywhere else these last two days.

It used to be vomit made me sick myself but tonight I barely notice. I'm disembodied from the speed I took to get me through my shift. And maybe from the speed preceding it the night before. At home I can lapse and only standards fail, but lapse before the 434's and I'd be cleavered off, neatly at the joints.

Last night I had to stay to three again. It was five before I knew I wouldn't sleep. I tried today to sleep between the heaves. Sometimes perhaps I did. But mostly I was mopping up. We are almost out of sheets and towels and now the last few clothes. I tried the laundromat at lunch tonight but it was full. Must be children everywhere are vomiting.

Did I say Suzanne was here? I called her in the afternoon. Joey is sick—Joey's always sick—but she quickly said she'd come. Too quickly. She thought she saw an opening, a victim's tack. Now we are a pesthouse here, failing children everywhere.

In her wake Suzanne has worked her usual disaster. Things even I'd got put away are once again strewn about. I

Mother's Day

stumbled through the door tonight to trip in the dark on pots and pans in the hallway. There are piles of soiled sheets riding the banister—though most of those are mine from earlier: I never quite got to organizing them for the laundromat. There is a pile of dirty towels on the steps.

They are all awake upstairs, crying out like seabirds in a storm. Thomas hasn't vomited all night, Suzanne tells me. He's lying on a stained mattress crying, instead. Maybe that means he's getting better.

I'm not. My ears are dulled from the machines, still the crying probes like razor shards. Speed has honed the brain raw. It cringes with the noise. Keturah is quieter by far. She's sweating still and printed in three colors from the comics I used instead of sheets. Suzanne's kids are squirreled in the living room downstairs. She said she tried to sleep with them on the couch till Joey heaved up there as well.

Somehow she is fresh and energized by this. Her cheeks flush high with red, like fever, and her Irish skin is smooth as milk. She moves beautifully as she ministers to the children. How can I think like this tonight? A wasted brain playing tricks on me. She went downstairs to check on her kids a while ago and came back up in a nightgown trimmed in whorehouse lace. Black fucking lace, for God's sake.

These children are dying, their father terminal. Still the centers twitch up here—like those frogs we pinned in bio lab. Twitch, spasm, twitch. I watch Suzanne's haunches hook the nylon as they move. Her nipples slide across the front, which flows around them.

Thomas is trying to push himself upright in his bed. He looks agitated. He casts his eyes about, as if he'd lost something. His look is intense and blank at the same time. With a quick loud groan he starts to heave his body forward off the bed. I'm by his side in time to feel the hot acid puke wash down my front. He heaves again trying hard to grip me with tight little hands. How much more can a small child puke? I am squeezing him hard to stop from pushing him away in sudden disgust. Suddenly I want to vomit myself.

Suzanne has brought a washcloth and Thomas has collapsed onto his bed. His skin is almost transparent, maps of blue veins on his forehead and his neck. He's shaking now and Suzanne covers him with a towel while I fumble with the buttons on my shirt. They're slippery with mucus and I get jumpy every time one slips. Just before he puked I almost crumpled to the floor. Without my knowing it the knees had given way. Now I am walking to the stairs like a stroke victim while my brain laps the distance back and forth, frenzied.

"The owl and the pussycat went to sea—" I began reciting and Suzanne giggled. We were so punchy we thought this would work. A sea of green towels around us in bed, the kids laid out against the wall on pillows draped with more towels. That way they can puke and we can just hold them, never having to get up again tonight. Somehow we imagined we would fuck each other, too. Somehow that seemed logical and appropriate.

Downstairs little Joey woke almost as soon as we began. Before, really, since Suzanne had come to bed with bra and panties in her contrary way. Only the top was off when Joey started calling. I held her fiercely for a moment, hoping he would go away, then she struggled loose and wrapped her arms around herself heading for the stairs. It's cold in here but both kids' skin feels hot. They are awake but deathly quiet, blessed quiet. They kick off any covers but I try again to wrap them in the towels. They look like they don't see me but their eyes are open wide, flicking around their sockets.

We added Joey to the bed with us, on Suzanne's side. That shut him up a bit. Suzanne scampered under the covers, energized by the cold. She tickled me to turn over facing her. The speed I took at work comes in surges and now I feel jangly again. I jumped as if she'd stuck an ice pick in me, almost knocking Joey off the bed. He cried again. When Suzanne turned to comfort him I slithered down and worked her pants off her hips. She tried to push me away with her feet but I pinched her hard till she stopped kicking. Now I have her by one cheek below and a breast above. I kissed her back, then firmly pushed against the skin with my teeth. She didn't move but tensed. My teeth feel tingly, as if tonight they've sprouted nerves along the edges. My gums itch the way they did when I was losing baby teeth. I can feel her nipple pulse against my palm. My cock stings from such intense swelling. Even my balls hurt, yanked tight against me. Suzanne started to straighten up and I gripped her harder. She stops again. I can hear her breathing below her skin, air whirring past the pockets in her lungs. I move my hand from her breast and slide it to her other cheek behind, squeezing them both hard. I'm afraid she may move and the kid will stir again.

Now one hand has hooked her hip in front to pull her toward me. She kicked at me with her free foot till I pinched her hard again and now she's arched her back and pulled her legs higher to her front. She hasn't said a word. Holding her cheek from underneath, with my thumb I can feel her lubricating. My cock throbs like a bruise and I can hear the echoes against the inside of my head. It feels hot like the kids' skin a minute ago. My brain is choked with amoebas, crowding for space. Suzanne is still on her side, facing away from me. I have a hand now on each haunch, fingers digging in the soft sides and the thumbs kneading her perineum. She's wet and the thumbs are slippery, skidding off to rest against one opening or the other. I push them hard inside the lips of her vagina, where it feels warm and spongy. Then I slide them up and push them hard against her sphincter. One thumb slides in and she pushes down against it. The muscle tightens. Then loosens.

I don't know when exactly Thomas began to fidget next to me but I was sliding the head of my cock against her lips when I heard her stretch an arm back over us to try to quiet him. He didn't quiet. He was trying again to get up as he did in his bed a while back. I could tell by the sharp bounces of the bed against his collapsing arm. He was shifting his weight about. I knew he was about to vomit.

I spun around and broached the covers like a wounded whale. Thomas tried three times to vomit before anything came up. I shoved him bodily against the wall to calm the violence and speed that burned in me. He stopped heaving just long enough to begin a piercing wail.

Suzanne was already struggling out of bed, snatching for her child who was about to fall off. I was quaking in my shoulders and my arms shook against Thomas and the wall they held him up against.

"Shuddup!" I hissed, but it came out a guttural growl. Keturah's eyes were open now but she wasn't moving. Somewhere behind me I heard Suzanne lift Joey, pick something from the floor, and head toward the door.

"Shuddup God damn it! God *damn* it!" Thomas was hiccuping now, and crying fierce bursts between the hiccups. I kept thinking if he didn't shut up he would wake the kids. An ancient mindless reflex but I thought it just the same.

Now he begins to scream. After all this fever I didn't think he had it in him to scream. High yipping screams like savages in dreams. This has got to stop. My ears are hammering inside against the back of my eyeholes. I am running now with Thomas into the nursery, like a wounded dog running to escape the pain. As I was holding him high in front of me by the arms, running, Thomas vomited again. The vomit is on my face, stinging my mouth and I'm about to vomit myself. I shake him hard and his feet lash out in fear.

Mother's Day

The toenails caught me in the cheekbone. They felt like spikes, and the bone thundered when they hit. In one motion Thomas was high above my head again then hurled towards his bed across the room. He hit the wall somewhere on his back and fell face down on the bed. Someone was pummeling him, screaming in my ear. My fists kept being thrown against the wall and corners of the crib, they kept being hurt. I have to get out of here, I know. I could get hurt, whoever this maniac is.

I've been asleep on this chair. I don't know how much time has passed but it can't be long. It's still dark out. It's cold and clammy quiet here. Keturah and Thomas. Keturah is on my bed in here, I can hear her breathing regular and loud. Thomas. Thomas on his bed.

I am on my feet and bumping into walls as I struggle to his room. He's lying on his face on his bed. His skin is burning and he's lying still. I turn him over and I can hear the breath creaking in the tubes. It sounds like wax paper on a comb. But he is burning hot now and his eyes roll white behind the lids I push up. He isn't even sweating, just hot and dry. Like an infection. Somewhere I have read about cold baths. Sponge the fever down.

I am holding Thomas under one arm, like a rolled up rug, turning taps which echo like a swimming pool. Where's that washcloth. Goddamn Suzanne left it somewhere weird, I know. A wet towel, that will do. I throw the towel in the water, pushing it under with my free hand. Now I have Thomas like a baby, one hand on the neck in back, the other cupping his behind. You lower them hind first, as I remember, and watch the head to keep it out of water.

First there is a piercing shriek from somewhere. It cuts across the front behind the eyes, poker orange. Then another shriek and Thomas is bucking now, half in the water, splashing icy fragments on me. The shrieks are pulsing now against the tiles, trapped and metallic.

"Thomas! Shut the fuck up, Thomas!"

He's not paying attention, this kid. He's not paying attention. I think he's out to kill me, too, to wake the lot of them again in this inferno. It's the third day or is it fourth and they are howling till the eyeballs bleed inside.

First I pushed him under water all the way, then pulled him up to see. The tiny creature is shrieking still, I didn't even hear a pause. So I pushed him down again, this time long enough. There, a pause. A distinct pause. Quite a nice pause, in fact.

How long's it been, this pause, you think? Got to have a decent pause. Pause two, this is, or is it still pause one?

It's very quiet, just the crackle of the water as I bring him up. I'm looking at him but he doesn't notice. I think he doesn't care. It's so quiet here I can hear the cold. Now he's cooled a bit. I think I'll wrap him now, this towel will be fine. He's cute now in this towel, all wrapped up. They don't always look this cute.

What we'll do is just hold this baby close awhile. We'll hold him wrapped like this, and just lie down awhile in here. My bed feels warm—how come? And Thomas rough as towel next to me. Rough as towel, small right now, and quiet as a mouse.

Keturah was sitting naked on the cold floor by the window, shaking a finger at someone. Her lower lip was pushed out and she was nodding her head, trying to look stern.

A whisper woke me. Whispers mean trouble. No kid whispers if he can help it. The bones around my eyes ache as I try to stare again at Keturah, so I close them. It was sunny in here, I noticed that before I closed them. Nice and sunny. But something feels wrong.

Shaking her finger. She used to do that at things I had forbidden her. I wish my eyes would work better. This time

Mother's Day

I'll go easy. Squint, adjust, then slowly open wide. Ah, yes, I can move my head as well to look.

There is Thomas, over in the corner by the chair. He has a towel around him.

"Thomas? Thomas? Come to Matt, OK?"

He looks at me with no surprise, a kind of quiet curiosity. "Hi, Matt."

"Hi, Matt. Hi, Matt"—Keturah chiming in. She's getting up to come. Thomas has been lining a pile of paperclips along a floorboard crack. He wants to finish, I can tell, because his tongue tip's sticking out and he's frowning with concentration.

"Finish your work, Thomas. That's OK."

Keturah's here, clawing to get up in bed with me.

"How's my Keturah? Oh, you're cold, my little mouse, you're cold. Come under here." I tuck her round a blanket next to me and she is wiggling like a puppy with pleasure.

"Cold, Thomas? Are you cold?" He doesn't answer he's so engrossed. Keturah's forehead feels cooler than it has for days. She pulls down my hand from her head and traps it between her chin and neck, squeezing it.

It's a watercolor April day out there. My window looks friendly and warm. The sun seems high for morning.

"Hungry, kidlets? Thomas—want an egg?"

"I want juice. And toast."

"Juice and toast. OK, but first we all need clothes—right?"

Only that's not easy. My capillaries ache and there is sand between my joints. Keturah is clinging to my chest. She feels like diver's weights. I'd be angry with her for the weight if I could, but I'm concentrating on getting up and over to Thomas. I cup his forehead with my hand. It's still somewhat hot. His hair is staggered to the left of his head, the way it dried. He looks lopsided.

"Cold, Thomas? Let's get some clothes."

"Wait, Matt. I'm working." I am looking for proof he's not

paralyzed or broken. He hasn't really moved since I woke up.

"Thomas? Feel OK this morning? No more sick?"

"No more sick." He carefully arranges another paperclip, then looks at me. "I got flowers, Matt."

"Flowers?"

"In the kitchen. Come and see." He is up, dropping his towel and walking easily toward the stairs.

"Wait, Thomas. It's cold. Let's get some clothes."

"Come see my flowers."

Dandelions. I haven't noticed dandelions yet. The kitchen is blinding bright and Keturah is struggling to get down, wiggling and pointing all her weight toward the filthy kitchen floor. The dandelions are lying on a chair. They seem impossibly clean and yellow.

"Dandelions. Beautiful, Thomas. Where'd you get them?"

"Suzanne gave them."

"Suzanne? Where is she? When?"

"Suzanne gone home. With little Joey and Jonathan."

"When did she go home? This morning?"

"After breakfast, Matt. She got the flowers in the grass."

I looked in the living room. Not a trace of them. I can't even see Joey's puke stain on the couch. It must be later than I thought.

CHAPTER XVI

Three days of watercolor calm. There are indeed dandelions. Keturah staggers around picking them by the heads. Thomas has nothing but disdain for that. He's grown up, he seems to be indicating, as he snaps them neatly by the stem. One year when he was tiny I remember crying out with horror because he had yanked the heads off every pansy we had planted. He had looked at me bewildered, then his face pressed itself into a circle round his nose and he sobbed. He lost his balance, sat down hard on the ground, and sobbed again in surprise.

Today we're in the remains of last year's vegetable garden, where the kids have played muddy and subdued since early morning. I sat on a fence post by the chives, which are already shooting new sprouts, chewing bits of it. Ruminating, I guess, is what I am doing.

Thomas has been industrious, digging a hole with a small plastic shovel he unearthed somewhere. He keeps calling me to come inspect it, which I do gravely about once every fifteen minutes. Keturah seems to have found things to eat—grubs or worms, I suppose, but I'm not much motivated to find out. Around this small fenced-in garden the grass is an impossible technicolor green.

Between inspections of Thomas' excavation I have been thinking about work. It amazes me how simple it has been not to work. I called in sick, that's all. So I'm sick sitting here warming in the sun, watching two tiny strangers playing in the mud. I wonder what I've been doing all these months that I haven't noticed how they've changed. Sometime between then and now Keturah has become a person. I've barely noticed her these last months, she was just something urgent I had to feed and haul about. Something that required picking up after. A mechanism for fatigue. I'm not sure there were even features on that face. Today, squinting in the afternoon sun, she looks like pictures of my grandmother. Grandmothers, I am sure, weren't permitted by fathers to play in April mud, but a picture my mother once showed me had captured this small-boned little girl in white standing by a hedge squinting and embarrassed. The sun was in her eyes, too, and she looked offhand and beautiful like Keturah.

The phone just rang next door, then the wife came over with a message. Cindy would be up this weekend with Don, her new friend. She's also bringing Joanne. The wife looks to see if I'm embarrassed to hear this. How can I be so shameless? I should be here nurturing my children; instead, I am apparently hosting adulterous orgies. What is motherhood coming to?

"Thanks," I am saying. "Friday night at eleven, huh?"

The wife is staring transfixed at Keturah in the mud. I wanted to tell her about my grandmother's picture but I couldn't figure out how. Her outrage made me angry—her acting as if I'd failed to meet some standard. The wife turned and headed back toward her kitchen.

Mother's Day 237

"Oh, by the way," I called. "Cindy say anything about the Vaseline?"

"What?" she shouted back.

"Never mind. Thanks anyway."

It is Sunday morning. Cindy and Don are sleeping upstairs. They've slept a lot since they arrived late Friday night. In fact, Cindy slept prematurely on the highway and winged a bridge near New Haven. They traded a right rear bumper for some metal stanchions.

They were giddy when they got here. Stoned. Joanne and Cindy have become firm friends. They have me in common. After New Haven they crouched in the back seat smoking dope and talking man to man. I think Don feels left out. He's the only one here who hasn't slept with me.

Friday night no one slept with me. It seems I've mislaid my libido. Anyway, Joanne was so stoned when she got here we couldn't even thread our way through the necessary disclaimers.

Just as well they were all stoned. I kept feeling like someone out of Poe. Couldn't they hear the screams up there, the horrible choking? After they went to bed I lay awake downstairs listening to the wind trying the doors. Later I woke to hear someone crying, but it was only Cindy coming. She never cried out like that for me.

It seems such a natural charade. Gentle doting father with his children. And the thing is, you fall for it yourself.

Joanne came down early Saturday with a stiff neck. It had rained during the night and she said a chill had gotten her.

"Serves you right for sleeping by yourself." I smiled at her to show I wasn't whining.

"Couldn't have done it without you, Matt. Don't try and give me that."

"OK, you're right. But I have my principles. I don't put out for just anybody darkens my door, you know. I don't want to be used, either...."

Something in the texture of that last remark surprised us both and Joanne looked at me concerned.

"It's just that a lot of things have changed recently, Joanne. And anyway, virtue is its own reward, right? I guess what I am saying is let's just not allow such a serious lapse another weekend—OK?"

I massaged her stiff neck as she sat at the kitchen table in her nightgown. She was looking at the spring flowers on the neighbor's lawn out back.

Then I had to massage Thomas' and Keturah's necks. They kept pushing themselves between me and Joanne, then looking carefully at both of us.

We walked the kids down to the stream where I'd found Thomas and the black dog last autumn. Everywhere the wholesale nattering of blackbirds who canopied the newly worked fields. In the hollow by the stream the grasses were already tall, tessellated with dandelions. We sat in a pool of hot April sun feeling botanical. The children toyed at the edge of the stream.

"Times like this it's hard to imagine anything else. It's hard to realize how few moments of joy I can think of from this past year, how much awful shit the kids and I have been through—"

"What's this? A new, improved *gloomy* Matthew Vole?"

"For good reason. I'm going to have to give them up, Joanne."

"Matt?" Joanne reached for my shoulder but I had to look away.

"I sit here watching two perfectly put-together little bodies playing by the water and I am sick for all the horror I've brought into their lives."

"Matt?" She wanted me to look at her instead of out over the trees by the stream. I turned and stared at the grass by her knee. "Matt, you're very special—you know that, don't you?"

"Specially awful, you mean?"

"Matt, I mean it. You're very important to all of us here, them *and* me. You're three-dimensional, not some cardboard cutout like other men. Those kids couldn't have asked for a better father—"

"It's the mother part worries me. Any asshole can be a father—unskilled part-time work, good hours, good benefits. But I've been a mother like those ogres in folk tales. Sometimes I think Cindy's ancestors were right: the gnashing of teeth is the true music of the spheres—and you might as well acquaint children with that from the beginning...."

Keturah was wrestling with her shoes, trying to follow Thomas into the stream. Joanne was up and helping her. I walked over by the stream and sat down. Thomas was busy piling wood and stones to make a dam, then Keturah began to flounder around, disrupting things in her eagerness to help.

"What's hard as any of it, though, is thinking about them with Cindy and Don—"

"I like her, Matt. We talked a long time last night in the car. She said she really wants them now. You need time to yourself. No one forgives a woman who abandons her children, but that's not fair. She's really trying to get herself together to be a better mother to them now—"

"A better father, maybe. I don't think she can ever be a mother to them."

"Whatever. I think she cares, and feels—"

"I don't know if any of those people can do that, Joanne. They're all cut off—your usual New York careerist coronary bypass."

"Stop it, Matt. I like you better when you're not being cynical. Now you're reminding me of Basil."

"Sorry. It's just all these petty-assed conversations with

Cindy on the phone. I suppose they mean she's caring about the kids but I can't accept that. All I feel is an assault on me. I *am* the children."

"What about them, Matt. Have you said anything to Thomas? What do they think?"

"They don't divulge that information."

We were back for lunch before Cindy and Don were up. Cindy had a toy each for the kids, so lunch was festive. We drank Bloody Marys. Don and I tried very hard to show we liked one another. And he kept picking up the kids the way men are supposed to do, roughhousing with them. But he spoiled it somewhat by checking his shirt cuffs after each bout.

Thomas spills his juice and I laugh tolerantly. Keturah's eyes gleam at new treasures left idly in reach by the visitors. I lunge about saving Don's camera, Cindy's cigarettes, Joanne's earrings. Don just left a cup of boiling hot coffee on the table edge when he went to the bathroom. I got there before Keturah's wild swipe at it, and hoisted her playfully onto the kitchen counter while they all laughed. I've whipped up meals all around, short order, feeding the kids gracefully in between. The kids know something is up and Thomas took a plate of spaghetti to the kitchen wall to see what I would do. A deep indulgent chuckle is what I did. Of course.

"I don't see how you can cope this way, Matt," Don is saying. "Really amazing." We are mixing late-afternoon drinks and Cindy and Joanne are watching from the kitchen table.

"Nothing to it," I smile. "I just beat the *shit* out of them all the rest of the time."

We all laugh.

Something's up and Cindy knows it. I never had her fooled. Joanne and Don are cooking supper and we are together bathing the children Saturday night. A couple of parents.

"Why haven't you been answering my calls, Matt?"

"I haven't had anything to say, I guess."

"That scared me."

"It scared *me*."

Cindy was drying Keturah's hair with a green towel. Keturah had leaned wet against her and her denim jumpsuit is stained dark blue. "Matt, what's really happening? Nothing seems normal this weekend. This place is tidy as a funeral parlor."

"What do you mean? I thought things were insufferably normal."

"OK, Matt. That's enough. We'll drop it."

What blind sacrificial urge keeps me from reaching out for help? I tried last night to say something to Joanne but then I knew she'd never comprehend. I don't think she'd even believe.

But Cindy might. All day I've wrestled this. I study the abject, naked thing I have become. What's to protect? What do I lose?

"Cindy? After they're in bed I need to talk to you."

"I'm not up for more word games, Matt. I'm not sure I want to."

"No more games, I promise. Strictly children's hour."

Both children have stopped their usual fussing and are looking at us gravely. Something in the tone of voice.

At first Cindy said nothing at all.

"What I just said, Cindy, was I tried to kill Thomas last Tuesday night. I tried to drown him out."

"I heard you."

We are walking on the gravel driveway by the house. The pebbles underfoot sound thunderous in the dark. Joanne and Don are cooking supper inside a cube of light over to our left. You can see quick movements across the windows. People move so fast preparing food.

"I knew you were faking, Matt. I knew it from the day Thomas was born. All that moralistic crap—how could I have believed it?"

"People do."

"Have they been to a doctor? Are they all right? What other things have you done?" She didn't seem to expect an answer. I tried to see her face in the reflected light from the windows but she had turned and was looking out in the direction of the fields. Beyond them, behind a line of black hill on the horizon, the sky glowed fluorescent gray from the lights in Montville.

"I haven't been back to work, either," I said—as if that had anything to do with anything.

"No, I suppose not."

The gravel crunches underfoot. It makes it sound like a summer night when you are young in bed and grownups are out walking. We haven't said anything for a long time. Now Cindy wheels on me and her face shines from the window lights.

"You never did love those children. I did and I couldn't stay because of it. I thought you were right. But you just didn't want me to have them. Just to hurt me."

"Cindy—" I don't know what I was going to say. We heard a loud mewing from a tree off in the dark to our left. We approached it across the lawn, following the noise. A small light-colored cat peered down from the top of an apple tree, mewing more loudly as it saw us approach. We watched it a minute, then I said something to Cindy about getting a ladder.

"Oh, Matt, you're so screwed-up. You always did worry about the wrong things, Matt. How many cat skeletons have you ever seen in trees?"

CHAPTER XVII

Late in April, two weeks after that weekend, the children went away for a week. Since then they've gone away three more times. Today they go for good.

That first time in April it was Don's vacation from the firm. He and Cindy had planned for Jamaica, I was told, but cancelled when they decided, Cindy said, that they couldn't face it if anything should happen to the children. Instead, martyrs to good sense, they invited the children to New York.

Actually I took the children there, trying that way to ease the passage. And hoping to find Joanne.

Saturday noon when I drove in, Cindy was at work. Don was out. There'd be a key with Don's neighbor, 18C, Cindy said. Don would be back in an hour, she said, after his match at the club.

No one said what I was to do with my car. How, for instance, I'd either have to leave the children at Don's alone while I parked, or trundle them blocks with their stuff to the apartment if they stayed with me till I found a space. So for the fourth hour that morning we sat in the car—Thomas crying that he had to pee, Keturah clinging in confusion—till Don returned.

Don beamed bionically as I handed the kids over but he seemed afraid I might touch him in the process. He got jumpy when I came too close, as if he'd catch some ominous social disease.

As well he might.

Joanne I never found, and on the drive back the sky was quilted gray like a vast padded cell. You could tell it was spring, though, because the dead animals were out on the highways again. I felt like a burn victim, all the nerve endings gone. I realized I should have been feeling something but I was inert, estivating somewhere.

Cindy returned the kids the following weekend and she's seen them almost every weekend since. One she missed because Don took her to Haiti to switch partners. I had signed a document, agreeing. Since then sometimes both proud parents come here together. Those weekends I have learned to go away. I'm not a graceful learner, as you know, and this is not an easy thing to learn.

The children make things small like them, but when they go on weekends the house grows larger. My emptiness echoes off clean floors and giant ceilings. My emptiness hides itself in painful tiny clothes and stray toys that stalk me from room to room.

It seems a lifetime I have craved free weekends, but now when they happen I hunker in corners of immense loss. By Sunday when Cindy brings the kids back, the emptiness shrinks to familiar obligation—and relief to be monopolized again.

"Matt, you're going to have to get out more on weekends." It was Sunday morning, she'd brought the kids back early and found me sleeping alone, the house immaculate from my agonies of loneliness Saturday night. "You're going to have to find some friends. It's useless like this."

"That's my business, Cindy. Not all of us need to snag the first Lacoste who comes along."

"OK, Matt. Forget it. I was just trying to help."

"All of a sudden *I'm* the one who needs help? I'm not the one ran out, you know. Just because Cinderella now has her prince and—"

"You don't need help? Trying to kill your kid is normal?"

"What do you want me to do—join La Leche? No, I'm not as a matter of fact hog wild about what I did. Why else you think I'd tell *you* and run the risk I have? I thought I'd made that clear. But I have learned something from it you could never understand."

"I don't believe it for a minute. I don't think you've ever learned anything, even the simplest facts about your character—"

"Now wait a minute. I don't think you *have* a character until you've mothered children—as you never have!"

"That's not fair, Matt. I've done everything I could—"

"And assumed I'd take care of everything else, right? Everything inconvenient, unstylish, ugly, awful, and destructive—while you get to find yourself for your greater comfort and convenience."

We stand facing one another in the kitchen. I'm holding Keturah on my shoulder, almost like a weapon. For the last few moments Thomas has been pulling at Cindy's hand in uneasiness, reading tone of voice. Now he snatches at her dress and yanks it urgently. Cindy has been freezing up as she always does in fights, stiffening with hurt. Distracted now, she brushes Thomas aside, shoving him away and glaring at him.

"You're deliberately trying to drive me away from them, Matt. I know you. You're trying to crowd me out again, aren't you? Only this time it isn't going to work."

"Always whining. It was bullshit last time and it is bullshit this time. If you can't handle this, for Christ's sake, how do you expect ever to have anything to do with these kids?"

"This isn't what I *have* to handle, Matt. This isn't having children. This is fights. You're great at fights. It's being a father you can't handle."

"It's not the father having problems here. It's the mother. You, me, the neighbor wife, your mother, my mother. These are mother problems, Cindy, mother-fucking problems. What I need is a husband to support me, buy me baby-sitters, pay some bills. No one can do this alone."

Thomas is pulling at Cindy, harder this time. She starts to shove him away, then notices what she is doing and pulls him to her. He takes her hand and wants her to see something in the living room. She turns to go with him.

"That's right, Cindy. Walk away. You always walk out when the going gets rough—right? Look, I'm trying to tell you something. I feel like I've been treading water for a whole year, struggling to keep our heads out of water. I can't do it much longer. That's why I told you that evening. I feel I'm drowning, we're all drowning."

"You always dramatize. If you'd just gotten yourself in order, if you'd just calm down and do what you need to do, forget all this crazy crap about fascisms and freedom, all this paranoia, you might have made it. The kids would welcome some order—even some fascism around here, I bet."

"They probably already get plenty on weekends, I bet. You bring them back and they're jumpy like puppets—"

"What has your perfect brand of freedom contributed to them emotionally? Look at them. Look what you did to them. You're sick!"

"Sick, huh? Maybe. But at least I'm capable of feeling. You're extinct—an abstraction, a figment of some ideology."

Keturah is crying now for some reason. Maybe I moved too violently as I shouted, scared her. I reach up to hold both her hands and she stops crying almost instantly.

"Cindy's had her blue-collar lovers, her expense-account lunches, her maxi-therapy, her doting attorneys. Now all of a sudden it is Mother's Day? What have you done for these kids by being a career person alone in New York? It might be time for you to think less of your polyvinyl-chloride self and more about these two innocent bystanders."

"Stop it, Matt. What do you want from me, blood? I've deserted them and now I have to pay? You're such a prick, such a pious moralist, I don't know if it is ever possible to get through to you. I want them now and that is all there is to it."

Cindy looked away suddenly and rubbed the back of her hand hard against the side of her face. She was breathing quick short breaths and her metal bracelet belt rattled as it shook.

"*Take them* then. Take them now. God knows I can't do anything for them here without money—and you and Don won't give us any.

"I can't take them now. I just can't. Things aren't ready yet."

"Redecorating, you mean? Color-coordinating your modular lives? You make me sick!"

"You make yourself sick. Always have. Now it's just backed-up resentment against the whole fucking world. Your infinite capacity for self-pity."

"Look, you know why I'm not fighting you about them? I may be desperate and brutal, but unlike your kind of people I don't think it's OK to toy with children's lives. I don't think parents should feed upon the flesh of innocent children."

"They *need* two parents, Matt."

"You're right. You don't know what you're talking about and you want these children as far as I can see for utterly irrelevant reasons—but you're right for once. Listen, I'm giving them up because I have to, not because you and Don are superior persons. I'm not sure you're persons at all. But right now you're more rested than I am and you've got someone else to help—larval, duly conforming type that he may be."

"OK Matt. That's enough. I don't have to hear any of this from you. You're not *giving* me the kids. I'm taking them. Your—ah—life-support problems are my grounds and the firm is drawing up the suit right now. I'm taking them and you can't stop me."

Now Cindy was whiter of face than the clown paint under her eyes. She was clutching Thomas to her as if I were trying to tear him away. Thomas is staring up at her fascinated. I don't think he's ever seen her without her composure. I reach over to stroke his head, wondering how it is we always seem to fight in front of the children. Cindy pulls away from us. Keturah has been quiet, probably rapt, watching over this like some bird of prey. I bring her down but don't dare look at her. Here we are haggling like speculators in commodities—and I have only weeks before this house will echo like an empty school.

Cindy turned her head and stared hard at me, looking for something. Her eyes widened slightly. I noticed they were a surprising clear blue, untouched. She was disentangling herself from Thomas now, trying to get him to let go. She looked like a new parent in day care, planning her escape.

"It's OK, Thomas. Mommy's coming back soon. Mommy's coming back." She reached for Keturah who was perched in front of me on the kitchen floor. "My *good* girl, Keturah. Kiss Mommy." Keturah smiled at something she understood and kissed Cindy rather primly, crinkling up her nose with pleasure. Then both kids turned and looked at me.

"Thomas, take Keturah and see the toys in the living room, OK?" New toys—and the kids began to move out of the room, not looking back.

"Matt?" Cindy's voice was very quiet. "You're going to have to accept the fact that you are not the only person in the world capable of loving. I love these kids at least as much as you do. And I hate them a lot less, judging from what you've said. And done."

We're standing by the porch next to the flower bed. Don keeps lifting his glasses to rub the sides of his nose, grinning idiotically. Thomas and Keturah are following me around more than usual. They came back last weekend with custom haircuts and identical Lacostes, so today they look like tourists at a yard sale poking among their old belongings. Most are staying here. The duplex hasn't room. And Cindy frets among the neighbor's pansies for a centerpiece. She seems nervous and keeps asking me dumb questions. The sun is hot and I am sweating with control.

Cindy wants to walk once round the house. Thomas and Keturah are busy picking flowers, suddenly no longer clinging to me. Out back by the swings, Cindy is smiling sadly at some thought, looking up at the nursery window where the paint is flecking gray across the sill. I can smell lilac from across the lawn behind her car, which is glinting angles in the sun.

Cindy is collecting their flowers in two bunches next to hers on the driver's seat when I duck into the kitchen for Keturah's bottle from the refrigerator. When I come out the four of them are standing by the car and Thomas is pointing at some packages still wrapped that Cindy said were for the ride to New York.

I hand Cindy the bottle and she bites her lower lip. "Jeez, I almost forgot it."

"Got Pampers for the trip? You want some Kleenex? And Thomas' blanket? Can't forget tha—"

"Matt, it's OK. I got it."

We look at each other for a moment, then she drops her eyes to Thomas and pulls him gently back against her by his shoulder. He wriggles free and walks around the car, running his finger along the chrome. Keturah has sat down in the driveway like a sparrow taking a dust bath. She seems to be studying something small between the pebbles.

Thomas stops by the front lights and turns to me.

"Why can't Matt come, too?"

"I can't, Thomas. It's Cindy's turn to come."

I thought I had prepared myself for everything a hundred times. Apparently I haven't. The glands below my ears begin to hurt and now my eyes have blurred with water. I turn away towards the house. The azaelea there is out today. Light pink, with bees.